Devotion in the Open Air:
A Cozy Affection Anthology

Edited by
Chyina Powell

This is a collection of fictional works. Names, characters, places, and incidents are either a product of the author's imagination or are used fictitiously. Any resemblance to actual persons, living or dead, businesses, companies, events, or locales, is entirely coincidental.

DEVOTION IN THE OPEN AIR

Inked in Gray Press

InkedinGray.com

Copyright © 2024

All rights reserved.

ISBN

Paperback: 978-1-952969-28-7

E-book: 978-1-952969-29-4

Cover Design by Psycat Studio

https://www.instagram.com/psycatstudio/

https://www.facebook.com/psycatDINM/

CONTENTS

"There is always something left to love. And if you ain't learned that, you ain't learned nothing."
— Lorraine Hansberry

Before You Read

Language Usage

Please note that some authors hail from outside the United States and have stories featuring UK English. Please don't be alarmed if you see some extra 'u's or an 's' where there would be a 'z' 😀

Trigger Warnings

Some stories contained within this anthology have trigger warnings. In full transparency, we will list them here if you need them. 🤍

Ministry of Moss: death of a sibling, death of a parent, history of American slavery

Collecting Dragonflies: Alludes to children's deaths due to sickness, war, accidents, and abandonment (though the causes are not explicitly depicted on page). Grief of adult family members left behind is alluded to but not fully depicted on page.

Sunna's Eclipse: Emotional Abuse, Miscarriage, Disownment, Abandonment, Generational Trauma

The Sacred Amid the Mirth: Racism, governmental oppression, loss of parents and siblings, hypothermia, refugee status, social isolation, brief reference to child trafficking.

Mother, Ghost, Bride: Infant death.

The Secret Keeper: Master/servant relationships and social class discrimination, though technically in precolonial Philippines — which the concepts of this story are based from — it wasn't considered slavery but a system of obligation and repayment through labor. Mentions of war, death, territorial disputes, and bladed weapons. Allusion to a sapphic love story, though one-sided.

Ministry of Moss

Kionna Walker LeMalle

The man's legs lacked ankles. Instead, his calves transitioned into feet as wide as his thighs, and his toes appeared gnarled into a pair of dusty sandals. Bea tried to imagine the man in a closed shoe, but always his twisted foot merely crushed the shoe beneath it. She giggled when she imagined a pair flattened under the weight of his too-wide, ankle-less feet. But as soon as the hint of laughter escaped her barely parted lips, she felt her mother's side-eye as if it were a jab just below the ribs.

"Hush, Bea," Norma spoke without turning her eyes away from the huge tree of a man.

Bea tried to focus on something other than the man's boughed arms and rooted feet. She thought his eyes would be safe, for no one's eyes could resemble a tree. But when she looked up to the man's face, he was holding Spanish moss above his head, his arms raised like branches. His skin was dark and uneven, rough like damaged bark. Bea blinked. For a moment, the moss seemed to be a part of him, seemed to be more than something he was holding. She wondered if this man was not a man at all but indeed a tree.

"Legend has it," he began, "that Spanish moss originated

from a woman's hair — a young bride who—" He looked over at Bea, took notice of the young child in the room and edited the rest of the story. "A young bride who cut off her hair and placed it high in a tree so that her groom could always look up and see her, even when they were far apart."

Norma Thompson frowned a bit and tilted her head at the man.

He motioned to her daughter and pursed his lips as if to say "Well Professor, you're the one who brought a child to the lecture hall."

Norma sighed. She would have to find a sitter as soon as they were settled in. They hadn't even completed the move yet and already she was making the wrong impression on the department's chair.

Professor Griffin went on to explain that long after the couple passed away, the bride's hair remained. It grayed, and it grew, and it spread from tree to tree. Bea stared at the man who placed the moss over his shoulders and let it rest there as he continued to speak. She watched as the moss made its way up to his balding head, like a toupee, and sat.

"Mama, look!" Bea pointed.

Norma gently lowered Bea's hand but otherwise seemed not to notice. She said nothing and resumed writing as quickly as she could. Her pen moved continuously across the page in an endless stream that Bea could not yet comprehend. She could only read her teacher's cursive with its perfectly sized and slanted loops. Her mother's handwriting zigged and zagged a bit, and it curled in unexpected places.

The professor was now talking about the historical uses of moss: Native American women used it to make clothing; the American colonists mixed it with mud to make mortar; those who were enslaved used it for mattresses, even long after slavery ended. One former slave sang a chant, expressing his refusal to use cotton. Professor Griffin straightened his body and held up his head. He sang: *We free, we free, liberty done come. We free, we free, slavery done done. No more cotton. No more cane. Only the moss for me, sunshine and rain.*

Bea liked the song a great deal and continued humming the melody long after the professor stopped singing. As she did, she drew, beginning with the man's feet, which spread across the bottom of her paper before moving upward into two thick, trunk-like legs.

"There is much debate over who first created a moss doll, whether Native American, African, Cajun, or Creole. It seems likely no one can claim doll creation. Little girls as far back as the first daughter of Eve likely created a doll with whatever was at their disposal." He shot a softened glance at Bea, as if imagining her at play, but her eyes were trained on her paper at the time, as she detailed the moss running down his shoulder. "There have been many legends about the origin of moss," Professor Griffin continued, "including the one you *and I* heard for the first time today." He shot a quick look at Norma, but her eyes were also trained on Bea's drawing, the precision of it. She missed both his joke and his confession. "But with all of the uses of moss, there are no legends about how these uses came to be. So, this summer's culminating project is a moss-themed anthology, and you will each have the opportunity to be published."

A buzz broke out in the room, which was filled with aspiring writers — young MFA students from LSU, the flagship university, and undergraduate creative writing majors from LSU Alexandria, which had only recently transitioned from a community college to a four-year university. They had each traveled to Alexandria for a summer intensive on the regional literature of the American South. There was something about the historical archives here in what the locals called CENLA that made it a writer's paradise, at least that's what the MFA students had been told. Behind closed doors, the story differed. Professor Griffin confessed that they needed a way to bring attention to their own fledgling program.

Bea looked away from her drawing, which now included

everything except the man's neck, face, and bald head. She had become consumed with detailing the strands of moss on his shoulders, which seemed longer every time she checked in again, trying to capture the realness of this strange man. Professor Griffin raised his hand, calling the students to attention. The moss now hung beneath his triceps, and Bea considered adjusting her drawing.

"Hold on," he said. "There is more. The stories will be judged blindly by university faculty. The first-place winner will receive a full tuition waiver for the MFA at LSU if a graduate student is chosen, or for the BA at LSUA, if an undergraduate wins."

Now the students seemed to shift from friendly elbow taps and knee pats to a forced distance. They each sat more erectly in their seats, hanging on to the professor's every word. Considering the stakes, there would be no discussion of these stories. One by one, they determined a refusal to workshop the anthology piece for fear that someone would steal the story.

A kid in the back of the room, a boy no older than Bea, maybe younger, and unaccompanied called out, "Can I write a story? A collection maybe? If I write a book, will you read it?"

Professor Griffin paused and looked around, as if trying to match the child with some present adult. But he said nothing to the boy. He simply addressed the room. "Are there any questions?"

Bea turned in her seat in search of the boy who she had heard but not seen. Hearing, she had known the voice was a boy's voice, not a man's, not even a young man's, like those in this room. This room was no place for a boy or for her, for that matter. The walls were a dirty white; the thin commercial carpet a rippled gray. They sat in seats with stained burgundy cushions, many torn, and there was a musty, papered smell, like that of library archives. Only the books that were once in this space had been moved elsewhere, leaving behind the peculiar scent of aged paper and the looming smell of forgotten lectures. This was a place for serious scholars, not young children, and especially not unaccompanied children. Where had he come from? And where was that boy now?

"Well, if there are no questions," Professor Griffin said, "Let us dismiss until tomorrow morning."

"But if I win—"

There was the voice again, and again Bea turned in her seat. She saw the boy's shadow, but someone blocked him from her view.

"Tomorrow morning, we'll meet outside this building under the oak tree." Professor Griffin pointed to his right, as if it were possible to see through the built in bookcases. "You are dismissed."

Movement began immediately, and when the person who was blocking the boy's shadow moved, he was no longer there. Bea frowned. She had hoped to see him.

"Wait," Bea said and raised her hand.

Professor Griffin smiled with his lips tight and his eyes closed. "Little Miss Thompson, I presume?" He opened his eyes and looked at her as if longing to reveal something taboo.

Bea shifted in her seat when her mother placed her hand on her knee, but she kept her head up and returned the eye contact. It was what her father had taught her. "Yessir, Beatrice Thompson."

Norma felt the heat of colleagues on the back of her neck. The writing students continued to file out, and she wanted more than anything to file out with them. She remembered being one of them, so filled with hope that she would complete her MFA and stories would somehow flow from her with greater ease. She remembered thinking she could crack the story code, that she could be the next Mildred Taylor, deep diving into trauma and drama and healing. Norma gently squeezed Bea's thigh, a subtle warning not to go too far, not to appear too smart, not to be the typical Beatrice.

"I'd like to enter the contest, too," Bea said. "You can hold my tuition, if I win." She looked back for the boy one last time, planning to smirk, but there was still no trace of him. There was no trace of anyone except Bea, her mother, and this living tree.

"But you are no more than eight," Professor Griffin began.

Norma squirmed in her seat.

"Nine," Beatrice said. "Nine and a half."

Professor Griffin smiled with a kind of half-hearted sarcasm. "Professor Thompson, a word please."

Norma leaned over and whispered in Bea's ear. "I'll meet you right outside this door in a few minutes. Don't go anywhere, and Bea please, don't—" She paused, hesitated to say anything that might give Bea an idea. "Don't do anything but stand or sit and wait. Okay?"

When Bea stepped out of the university's library, before her was a beautiful fountain, and to the right of that fountain was a huge oak tree, surrounded by black iron benches. Somehow, when she came in, she had not seen this tree at all. How had she missed it? Its canopy stretched out enough to gift more than fifty people with its shade.

Bea walked over and placed the palm of her hand flat on its trunk. With her fingers spread wide open, she patted the tree and said, "You have lots of stories to tell, don't you?"

"Yes, yes I do," a voice said.

Bea jumped before the familiar voice broke into laughter.

"Scared you, didn't I?" The boy had again appeared out of nowhere.

"Who are you?"

"I'm Odu Ahmed," he said.

She squinted and looked the boy directly in the eyes. There was something familiar about him, something just out of her reach. "I'm with my mama. Who are you with?"

"Well." he hesitated and looked toward the library. "I guess you could say I'm with him." He motioned toward the window, and Bea could see Professor Griffin and her mother talking.

Professor Griffin's hands flailed wildly, as if explaining something urgent. The moss now extended from his shoulders to his wrists. If Bea hadn't known it were impossible, she would have believed it was growing on his skin. Her mother seemed not to notice.

"Is he your uncle or something?"

"Or something," he said, smiling.

Bea tilted her head at him and wondered about that. Odu was cute, his skin dark and smooth. He looked too young to be Professor Griffin's real nephew, unless he were a great nephew or maybe a play nephew. That could be it. She had a play uncle herself. Uncle Scott was her dad's best friend. He'd helped her mom settle into their new home, but he was back in New Orleans now, which made her miss her dad even more.

Odu bent over and picked up a small twig then sat on one of the black iron benches.

Bea sat next to him and poked her fingers through the gaps between bars. "So Odu, you like telling stories?"

"Yeah," he said. "But no one will listen."

"I'll listen," Bea said. "What's it about?"

"It's about moss. I know why it's here, why it's all around us."

Bea laughed. She thought of telling him he couldn't possibly know but decided against it.

Odu smiled. His beautiful teeth were perfectly straight and white, nothing like Professor Griffin's yellow sap teeth. He most certainly must be a play uncle, maybe even a neighbor.

"Is that what you want to write for the contest?"

"Yes," he said. "But I can't write it. I need your help."

Bea didn't understand. Why had he said he would write a book if he couldn't write?

He read her mind. "I saw you," he said. "I knew you could write for me."

"What does that even mean? You can't write? I can write for you?"

"Will you?" He faced her now, and his face looked older for a second, much older, like a younger version of Professor Griffin. She was back on the real uncle idea.

Bea extended her hand — a gesture she had seen from her mother. "If you tell a good story, I will write it down in my very best cursive."

Odu grabbed hold of her hand. His grip was firm, confident. He held her hand a few seconds too long.

Just as she attempted to pull away, she felt a surge through her body. She flinched. "What was that?"

But Odu was gone, and when she looked at her hand, there was a full tree branded into its center.

PROFESSOR GRIFFIN SPREAD the Magic Shave over his head and set a timer for six minutes. While he waited for the timer to go off, he shaved his face, checking carefully to ensure no stubble remained. Somehow in this fourth life, the tiniest bit of hair was fertile ground for that awful plant. He could love it — the uniqueness of it, its soft texture and nearly invisible gray scales, its overall practicality in every life he had lived. But now, it threatened to get in the way of his living as normal a life as someone with his wealth of experience could live. And yet, with all of the living (and dying) he had done, he had yet to understand the plant's attraction to him.

No matter where he awakened after some untimely death, Spanish moss was sure to find him, even if it had never grown there before. It had been in his hair when he washed ashore on the bank of the Red River, his head pounding painfully, his ears ringing, his lungs aching with water. A woman had pulled him through the trees and onto a small plot of land with a small white shack — a room really, where far too many kids lived. She had pumped his lungs and made him cough something awful, and then she placed her thin lips over his and sent breath into his body.

"What's your name? You from the Magnolia farm?" She was a shapely woman wearing a rather plain blue dress.

He had tried to answer her but could form no words. He didn't know his name.

"Well, use your tongue." The woman craned her neck and bent down a bit, trying to see into his mouth.

He moved his tongue around, but he had no idea how to use it. Nothing happened, except a welling of spit in the back of his throat. He found himself coughing again.

"Well, I reckon you the one we been expectin' — Leston Griffin. From that Magnolia farm. It took you mighty long. I thought maybe ya was dead." She frowned then smiled. "If I wouldn't've pulled you out of that water, you would be just that. Dead." She laughed then. "But the trees, they always talk. I know'd you was here when the leaves all blew to the river. That's how they told me to go see what was there, and there was you. Face down, dying, almost dead — our long lost Leston Griffin." She said all of this while bent over, trying to meet him eye to eye. Her thick sandy-brown hair was pulled back into one thick braid then pulled forward so that it didn't hang, rather it sat on the center of her head like a strange but beautiful hat.

He shook his head, slowly so that it wouldn't hurt. His mind flooded with questions. Why would he have been running? Who was she, and where were they? He placed his hand on his throbbing head and winced. The knot felt like a smooth rock.

"Come on," she said, taking him by the hand. Against his, her hand looked pale and felt soft. "I don't let nobody stop here on their way to freedom and not eat. Of course, you ain't got no cause to move on from here now no ways. The war almost over. We soon be free." She held his hand up and examined his fingertips. There was dirt caked beneath his nails. "Your hands need a good wash," she said, leading him inside the shack to a pale of not so clean water. Several kids dressed in shades of tan and green stared at him. A little girl waved. "Hurry up. Millie be bringin' the food here soon, and John gonna bring us a word from the Lord."

Her name was Norma, Norma Thompson, which was the thing that drew him to the new professor he'd hired: another Norma Thompson, one hundred sixty years and five lives later. The first Norma had been what they called mulatto then, what they call biracial now. If she were ever a slave, she never behaved like one. Rumor had it that she was favored because she was Paul Laurent's only child. His wife had been barren. As far as he could tell, it was Norma who ran the house. After the war, she did what they called a remaking of the place and gave the emancipated slaves paid jobs or a plot of land right there on the plantation. The land had to be worked; the house had to be run, and Paul and Lauretta Laurent were in no shape to do it. Their spirit had been broken by the war, but there was no breaking Norma and no breaking the children she saved and raised. And this meant there was no breaking him, no breaking Leston Griffin — not in this life nor the last nor the two before that.

How could he not hire Professor Norma Thompson? He made up his mind when he saw her name, and he solidified his decision when he read her vitae. But to his surprise, when he met her in person, he felt no connection. Her daughter had been the one to assure him he'd made the right move. She had seen him as no one had in his other lives — the tree, the unrelenting moss, the secret that even Ma Thompson had never seen.

———

The tree had been seared into Bea's hand a full two weeks and still her mother had no idea. Every time Bea attempted to show her, the branding disappeared, and Bea was left looking like she'd just made up another strange story.

"And then what happened?" Norma asked, turning away from Bea and pulling the next story from her stack of papers. "Can you feel the tree? Does it glow at night? Does it have magic powers?"

"That's the thing, Mama. It doesn't hurt. It doesn't glow. It's just there. And that boy, Odu, the one who gave it to me, I can't find him. So, am I just stuck with this tree in my hand?"

Norma turned to face Bea. "Well, that doesn't make for a very interesting story. Something has to happen. If there's an inciting incident, like a tree showing up in your hand, it has to lead to something happening. Otherwise, what's the point?"

Bea looked down at her hand and, seeing the tree clearly, placed her open hand directly on top of the story her mother was reading. "Mama, look! I'm not making this up. It's an actual tree!"

Norma smiled. "Well, you're convincing, that's for sure. Now go back and think about what's going to happen with that tree. Maybe you can tell me the rest of the story during dinner."

Bea shook her head. How could her mother not see the tree? She traced her fingers over its trunk, its leaves. The branding — or whatever it was — was deep enough to feel grooves, as if she had been carved. Bea turned to leave the room, her mind focused on how to make the tree visible or how to get rid of it, whichever proved easier.

"Okay," Norma said, taking hold of Bea's arm.

Bea turned to face her mother again.

"I understand that you want to enter the contest—" She took hold of Bea's hand and traced its palm with her fingers.

Bea smiled and relaxed her shoulders. Her mother could finally see it.

"But Bea, you have to understand that it's for college students only. There's just no way you can enter." Norma clasped Bea's hands into her own. "And I know I haven't been taking time to listen to your stories lately, but I will. Just let me get through this stack of stories and you can tell me what happens after Odu — that's his name, right?"

Bea nodded and sulked, somehow simultaneously.

"After Odu brands you, or rather your character, with that tree."

"But Mama, I'm trying to tell you—"

Norma turned back to her work. "I know!" she said, looking

only at the paper before her. "How about you go and take Muffins for a walk? Sometimes when I have writer's block, going for a walk makes all the difference." She handed Beatrice a sage green leash and returned to reading.

Muffins, who had been lying near the door jumped up at the word *walk* and tugged at the leash.

"Okay, okay," Bea said. "Let's go."

Once outside, Bea let the mild wind calm her a bit. What was it that her father used to always say? "*No* is only the beginning of negotiation." So what if Professor Griffin wouldn't let kids enter the contest? She just had to figure out how to get him to read kids' stories, then surely Odu would return to have his story read, and then maybe she could get rid of the tree print in her hand.

"I like the way you think," a voice said.

Odu! Muffins pointed her tail and growled. She could see him!

"Will you stop sneaking up on me?" Bea said. "And why did you disappear on me like that? My mama thinks I made you up. And how are you in my head?"

"Your mom isn't ready to see me," Odu said. "*You* are. And can you ask one question at a time?"

"What do you mean she's not ready to see you? And I am?" Beatrice knelt down to eye level with Muffins. "Hush girl." She paused and took another look at Odu. There was that genuine smile of his, so white against his dark skin. "It's okay. He's a friend," she said, stroking the dog's head.

"Sometimes," Odu said, "people just don't see what's right in front of them. They're too—"

"Busy?" Bea asked, her eyes still focused on Muffins.

"Occupied." Odu spread his arms wide as if the gesture defined the word.

Bea looked up then. Occupied. It was her father's word — one of his words, anyway. "You sound a little like my dad," she said, standing to face Odu. She looked closely at him, not in his eyes but at his lips. His smile.

"Is he here?" Odu started walking toward the tree line.

"He passed away," Bea said, following him. "Last year."

Odu paused and faced her. "So is he there?" He pointed to her heart. "And there?" He pointed to her head.

"Always." It was another of her father's words. *Do you love me, Daddy? Always, baby girl. Always.*

A falling leaf brushed against Bea's arm. She looked around. The nearest tree was half an acre away.

"Then, he's here," Odu said, twirling around with his arms spread. "He's everywhere you are!" Odu started running toward the treeline. "Come on," he said. "Let me show you something."

Muffins took off in a sprint after him, almost causing Bea to fall. She regained her balance and ran to keep up.

Bea had never seen a backyard so big. Their new home was an old two-story house set on five-acres of land, divided from neighbors by a line of trees. It had been in the Thompson family for generations and had landed in her mama's hands after the death of Bea's great great-grandmother, which had followed the death of her father. And now they were here in this new place where men looked like trees, Bea had somehow been branded, and leaves fell from the sky. It made no sense, and yet she ran with Odu — a boy she wasn't sure anyone else could see.

When they neared the tree line, Bea could see that it was made up of five or six rows of trees — a mini-forest in her backyard. Odu dropped down to his belly and crawled along the ground instead of continuing to run. Bea paused. What was he doing? She wasn't dressed for this. She had on white shorts and a pale pink shirt. Her sandals were a light khaki.

"Come on," Odu said. And now, he was looking closely at the base of the trees, as if they held some secret.

"Okay, Muffins, let's go," Bea said, dropping down to the ground.

Muffins paused and scratched at the base of a tree.

"Come on, girl," Bea said. But then she noticed that way down at the base of the tree, the bark was carved out into what looked like an arrow pointing to the next tree. This etching was so low on the tree, it'd be impossible to see, unless you were scouring the ground. She looked ahead, but she could no longer see Odu. She could only see the carved arrow and the forest of trees. Bea followed the arrow to the next tree and found another marked the same way and another and another. Each tree pointed to the next one as if telling her where to go. So, that's what Odu was doing. He was following the arrows.

Bea crawled on her belly, her fingers combing the ground, pulling back the grass at each tree's base. She was looking for the next arrow when Muffins caught eye of something, pulled the leash from Bea's inattentive hand, and took off zig-zagging through the giant trees. Bea ran, trying to keep up with her. Then, suddenly Muffins stopped. Bea slowed down and came up behind her. She was standing in front of a barbed wire fence, all rusted out. On the other side, she could see Odu, standing on a small plot of cleared land surrounded on all sides by large oak trees. The only thing on the land was a small white house, no more than a shack (maybe even a single room). Its wood was streaked with gray and black, the windows covered in caked up dirt. Behind the small plot of land was a river; a small boat leaned against the shack, but it looked like it hadn't been moved in years.

"Cross over," Odu said, waving his hand.

Bea squinted. The opening was so small, she wasn't sure she could fit through without hurting herself. "I don't know," she said.

"Cross over," Odu repeated.

"Why should I?" Her hands were on her hips as if she felt confident, but her heart beat rapidly, and one of her knees trembled.

"I want to tell you my story."

Bea turned around and started to head back home. Odu's imagination had hers beat, and she wasn't sure she wanted to keep up. "Come on, Muffins," Bea said. "Let's get out of here." Midway across the tree line, she could see the grassy field that signaled home. She quickened her step, but then a wisp of wind moved across the grass, in a straight line, as if God had blown in one spot. Bea stopped dead in her tracks. Muffins stopped walking too and moved in a circular motion, sniffing around. When Bea's eyes focused, she saw that the wind left behind an imprint in the grass — not a line but an arrow, and it pointed back to Odu. Muffins turned then and ran back to the barbed wire fence. She started to dig.

Bea ran behind her, her heart now racing at full speed. "Muffins, stop that!" She reached down to grab the leash. But Muffins found an opening in the fence and squeezed through before Bea could stop her.

Odu greeted Muffins with a warm pat on the head. "Your turn." He beckoned to Beatrice again.

Well, what was Bea to do? She couldn't go home without Muffins, so she knelt down and felt around with her hands until she found the opening in the barbed wire. When she slipped through, she stepped smack dead in a muddy puddle. Odu's story had better be worth it, she thought, because she was about to get in trouble big time.

It occurred to Norma that the sun had gone down and Bea had not yet returned to the house. But what was there to worry about? They lived several miles from the busyness of Alexandria, and Muffins would never let anything happen to Bea. She was docile most of the time, but when necessary, her Rottweiler instincts kicked in. She had saved Frank's life once, when a carjacker tried to steal his 1969 Mustang. Built the year Frank was born, his father had gifted it to him as a wedding gift. Muffins had been asleep on the back seat; the carjacker had no clue what he'd gotten himself into. Norma chuckled then sighed. If Frank were still here, Bea would not be wandering the property alone. By now, he'd have taught her to identify the trees. She'd heard there were oak, pecan, and even plum trees on the land. But she had yet to go out to explore. She had only three more stories to read, and then she would call Bea in to bathe and eat dinner. She would have to think of a new rule to signal that it was time to come inside. There were no street lights where they lived now, and the bright stars lit up the sky in a way that made you feel safe outdoors long after dark.

Norma needed to get through the students' drafts. She needed to do well on this job. Her last book hadn't sold, and after Frank passed, teaching adjunct hadn't been enough to pay the mounting bills. Then, the call came. Bea had inherited what used to be the big house on the Laurent Plantation. She was the next in line after generations of one-child families, carried through the Thompson lineage. Apparently the Laurents — those who were allowed to claim the name — had died out prematurely.

At first, Norma had no immediate plan for the property. She thought she would simply wait until Bea was old enough to decide what she wanted to do. But then, her agent called. There was a university in Alexandria. They were looking for a visiting writer. They couldn't afford much, but it would be a good change of pace with Frank gone and all. It could get her back on the map. God bless Marissa. She was not only an agent but a friend. So now, Norma was sitting in the living room of an old plantation home, reading moss story after moss story, her daughter claiming to have a tree on her hand and exploring who knows what on the land.

She shook her head. "Of all topics," she said aloud, "Why moss?"

She took another sip of tea, continued to read, and hoped the next story would be better than the last.

"SO YOU'RE TELLING me you got here in that little boat." Bea pointed to the small pirogue leaning against the shack. "When you were ten years old 160 years ago?" She laughed. "And I thought I had a good imagination."

Odu leaned against the largest oak tree. Its thick branches extended so far that its canopy nearly covered the shack. His bright smile faded. "I thought you'd believe me."

"Come on, Odu. It's a good story. I mean, I was with you the whole time. And this boat!"

Odu was quiet. After a while, his silence broke through Bea's laughter. She stopped and looked into his eyes. It was the first time she had really looked at him, not at his teeth, but at him. His eyes were not young. His eyes were not beautiful. His eyes were an old man's eyes. They were the same as Professor Griffin's. Bea gasped but pretended not to see this reminder of the old man.

"Okay, let's say I believe you—" She walked over to the shack and took a closer look. The outside of the boat still looked like the log from which it had been carved, or rather the tree from which the log had been cut. When she ran her hand along the bark, it flaked off and fell to the ground.

"My dad used to take me fishing on his boat," she said, thinking of her last time on the water. "Let's go out on the river." She turned the boat on its bottom. Traces of moss clung to the inside; there was an obvious split in the wood.

"No!" The strength of Odu's voice shocked her. "It's not safe," he said, walking toward her. "I told you, it flipped over. Hit a big rock or something. I hit my head. And Sofi—" he stopped and looked towards the river.

"Who's Sofi?" Bea looked at Odu then back at the boat. "Is she like a character in your story or something?"

Odu shook his head and croaked out two words through slightly parted lips. "My sister."

Bea thought of how desperately she wanted her mother to believe her and remembered how defeated she'd felt when accused of making up Odu. She laced her fingers and traced the tree in her right palm with her left thumb.

"Is she here?" Bea said, looking around. The oak trees surrounded the small plot of land, like a barricade.

"Only here," Odu said, pointing to his heart. "And here." He pointed to his head.

Bea nodded. "Let's say I believe you."

Odu smiled.

"What does your story have to do with moss? How will we get Professor Griffin to read it?"

"Let me show you something." Odu led her to the shack's door and pushed slightly. It creaked. He pushed just a little more, slowly as if afraid the shack would fall.

Cobwebs lingered between the door frame and door. Odu waved his hand to break their hold. "This is where we hid until the war ended," he said. "Ma Thompson would sneak in scraps of food, and we shared whatever there was."

Inside, there were pallets of moss on the floor and a makeshift table that resembled a tree stump and a black kettle filled with what looked like ashes. Bea counted the pallets. Ten. "You keep saying we. Who was here with you?"

"There was Jack and Jill, Gloria, Adrienne, Samuel, Sampson, Tet, and Amanda." He tapped a finger with each name, as if counting to make sure no one had been forgotten. "These are their memories." He plopped down on a pallet of moss and closed his eyes. "This was Amanda's. She was short and kind. Her father owned the Magnolia plantation. He lavished her with gifts and kept her work light, but his wife was plotting to kill her. So, she ran away."

He moved over to the next pallet. "And this was Sampson's and before him Adam's. They were brothers. Their mama was a slave at the Kent House. She sent them a year apart. Adam left here and went north before Sampson came. Sampson stayed and helped Ma Thompson long after the war." He moved through pallet after pallet. Jack and Jill were best friends sent together from the same plantation. Gloria had the most amazing smile. Adrienne was the storyteller, always sharing tales her grandfather had passed on from Morocco. Samuel knew how to read and had somehow managed to sneak a Bible off the Bayou Boeuf plantation. He read from Exodus every night, and it was he who taught Odu how to read. The last pallet Odu moved to was Tet's. He lay back on that one and let his head rest on his folded arms. "Tet," he said, "was always getting us in trouble. Once he caught a toad and hid it in Ma Thompson's dress pocket. She screamed something awful when she reached in and felt that toad."

Bea laughed. "And Sofi!" She plopped down on the final pallet, which was smaller than all of the others. Immediately, she knew this was not Sofi's pallet. She saw Odu in a boat — the same boat she had touched only moments ago. He lay beneath layers of moss, a girl beside him. Heavy rain rocked the boat. Two men who appeared white, one on each end of the boat, struggled with the oars. Then, the boat flipped. The moss, then Odu, then the girl fell into the water. He began swimming. The girl went under. The men held onto the boat until one of them slipped. Then the other went after him. Odu dove under the water, looking for the girl. He came up screaming. "Sofi!" Bea jumped up! She looked at Odu. "You're telling the truth!"

Her right hand vibrated. She looked at the tree in its palm. "I have an idea," she said.

"PROFESSOR THOMPSON?" Leston Griffin leaned forward in his office chair and motioned for Norma to take a seat.

She sat slowly, timidly. Had she rejected too many of the stories? Had she asked too much of the students?

He handed her a stack of flyers — some wrinkled, some damp, one torn across the center and retaped, another missing a corner. Each of them uniquely illustrated in pencil with intricate detail — sometimes a forest of trees, sometimes a house and a single tree, sometimes a pair of trees, a dog next to a tree, a kid climbing a tree. Every tree drawn was adorned with Spanish moss, and every flier said the same thing:

Norma gasped. Even without Bea's name anywhere on the flier, she recognized her daughter's imperfect cursive and perfectly detailed drawings. Her neck tightened, and there was that vein again, pulsating in her left temple. "Dr. Griffin, I assure you. I had no idea."

He stood, and the shadow of a tree fell on the wall behind him.

Norma looked for a window or a potted tree in the office. The only window was behind her, and there was no visible tree — not outside, nor inside.

"This is your daughter's doing. No?"

Norma nodded and pulled in her top lip.

"The thing is, Professor Thompson, your daughter's story time is now the talk of the town. There have been rumors about that missing bank for over a hundred years. These flyers have garnered the attention of the mayor, the school superintendent, the head librarian." He paused. "And do you know what's scheduled for July 31?"

Norma felt herself sink down in the chair. Her voice came out soft and hollow. "The pre-release reading for our Origins of Moss anthology."

"Exactly. So how do you suppose we are to compete with your daughter's event?" He sat back down and leaned forward, looking into rather than at Norma. She felt the weight of his eyes.

"I-I'll tell her to call it off," she said. "I'm sorry. Bea's dealing with a lot. Her father passed, then we moved. And I'm working so much."

Professor Griffin raised an eyebrow.

"Not too much. That's not what I mean. It's just that everything has been hard for her."

Professor Griffin leaned back in his seat. "I gathered that. And that's why I don't want her to cancel it. We're moving the reading to the tree line behind your house. Mrs. Throwberry, the librarian, says there are stories about a section of the Red River near Shreveport that was part of the Underground Railroad. And well — if that land behind your property was somehow connected to that time in history, I think we all want to see it." He stretched, and again tree branches appeared in his shadow. "Besides, I for one am wondering what moss has to do with this story. Are you not?"

Norma was speechless. But she had to admit to a budding curiosity, though it was mixed with worry. Had she let Bea wander so much that she'd created flyers and posted them all over Alexandria? And had Professor Griffin said Marksville as well, and Cocoville, and Mansura? There was no way Bea could have gone on foot to all of those places. She had to have help.

Odu, she thought, recalling Bea's words. *He's a real boy, Mama. He put this tree in my hand.*

"Professor Thompson," Professor Griffin fanned her with a flier. "Are you okay? You look like you've seen a ghost."

Norma managed a smile and a false nod.

"All right then." Professor Griffin approached the door. "I'll be there tomorrow to assess the space. Please send a message to our students with the new location."

Norma nodded and crossed the threshold into the hallway.

"And Professor?"

"Yessir?

"We have an anthology to publish. You have to stop rejecting the stories. We are down to three weeks before this reading, and the anthology releases in five. You understand?"

Norma pursed her lips, but there was laughter in her eyes. She had been rather hard on the students, hadn't she? "I'll start rereading tonight," she said. "Right after I have a conversation with little Miss Beatrice."

Norma prepared pastries and sweet tea to welcome Professor Griffin to her home, but he had no interest. He pulled onto her gravel driveway in a large pick-up truck and stepped out wearing work boots and overalls. She had never seen him like this — sandals yes, but boots? Overalls?

"Sir, would you like an apple fritter," she asked. "And tea?"

He shook his head and headed toward the tree line.

She followed him. "Or coffee. I have coffee."

"I'm fine, Professor. Let's just see the space."

Norma was nervous. She had gone herself the night before and found nothing but an old shack. She'd suggested cleaning the place, but Bea had begged her not to.

"He has to see it just as it is," Bea pleaded. "Please Mama. Odu says it has to be just like this, pallets and all."

And here was Odu again, a boy she had never seen. According to Bea, he led the way now. The girl's imagination had gone too far. When they got to the tree line, Bea dropped down on all fours. Professor Griffin looked at Norma.

"You don't have to go in like that," she said. "I just walked through last night. It's tight though. Lots of raised roots. Be careful."

Professor Griffin eyed Bea closely then bent down to see what she was following. When he saw the arrows, his eyes lit up. He dropped down like a ten-year-old boy and followed Bea from one arrow to another.

When they reached the barbed wire fence, he paused. "All of this. It feels so familiar, like I've been here a thousand times."

Bea was on the other side of the fence now. "Cross over," she said, beckoning. "I have something to show you."

Professor Griffin squeezed his body through the opening in the fence.

Norma followed, slowly. "Sir, I'm sorry," she said.

But he didn't hear her. He was focused on the shack, the boat, the trees.

"This," he said. "This is what I've been looking for. Life after life after life."

Norma looked at Bea and mouthed the words "Life after life."

Bea opened the door to the shack. There were no cobwebs blocking the door now. Professor Griffin followed her in.

"Sit here," Bea said. She pointed to the smallest pallet.

"I've been here," he said. "But how?" He sat on the pallet, which was shorter than the length of his long legs.

Bea saw the visible shock on his face, then the streaming tears, then the joy.

"I'm not Leston Griffin," he said. "I am Odu Ahmed. My sister was Sofi."

With those words Odu appeared, visible to both professors.

Norma stepped back at first, then calmed when her boss said, "You're, you're me. You're Odu Ahmed. How did I forget you?" He touched the pallet next to him. "Tet! This was Tet's." He got up and touched pallet after pallet, remembering each of his friends from more than a hundred years ago. "So the moss holds memory?" His eyes were filled with satisfaction.

Odu spoke then for the first time. "Yes, all moss everywhere is a lost memory, waiting to be found."

"You've been following me," he said, walking to Odu. "For hundreds of years across multiple lives. I never understood why my spirit wouldn't rest. But it was you trying to find me, trying to tell me that I have never been Leston Griffin. I have always been Odu Ahmed." He reached out and embraced the boy with a huge hug.

The shack trembled. Norma grabbed hold of Bea, but Bea was pulling away running toward Odu, as he and the big tree of a man became one. They were neither old nor young but something else, something that superseded age, something beautiful, something whole. She reached out to touch them but captured only a handful of moss.

They were gone, but they were not forgotten. She would remember them as she remembered her father. Always.

About Kionna Walker LeMalle

Kionna Walker LeMalle is an executive writer by day, a fiction writer by night, and an occasional poet. Her work has been featured in The Southern Quarterly, Delta Education Journal, table//FEAST, and The First Line. In 2023, she won the Lee Smith Novel Prize for Behind the Waterline (Blair Publisher, 2025). Kionna has been married to her pastor and best friend, Averri LeMalle, for twenty-six years. Together, they have four children and one granddaughter to whom she hopes to leave a legacy of faith, love, and story.

facebook.com/kionna.lemalle

 x.com/KionnaLeMalle

 instagram.com/kionnalemalle

COLLECTING DRAGONFLIES
STEFANIE CONTRERAS

Death was not to be feared, so Jacinta was extremely meticulous about her wardrobe when she dressed each day. She donned trousers that were well-loved and a simple knit sweater that had no stray threads or holes. Her boots were warm and broken in. The cloak she donned next was a luxurious dark amethyst with embroidered silver leaves along the shoulders and head covering. A black rose brooch secured the cloak at her neck. It was designed to match the black leather belt she looped around her waist. She left her dark hair loose, though she had a hair tie around her wrist if she should need it. Knowing her travels to the realm of the dead sometimes encountered vicious winds, she was always circumspect about being prepared.

"Jacinta, your breakfast is getting cold," called a sweet voice from downstairs. It made Jacinta smile at herself in the mirror.

"Today will be a great adventure," she said to her reflection.

"Hermana, stop muttering to yourself and come downstairs!"

As the eldest sister, Jacinta did not dignify that statement with a reply. She put a handkerchief in her pocket and went to the stairs. As she descended to the first floor, she could hear both of her sisters talking to each other in cheerful voices. The girls were discussing what color to paint the chicken coop, and whether the color might affect how many eggs each hen laid.

"What do you think, Jacinta?" Araceli was her baby sister. Her dark hair framed her delicate face in ringlets that she claimed were untamable, but they always looked like perfect curls to Jacinta. When she smiled, a dimple appeared in her left cheek.

"She's going to vote for purple," Paloma said. Paloma was the practical sister who always kept her dark hair up in a bun. She made sure that Araceli never left their home in mismatched clothes or that Jacinta never left without breakfast. But if Jacinta or Araceli tried to do something for her, Paloma scoffed and waved them away with a scrunched nose and a twinkle in her eye.

"What colors do you two want?" Jacinta asked them. She didn't particularly care about paint colors, but she was happy to support whatever decision they wanted.

Araceli shrugged. She always looked to Jacinta as the final say, but she had a determined look on her face. "I think we should paint it green and brown, so it matches the trees around our home," she said. "That way the coyotes won't recognize it and try to get in."

Paloma scoffed. "Coyotes can tell colors now, can they?"

Araceli looked at Jacinta for help, but Jacinta didn't know if coyotes could tell colors. So she said quickly, "What color do you want, Palomita?"

Paloma lifted her chin. "I think we should paint it white so that when it's hot, the sun's rays will bounce off the walls instead of going inside to make our chickens uncomfortable."

Jacinta and Araceli blinked at her in surprise. Paloma normally didn't care what happened with the chickens. In fact, Jacinta and Araceli knew she was afraid of them, especially when they flapped their wings. Jacinta liked the chickens but Araceli loved them. They were Araceli's little friends. So, it was surprising to hear Paloma had given them consideration when thinking about the color to paint their coop.

"Don't look at me like you're surprised," Paloma scolded, startling them both. "And Jacinta, eat your breakfast already before it gets cold!"

"Stop ordering me around," Jacinta grumbled. Paloma acted as though Jacinta was one of the little chickens clucking around in the yard, instead of a woman with twenty-six winters under her belt *and* the head of the house.

As Jacinta went to the breakfast table, she thought she saw Paloma stick out her tongue.

"I suppose white is a good color after all," Araceli conceded.

On the table sat a chipped mug of coffee with milk and a bowl of oatmeal with brown sugar and cinnamon. Jacinta's favorites. When she sat to eat in one of the three chairs at the table, her sisters came to sit with her too, even though they'd already had their breakfast.

The first spoonful of oatmeal was a warm, sweet mouthful that made Jacinta smile. It was such a simple meal, but for some reason when Paloma made it for her, it tasted the best.

"I know you have to go to work soon," Araceli said hesitantly, "but I wanted to ask you about something." She glanced at Paloma, who gave her a reassuring head nod. The two looked at Jacinta with such serious expressions, it made her put down her spoon and focus her attention on Araceli.

"Tell me," Araceli said to her sister in a soft voice. They never had secrets between them, so Jacinta wondered what could be on her mind.

"I was wondering if . . . one of these days, perhaps, I could . . . go with you to work?"

Jacinta frowned at her for a long moment, wondering what brought this about. Her sister had never asked to go with her before, though she'd accompanied Paloma many times. Paloma had gone with Jacinta once, and said she'd not like to do that again.

"Forget it," Araceli said quickly, when Jacinta's pause lingered too long.

"No, you'd be welcome," Jacinta assured her. "I'm simply surprised that you're interested. What brought this on?"

Araceli looked down at the table in embarrassment.

"It's just that I never thought too much about what you do but then . . ." Araceli trailed off. Her cheeks grew pink at the edges.

"Yesterday she helped me with the laundry and noticed some strange things in your pockets," Paloma filled in. Understanding dawned for Jacinta. She knew exactly what Araceli had found in her pocket. She'd been so tired when she came home, that she hadn't emptied them into her chest of drawers before Paloma came to collect her things for the wash.

Jacinta nodded. "Very well, you can come with me. Collect your things so we can go, and dress warmly."

Araceli's expression brightened, and without another word she jumped up from her chair and dashed to her bedroom.

"I know you'll take care of her," Paloma said while Jacinta finished her coffee and oatmeal. "I've packed you both some food for later."

"Gracias, hermana," Jacinta said. "I appreciate you always looking out for us."

Paloma smirked at her. "It's what I do," she said.

Jacinta took her empty cup and bowl to the sink, but her sister waved her away and told her to gather her things as well. Araceli came barreling back into the kitchen dressed in a blue woolen dress with thick leggings and boots. She did not have a cloak but there was a satchel looped over her neck and shoulder. It hung at her side and looked like it had a book stuffed inside.

"Bring your cloak," Jacinta said. She collected the bag of food items Paloma had packed for them and attached it to her belt. Then she hugged and kissed Paloma goodbye and stepped outside their casita. Araceli was on her heels, but she hadn't grabbed her cloak.

"You should have seen it, Jacinta, yesterday when I was in the garden, I swear to you I saw a fanged beast trying to eat all of our tomatoes," Araceli said. She turned and pointed at the garden, as if that would help illustrate her story better. Jacinta suppressed an eyeroll and turned back to the doorway, to find Paloma already there with Araceli's cloak. Araceli didn't seem to notice Paloma, and continued talking even though Jacinta wasn't paying attention.

Jacinta shared a look with Paloma, who handed her the cloak but did not interrupt the one-sided conversation. Jacinta draped Araceli's cloak around her shoulders and tied it closed at her neck while Araceli yapped about their next harvest. With a wave to Paloma, Jacinta took Araceli's hand and guided her down the path to their fence. Beautifully colored dragonflies zoomed over their heads, darting here and there in little swarms. Once the gate was latched behind them, Jacinta pulled up the hood of her cloak and closed her eyes. She held tighter to Araceli's hand and transported them both to their first stop for the day. Araceli's speech about growing patterns immediately dissolved into a surprised shriek as they traveled through time and space together. Jacinta may have had a slightly mischievous smile on her face, but it was gone by the time they arrived.

"You could have warned me!" Araceli hissed at her when the two appeared in a child's nursery.

"But what's the fun of that?" Jacinta whispered back. She let go of Araceli's hand and turned to the small figure in the bed. A woman leaned over the child with her ear to the child's chest. She looked somber as she sat up and half-heartedly smiled at the child — a small girl of maybe seven years with big blue eyes in a gaunt face.

"I'll be right back in a moment, dear," the woman said. "I'm going to speak with your family for just a moment."

The child didn't reply and the woman didn't wait to receive one. She turned away from the bed and left the room, closing the door behind her. The woman didn't see Jacinta and Araceli standing by the wall, but the child did. Her eyes widened as Jacinta stepped forward from the shadows and lowered her hood.

"Hello," Jacinta said softly. The child's eyes roamed over the detailing on her cloak with interest.

"I know who you are," the child whispered in a weak voice. Beside the bed, Jacinta saw a tray on a small side table with a bowl of untouched vegetable soup. Next to the bowl were some pretty rocks and a full glass of water. She sat on the edge of the bed where the woman had been.

"I've come to bring you home," Jacinta said. Through the closed door, she could hear the woman telling this child's parents that there was nothing more that could be done for the child except wait for Death to come. The child heard the woman too, and tears pooled in her eyes when they heard another woman's voice cry out in sorrow.

"Don't be afraid, beloved." Jacinta picked up one of the rocks on the side table and offered it to the girl.

The child's mouth turned down at the edges as she fought to keep her sobs at bay. But she fisted the rock and pressed it under her little chin.

"I'm not afraid," the child said. "I'm gonna miss my Mommy."

Jacinta smiled at her. "It's not Mommy's time yet, but you will see her again. I promise you that."

The girl sniffled and tried to wipe the tears from her eyes but she had no strength any longer. Her tiny body had nothing left to give. Jacinta pulled her handkerchief from her pocket, and slowly leaned over the child. The little girl watched her carefully as Jacinta gently dried her eyes and tucked the handkerchief away.

"I'll see Mommy again?" The child stared at her seriously, measuring Jacinta's words for truth.

"Yes, I promise," Jacinta said. "I know you have been very sick. That's why I came, because it's your time to go. Are you ready to come with me?"

The little girl glanced at her closed door once more. She could hear her mother crying, and someone else attempting to console her. Jacinta held her arms out for the girl, leaving it up to her to decide. The child took a moment to look around her room. There were dirty shoes beside the door. Dolls and books on a shelf. Pretty dresses hanging in the closet. Extra blankets at the foot of her bed.

The child sighed. Then she sat up and opened her arms to Jacinta. Jacinta collected the small child in her arms and stood up with the child's head tucked against her shoulder. Araceli wordlessly came to her side and took one of her hands. Jacinta thought she saw tears in Araceli's eyes, but her sister looked away.

Before Jacinta transported them from the room, she heard the child softly whisper, "Bye, Mommy."

IF IT WERE a normal day of work, Jacinta would drop off the little soul in her arms with Araceli and leave for her next destination. But since Araceli was with her today, the two went to Araceli's domain together. They found a calm pool of water where several souls lounged on the shore, enjoying the breeze and moderate sun. Jacinta set down the soul in her arms and let her look around. Away from the human world, the soul was already shedding ties to her childish form, and reclaiming her lost memories of all the lives she'd lived before. The soul peered up at Jacinta and Araceli.

"I remember you now," she said with joy.

"I'm traveling today with my sister, but I'll return soon to make sure you're comfortable," Araceli said. "You can take some time and decide what you'd like to do in your next life and when you feel like returning. There's no rush. Spend time with our friends and let them hear your story."

The soul smiled and didn't hesitate. She skipped away from the sisters and embraced the souls one by one. Several of the souls came to say hello to Araceli, happy to see her again. A few approached Jacinta and affectionately greeted her. These souls had known her a long time.

The itch to keep going prickled at her. Jacinta turned to Araceli. "Are you sure you want to continue?"

Araceli nodded firmly. "That was beautiful to see, but I know there is more."

Jacinta held out her hand, and her sister took it.

<hr>

They appeared in smoke-filled rubble. Here it was nighttime, and the stars peeked through the torn, thatched roof over their head. Outside the building, the world was filled with the sounds of battle, but in here it was too quiet.

"What happened here?" Araceli whispered.

Jacinta frowned at the destruction around her. "War."

She turned in a slow circle until she found what she was looking for. A boy, maybe around nine or ten years, crouched beside a pile of rubble that covered where his bed should have been. Jacinta went to his side and crouched beside him. The boy startled when he saw her and threw his body to the side, away from her.

"Where did you come from?" he demanded.

Jacinta pulled a slat of broken wood from the pile of rubble and tossed it away.

"I came for you and your brother," she said. "I can help you find him."

The boy was quick to set aside his worry. He scrambled to her side and helped her move the debris. Araceli joined them, her presence causing the boy to gasp when he saw her too. Jacinta saw the way he turned to glance at the sagging wall where they'd come from, too many stories high for a normal person to climb over, and then at their cloaks and faces. He knew. He knew why they were there, and it made a sudden sob rise in his throat.

Jacinta and Araceli didn't stop working. Piece by piece they worked until they uncovered what they were looking for. Beneath the fallen roof and the fragments of a broken bed, lay two figures.

The boy beside Jacinta shook his head when he saw that one of the figures was himself.

"I'm dead," he whispered in disbelief.

The other figure stirred at his brother's voice and opened his eyes to stare at them all in wonder. This boy was younger and smaller. Jacinta held out her arms to him and watched as his soul shook free from its body and came to her with a happy smile. Beside her, the boy put his hand on her arm.

"Don't take him, please," he pleaded. "Let him live."

"It's too late for me, Osiris," his brother said. He accepted Jacinta's hug and wrapped his famine-thin arms around her neck. Jacinta pressed her cheek against the boy's head and felt him relax in her embrace.

"So it was for nothing." Osiris glared at the way his body tried to cover his brother's from harm.

"It wasn't for nothing," Jacinta said sharply to draw his attention back to her. "You tried to save your brother because you love him. His soul will always remember that."

"And I love you too," his brother said. He shifted in Jacinta's arms and held out his hand for Osiris. Jacinta held out her hand too. Osiris didn't hesitate, he crashed into their embrace and let Jacinta hold up his weight while he clutched his brother close.

"Come on, brave souls, I've got you," Jacinta promised them. She stood with both boys in her arms and waited for Araceli to grip her hand. Then she brought them all to peace.

<hr>

"When you collect souls, you don't just take them from their lives, you take away their pain and fear," Araceli said.

The sisters watched as the two brothers made their way to other souls they recognized and embraced. Jacinta liked it in the peaceful realm, and she liked hearing the souls' stories of all the lives they'd lived so far.

"I do it so you don't have to," Jacinta said. This was Araceli's realm. She was responsible for helping the souls adjust from their lifetime and decide if or when they wanted to return. Jacinta often saw Araceli walking among the souls and caring for them with great thoughtfulness. She was proud of her sister's work.

"But why?" Araceli asked. Her eyebrows knit close together as she frowned at her older sister in confusion. "I'm perfectly capable of helping them that way."

"Of course you are," Jacinta agreed. "Before a soul is ready to come here, they're already afraid or in pain, and then they see me and their fear escalates when they realize why I'm there. You've created a peaceful garden here for the souls to rest. I wouldn't want to bring you a soul in turmoil who unknowingly disrupts the peace for the others."

Araceli nodded thoughtfully. She put her arm around Jacinta's waist and squeezed in affection.

"Where to next, hermana?"

Jacinta wrapped an arm around Araceli's shoulders and clutched her tight.

"Wherever the children need us."

A baby lay in the marshes without any swaddling blankets. Araceli gasped and cried out when she saw it. "How did this baby get out here like this?"

Jacinta went to the baby and gathered it in her arms. Its breathing was jagged and irregular. She swept her fingers over the soft downy texture of its hair and cooed to it when it opened milky eyes to try and see her. Its face was an unnatural shade of blue.

Someone had left this baby out here on purpose. It came into the world unloved and uncared for, but it did not have to leave the same way. She stood and tucked the baby under her cloak so that it would feel the warmth of her body and hear the beating of her heart.

Jacinta looked around them. The marsh where they stood had a few large rocks clustered together. It appeared the sun was at midday here, but it wasn't warm. There was a soft breeze through her hair. She listened to it as the wind rustled her cloak. Her shoes made a soft splashing sound as she crossed to the rocks and sat down on one of them. With her free hand, she pulled at the ties that kept her lunch sack attached to her belt. It was a bit of work to do one-handed, but she managed to silently unwrap some of the items Paloma had packed for them. Her eyes were unfocused as she looked out over the marsh.

Araceli watched her for a long time. Jacinta could feel her sister's eyes on her and the small bundle under her cloak that she held close. She knew Araceli was upset but she did not comfort her. Not yet.

She ate an apple with peanut butter. As she savored the flavors, her eyes caught on a dragonfly hovering nearby. Under her cloak, the baby wiggled and sighed one last time. When it stopped breathing, Jacinta pressed her cheek to the top of the baby's head and closed her eyes.

"You're at peace now, sweet one," she assured the soul in her arms.

Araceli's cheeks were wet when she came to sit beside her sister. Jacinta handed her the bag of food. Araceli took it without question, and rummaged inside, but her mouth was turned down in a pout and she seemed to give up looking rather quickly.

"I'm not hungry," she said after a moment.

Jacinta nodded. She thought in the distance she heard the sound of an ocelot's growl, and it made her sit up straighter.

"What was that?" Araceli raised her head and looked around too, but it was difficult to see over the marsh grasses that surrounded them. Jacinta stood and tried to see into the distance but it was no use. A roar, louder and closer, pierced the solitude of the moment.

"Soul reavers," Jacinta said. Her body tensed for a fight. "They feed on souls if they can find one before I do."

Araceli gasped.

"*Soul reavers,*" she repeated in shock. "I've never heard about them before."

"I've had to fight them before," Jacinta said. "They are cunning and fast, but they are not a match for me. I've not fought them when I had someone with me, though, and I do not want to risk you or the soul encountering them, so it's best we're off. You collect the food and then take my hand."

Araceli scrambled to snatch the food bag and tie it closed. She quickly grabbed Jacinta's outstretched hand. Jacinta watched carefully to make sure she wasn't too late, but she held tight to Araceli's hand and the soul in her arms and was able to transport them all before the soul reavers could arrive. The sound of several feral vocalizations followed them across the plane, but all was silent when they appeared in Araceli's peaceful realm once more. Knowing everyone was safe now, Jacinta slowly loosened the tension in her shoulders and jaw.

"Does Paloma know about the soul reavers?" Araceli immediately demanded. Jacinta gently removed the soul from under her cloak and passed it over to Araceli. Araceli was just as careful with it as she cuddled it close and cooed to it.

"I believe so," Jacinta said. She truly couldn't remember if the two had discussed it or not. Paloma most likely dealt with the soul reavers in her work too — she was responsible for taking the souls from Araceli and bringing them back to the living world. Soul reavers could eat the new souls before they could take root in a new body, but it was much more rare than finding a soul leaving a body at the end of its life. "She likely has fought them as well."

Sometimes she and Paloma unconsciously worked together to protect Araceli from things they didn't want her to worry about. The disbelieving look on Araceli's face, that she didn't know about soul reavers, told Jacinta that this was going to be a prime topic of discussion tonight when the sisters were back together.

"Hold that thought," Araceli said. She spun on her heel and went to introduce the soul in her hands to the others who waited here. Jacinta watched as the soul was welcomed and embraced by the others.

She felt a tug on her awareness that warned her a new soul needed retrieving. With the threat of the soul reavers at her last pickup, she suddenly felt the urgency to get to the next.

"Araceli, I have to go," she called out.

"I'm coming," Araceli yelled. She hustled away from the souls that gathered around her and took Jacinta's hand.

"Are you sure you still want to go?"

Araceli scrunched her nose in annoyance. "Why are you asking," she demanded.

"I saw how sad you were when you saw the baby in the marsh," Jacinta said. "I know it's not easy, I just wanted to make sure you're still interested in going with me. I would never blame you for not wanting to witness this."

"I want to continue," Araceli assured her. "Let's go."

Jacinta didn't wait any longer. She focused on the tug that was calling to her and traveled there with Araceli in tow. The two appeared in the garden of a great estate. Looking around at the immense grandeur surrounding them, it seemed as though they'd come to the castle of a king.

"I notice that *you* didn't cry when you saw the baby in the marsh," Araceli said. "Have you become impervious to such things?"

Jacinta snorted. "Not yet," she said. "I try not to grieve them until the day is done."

Her feet moved forward, seeking the soul she needed to retrieve. Araceli followed as she went inside the castle and brushed past many people running frantically here and there. Most of the people wore the same colors, as though they were part of the castle staff. They did not see the sisters walk among them, but they may have noticed goosebumps for no reason or the feeling like someone was watching them. The staff moved out of their way without truly understanding why.

"How do you know where to go?" Araceli asked as Jacinta led her up a grand staircase.

"The souls call to me," Jacinta said. "I feel them pulling me to them like a beacon in the dark."

"Can I feel them?" Araceli seemed to wonder to herself. Jacinta glanced behind and saw her sister frowning in concentration. Her forehead was pinched adorably as she followed Jacinta to beautifully decorated living quarters.

They were in a well-appointed nursery. Jacinta saw the piles of toys and building blocks in the far corner, as well as short tables and chairs that a child could sit at for meals or lessons. On the opposite side of the room was a canopied bed with oversized pillows and a mountain of blankets surrounding a young, sleeping boy of perhaps four or five.

"He should not have been unsupervised in the stables," hissed a man with a crown atop his head. The man could not have been older than thirty years or so, yet he held himself with great authority and presence. Jacinta barely glanced at the person whom the king was berating. Her eyes were only on the child.

"Hello," she said to him, though he did not immediately stir. The child's head was wrapped in bandages. He did not open his eyes, but his small fingers wrapped around hers when she took his hand.

"Oh!"

Jacinta turned her head to see an older woman in the doorway. She had an ornate cane that she used to walk. Stark white hair was plaited into an elegant braid over her shoulder. She stared directly at Jacinta with piercing eyes.

"Hello, dearest," Jacinta said to her.

The woman stumbled backward to sit down in a chair by the door.

"Mother?" The man with the crown rushed to the old woman's side, but she didn't acknowledge him. She didn't drop her eyes from Jacinta.

"I'm not here for you," Jacinta promised.

"You're not?" The woman pressed her hand to her heart. "But then . . ." Her eyes jumped to the boy lying in the bed. "Please, not him."

"I'm sorry," Jacinta said. "His time has come, and he will be at peace."

The woman choked out a sob and buried her face in her hands. A dragonfly landed on the top of her cane and twitched its wings in greeting. The two others in the room tried to comfort the old woman and ask her what was happening, but Jacinta turned away to look at the boy. He stared at her with a small smile on his face.

"You're here for me?" he asked Jacinta. She nodded. The boy sighed in relief. "I don't wanna hurt anymore."

"Come with me, and you will feel no more pain," she promised with her arms outstretched. The boy sat up and hugged her without hesitation. She picked him up from his bed and turned to find Araceli, but realized another presence was in the room. A reaper had appeared with a cloak black as night.

"Hello, Jacinta," the reaper greeted.

"Welcome, Nayeli," Jacinta smiled at her. "I haven't seen you in so long."

"Too long," Nayeli agreed. She gestured at Araceli. "You have your sister with you. No wonder the soul reavers are out in force."

"You know me?" Araceli asked. "Wait, what do you mean?" She grabbed Jacinta's sleeve. In Jacinta's embrace, the boy's arms tightened around her neck.

"The soul reavers eat souls," Nayeli said, her voice low and vibrant like a stringed bass. "What better place to eat souls than in the peaceful realm?"

Araceli gasped. Jacinta felt a chill go through her. She grabbed Araceli without hesitation and concentrated. She saw the way Nayeli turned her attention to the old woman but they did not linger. In the blink of an eye, they were back in Araceli's realm. Jacinta gently transferred the soul in her arms to Araceli and backed away.

"What are you doing?" Araceli asked, her big brown eyes wide in surprise.

"I have to move fast and collect the rest of the souls," Jacinta said. "I'll meet you at home for dinner."

"Jacinta, wait," Araceli cried. "What will happen with the soul reavers?"

"I will fight them," Jacinta promised. "Do not fear. I will never let anything harm you or my souls."

"I can help you," Araceli protested. "Please don't go without me."

"Hermanita, you are peace," Jacinta said. "You should be here to look after your realm. Taking you with me could give the soul reavers the opportunity they need to breach your realm. If I need someone to help me fight, I'll call for the other reapers."

"Promise me you will ask for help," Araceli begged her.

"I promise," Jacinta said. She kissed the top of her sister's head and pressed something into Araceli's hand. Then she disappeared before Araceli could say anything else. When she was gone, Araceli looked at what she held. Jacinta had left her their satchel of food. Tied around one of the straps was marsh grass looped together with a bit of twine. Araceli wondered if it was a memento from her sister's quiet lunch with a baby in her arms.

The moment she appeared in the realm of the living, Jacinta's neck prickled. Her body moved instinctively as she ducked and rolled out of the way. Gnashing teeth and a slash of claws bit through the place where she'd stood moments ago, but they did not find their home. From her belt, she unsheathed a wooden stick. Clutched in her fist, it expanded in length, responding to the pulse of magic in her veins.

She stared at the soul reavers that ranged around her. There were eight of them, beautiful catlike creatures on four legs with golden fur, black leopard-like spots and two stripes that traveled from their noses, up between their eyes to the tops of their heads. Their white whiskers twitched in agitation as they bared their fangs. They stared back at her with deadly gazes the color of honey and rumbled a vicious sound in their chests that made her hair stand on end.

"You seek to steal the souls that I protect," she said to them. "I hold no ill will toward you, but you will not be fed today. Go home."

"We do not answer to you, *Reaper*," one of the soul reavers spat. "We hunger."

The other soul reavers supported his statement with hissing growls of their own.

"We used to be allies," Jacinta cried out. "The reapers never treated you poorly. Please turn back from this path."

"It's too late for that," the leader said dismissively. "We've acquired a taste for them. We spent so long protecting them, not knowing how *delicious* they'd be. Think of all the souls we could have eaten when we were so foolishly working beside the reapers."

Jacinta shook her head in dismay. Sorrow threatened to distract her but she refused to allow it. She saw the way the soul reavers widened their stances and flattened their ears. She shifted her weight to the balls of her feet, resigned to fight them and drive them away once more. These were once her friends. The weight of their transgressions was a burden she could not bear.

The tension in the air was almost palpable as the soul reavers lowered their heads and shifted to her right and left so some could circle behind her. She stepped backward too, matching their movements and refusing to let them gain access to her unprotected back. Two pops of air at her side made her quickly assess who had appeared to join the fight.

"I'm here," Paloma said from her left. She lifted a golden sword. "Araceli called me."

"I wouldn't miss this," Nayeli said from her right. In her hands was a reaper's scythe. "I've alerted the other reapers to be wary."

"Were you just going to face this on your own?" Paloma sounded angry with her. "When are you going to learn how to ask for help?"

Jacinta winced. When Paloma was upset, it was usually for good reason. She had a "say sorry immediately" policy when it came to her sister, but now was not the time to get distracted. She had prepared herself to take on the soul reavers alone. Now she had two others she needed to keep an eye on and protect. Paloma and Nayeli could no doubt hold their own, but Jacinta would cover them to make sure they remained unharmed.

The leader of the soul reavers coiled his muscles and launched his body at Jacinta. She swung her fighting stick up, catching the reaver's jaw, and then twisted the stick around and smacked the stunned reaver backward. The other reavers did not hesitate. They joined the fray, leaping for Paloma and Nayeli. Sweat beaded on Jacinta's brow as she fought the soul reavers, fighting with Paloma or Nayeli if either seemed to be overwhelmed. She saw a soul reaver scratch a deep wound in Paloma's arm, but her sister did not falter. She hissed something between her teeth and battled on. Jacinta stayed close to her side until the last of the soul reavers gave up and turned away, screaming into the sky and barreling through a cloud of dragonflies in their retreat.

THE SISTERS' cottage was bathed in moonlight when Jacinta returned. Warm lantern light and her sisters' voices filtered through the open windows, welcoming her home. After the battle with the soul reavers, she'd thanked Nayeli and helped Paloma bandage her arm, but the call of souls in need of collection had tugged at her until she was forced to leave Paloma sooner than she wanted.

The soul reavers had not reappeared. Jacinta wasn't sure if it was because Araceli no longer traveled with her or if they were regrouping to fight another day. She knew she'd see them again, but she hoped she'd always be stronger and faster and able to protect the souls in her charge.

As she latched the gate shut, a dragonfly landed on her hand. She carefully lifted it up to the level of her eyes and smiled at it.

"Hello, little one," she said. "Thank you for greeting me."

The dragonfly twitched its wings and then fluttered away to join its friends. Jacinta loosened the brooch on her cloak. She was tired, and hungry, and she wanted to see how her sisters fared. But she needed a moment to herself. Just a few minutes to silently reflect on the souls she'd collected today.

The girl with sickness.

The brothers of war.

The baby in the marshes.

The king's son.

After the battle with the soul reavers, she'd gone to collect seven more souls. Seven more children whose time had come. From her pocket, she pulled out the trinkets they'd left behind and silently honored their memories. She had a well-loved rock. A girl's hair bow. A necklace with an animal's tooth strung on it. A broken blue crayon.

"Hermana?" Jacinta wiped at her eyes and turned to see her sisters in the open doorway. Araceli held Paloma's hand. Jacinta eyed the bandage wrapped around Paloma's arm and sniffled to clear her nose.

"Dinner is ready," Paloma said. Her tone was firm but her gaze was soft. "Get in here before it grows cold." Jacinta laughed at the audacity of her sister's tone as she followed them into the cottage. Death is not to be feared.

Just ask her sisters.

About Stefanie Contreras

Stefanie Contreras is a Latinx author of The Merry Maids sci-fi trilogy and two published short stories, Pestilence from the Autumn Nights anthology as well as The Warlock and the Crow from the Rituals & Grimoires anthology. She was born and raised in Phoenix, Arizona and graduated with an M.S. in Communications from the University of Oregon and a B.S. in both Journalism and Advertising from Northern Arizona University. She also is a board member for WriteHive and an officer with Geek Girl Brunch. For more information, visit her on Instagram and Tiktok @latinageekgirl or at latinageekgirl.com.

instagram.com/latinageekgirl

tiktok.com/@latinageekgirl

Don't Look Under the Bed
Chere Taylor

Don't look under the bed.

Kendra Wakefield stared at the glowing message from her iPhone in the comfort of her flower themed bathroom. Every morning, she inspected her gold and black braids for frizz, then she did her stretching exercises and finally caught up on emails with her phone. Kendra liked to perform all these actions before starting another glorious day as the Sweat or Regret's fitness instructor and owner.

But this morning she was greeted with that strange message coming from her Notes app of all places. How odd . . .

It's Jeremiah, she thought. *He snuck in here last night, wanting to apologize by leaving me a gift under my bed.*

Kendra squealed with delight and ran into the adjoining bedroom. She scrambled across the pink and purple comforter to poke her head underneath the bed frame.

Then the impossibility hit her. How could Jeremiah sneak into her bedroom when her apartment door was locked overnight? Jeremiah hadn't earned her key privileges yet. And wouldn't it be more convenient to simply text her instead of leaving an awkward message on her Notes app?

So who wrote that message?

Her head dangled upside down as she laid on the mattress, her long braids coiling onto the floor like miniature snakes. It would be an easy thing to lift the rose patterned bed skirt and confront any surprise waiting for her there.

Don't look under the bed.

Instead, Kendra scooted herself back into a sitting position, grinding her teeth in irritation that she was actually obeying the anonymous note. Where was the fearless black woman who defied all odds by owning and operating a gym at the tender age twenty-two? The Kendra that wore the label of *hard-headed,* and *an obstinate child* from foster parents and teachers alike with a sense of pride? Where was that Kendra Wakefield?

What stupid shit are you talking about? I'm not afraid to look under the bed. Wake up, Wakefield!

On second thought, she returned to reading and responding to emails before sliding out from under the blankets to take a shower. She left the bed unmade (Kendra's house cleaning skills left much to be desired) and when she stepped painfully on her finger barbell, she angrily kicked it back under the bed. The notepad message was forgotten.

Almost.

KENDRA GYRATED her hips to the Sweat or Regrets exercise music while urging her class to make those same bends at the waist. *One, two, three, four. Come on ladies, give me more!* All the while she secretly envied the wonderfully curvy bodies of her clientele. Kendra's own body was flat-chested, hard, and lean like a male's.

The hardness that was her body, and in her mentality as well, had always been a part of her. Ever since her fifteen-year-old mother tucked Kendra's premature newborn body into a shoebox along with the afterbirth and then packed said shoebox into the closet. *My God, Michaela! You were pregnant?* Kendra imagined her grandmother screaming upon her rescue, examining the premature infant with the bony limbs and thick skull. The tearless infant that had refused to cooperate in her own would-be demise. *Oh God, Michaela. Oh. My. God.*

So her hardness, her determination, became the key to her survival, and she cultivated it, nurtured it like a sapling until it grew into an Olympian-sized tree. But Kendra's rooted firmness couldn't distract her from thinking about the ominous message. What did it mean exactly? Its purpose? Was it a warning? From whom?

Kendra chanted again, "One, two, three, four! Pushing limits, wanting more!"

As if in direct response, the thought occurred to her . . .

I really should ask Jeremiah's opinion about this.

True, he had been acting a little strange lately, not always returning her phone calls or texts. But Jemmy was still her closest friend, romantically involved or not. He felt like a solution of some kind.

Abruptly Kendra walked out of the studio for a so-called bathroom break. She heard groaning and complaints from her students. Though one or two might have collapsed to the ground with relief.

While in the stall, she texted Jeremiah.

Lunch at the Magical Mall at 12:30?

He responded with a green check mark. Grinning Kendra re-entered the dance room.

Blissfully they returned to punishing their bodies together.

JEREMIAH ARRIVED in his business attire as always, wearing his smooth, bald head and beardless cheeks and chin with the confidence of a male model though Jeremiah had no particular interest in fashion. He worked as a paralegal for the Caracy Law Firm.

Kendra offered her lips to him and he barely grazed them with his own before plopping his food tray and soda down on the table. He turned the chair backwards and sat in that cool dude fashion of his.

"So?" he asked and took a giant bite from his foil-wrapped burrito. Kendra wrinkled her nose. She could smell the calories from across the table.

"That's all I get?" Kendra replied. "No hi or hello?"

Jeremiah sighed. "What exactly is it that you want, Kendra?" His eyes were cold.

Yes, our breakup is imminent, Kendra thought, *if it isn't already here.* Something fluttered inside her chest and she squashed it. There were real threats out there, like from whoever sent that stupid note, for example. She refused to feel fear over losing a man.

"You see this?" Kendra scooted her cell phone towards him. She tried to imitate his distant, business-like style.

Jeremiah glanced at her phone without picking it up.

"You wrote it?" she continued.

"Nope."

"Who do you suppose did?"

"How the hell should I know?"

"Do you think it's a stalker?"

Jeremiah shrugged and then made an elaborate show of checking his watch.

Kendra turned her eyes towards the floor. "I wish I understood why you hate me so much."

"I don't hate you, Kenny. I just can't play this game with you anymore. That nothing's happened between us. That there's no him!"

Kendra stood up so forcefully she almost knocked her chair over in the process.

"Because there *is* no him! The guy you're so jealous of came to visit the gym once, Jem. Once! I demonstrated the Back-to-Back twist to him. If you insist on reading more into it, well I can't help your paranoia."

Jeremiah laughed, a bitter sounding chuckle, and shook his head. "You just don't get it, do you?"

"What is there to get? Nothing happened. I don't even know the guy's name."

"Okay, I'm done." Jeremiah stood up and threw his napkin on his plate. "Please don't contact me again unless it's an emergency. I still care for you Kenny, in my way, but I just can't take this denial anymore."

And with that he was gone, the twice-bitten burrito still left on the table. Kendra blinked.

Well, fuck him too. She didn't need Jeremiah. She didn't need anybody. A child who had been abandoned to a shoebox knew how to survive. The answer was obvious anyway. Delete the note, and when she arrived home from work, look under the bed. Mystery solved and game over. It was as simple as that.

Kendra took out her phone and gazed at the message one last time . . .

Don't look under the bed.

. . . then she tapped the trash icon and the note melted away. It was a shame all of life's problems couldn't be as easily solved, with a single finger tap.

Kendra tossed the remains of Jeremiah's burrito into the wastebasket on her way to the car.

THE NOTE TRIED to re-insert itself in Kendra's thoughts and she squashed it with the same irritation and efficiency she did when swatting mosquitoes. In other words, not terribly efficient at all. Funny how she had assumed Jeremiah's uncouth breakup would be forefront in her mind. Instead, it was the note, its almost playful warning. *Just goes to show how mixed up my priorities are*, she thought with a grim smile.

When Kendra arrived home that evening, she went about her apartment switching on lights. The ceiling lamp in her bedroom tore the darkness with a savage brightness, as if it were a blazing spotlight shining on her unmade bed, daring her to touch it.

She tossed her gym bag on the bed and it landed with a soft thump. All the while she was holding her breath. Why? What was she waiting for? A cloud of flies to come swarming towards her from underneath the mattress, along with the melodramatic stench of death?

Kendra marched towards her bed, knelt down and pressed her head against the bare floorboards and peered with one eye closed. She could only see an inch of darkness. The bed skirt covered the rest.

Don't you normally relax with a glass of Sauvignon Blanc before dinner? Isn't that your normal routine? You don't have to do this right now.

Squeezing both eyes against the dark, she stretched her arm into the blackness and felt about with her finger tips.

Something thin and vile slipped around her wandering fingers.

Kendra screamed, a piercing, rat-like screech. She backed away from the bed, scraping her arm against the heavy bed frame in the process. The bed frame cut into her arm causing it to sting with pain. But the thing was still attached to her hand. It refused to let her go. She lifted her arm towards her face intending to strangle the creature . . .

. . . only to discover it was her bra strap wrapped around her fingers, the cups gently grazing her wrist.

She giggled out loud noting a slight edge of hysteria to her laughter. *That's what I get for being such a lousy housekeeper.* The truth was that there was nothing under the bed. Nothing. Except for dust bunnies and perhaps some more scattered underwear.

Kendra examined the top of her arm that was raw and red. Undoubtedly there would be a nasty scar once it healed.

Maybe nothing is under the bed . . . but I was damaged nonetheless.

She stood up and dusted herself off, deciding that that was enough drama for the day. It was now time to rinse her wounded limb and perhaps enjoy that glass of wine after all. There were no boogies under the bed, the same way Jeremiah was no longer in her life. It was time, in a sense, to get out of that fucking shoebox and return to the safe and comfortable blandness of her existence.

WHEN KENDRA RETURNED to her bedroom, dressed in her sleeping gown, phone already plugged and charging for the night, she was surprised that the spotlight sensation had not gone away. Indeed, it was more intense than ever, as if her bed were on a stage and she was part of a live performance. *Ladies and Gentlemen, watch our heroine as she fiercely defends herself from the terror lurking beneath the furniture in today's episode of . . . Below the Mattress!*

Come on Kenny, you can't afford to go to pieces like this. Besides, we've already established that there is nothing under the bed.

Wrong! We've established that there is nothing in the area that you've explored with your fingertips. We have not searched all the darkness underneath.

It was always a bad sign when she referred to herself as "we." As if there were two separate individuals hiding inside her head. One, an athletic, perfectly normal (well, normal-appearing anyway) woman with the strong desire to persevere no matter what, and the other a cramped and warped fetus, still struggling for every next breath. An individual who in her private, personal way, had never left the shoebox.

Uh-huh. Let's move this fucker once and for all. No more secrets and no more bullshit.

Grunting, she attacked the bed, a bulky, king-sized monstrosity built in an era before wood or light-weight metal were considered material for frames. She shoved, pulled, and pushed. Her wounded arm bled again on her dark skin. Eventually, she was able to shift the heavy furniture about ten inches.

In the process a small, bulbous piece of plastic rolled out from underneath the bed skirt. It made a circular turn and gently nudged Kendra's bare foot.

It's the finger barbell, remember? The fluttering sensation had woken in her chest again. *One of Jeremiah's gag gifts along with the finger towel and the finger sweatband. We don't need to concern ourselves with that now.*

She did however, pick it up, examining it more closely. No, this was no gag gift, but a child's toy. A garishly colored purple and green baby's rattle to be exact.

I just can't play this game with you anymore . . . Jeremiah's words slammed into her heart at warp speed.

No. Oh no, no, no no, no.

That nothing happened between us. That there's no him.

His name was Jay, short for Jeremiah Jr. A child who was loved by both his parents. Jay, who was not shoved into a shoebox out of youthful ignorance, but birthed by c-section in a hospital like a normal child.

He had always been a serious infant. Rarely smiling, even when she cuddled him and called him her Itty Bitty One. He had a habit of clinging to a strand of her long, braided hair with a chubby fist. As if even he knew what kind of monster he had for a mother. *Don't forget me, Mama,* those solemn, unblinking eyes said. And she never did. No ma'am and no sir. Not until that Saturday morning when she was compelled to open the Sweat or Regret fitness center personally because her regular manager called in sick. Instead of dropping off her six-month-old infant at his father's house . . .

No, no, no. Kendra dropped the rattle and pushed both hands against the sides of her head as if she could force the memory out of her skull.

. . . she had accidentally left him dozing in the car seat at the Fitness Center's parking lot. It was a warm summery morning that weekend, and the temperature inside her car rose to an astonishing 140 degrees.

No, no, no, no, no, no, no.

She dropped to her knees with misery so great that all she could do was whisper "no" in the face of it. No, she didn't forget her most precious possession in the world. No, she wasn't the irresponsible parent her own teen mother had been.

What did you do to him afterwards, you fucking bitch? Did you stuff him under your bed in a shoe box? Is that why you're so scared to look under the bed?

Suddenly, Kendra became sure that this was exactly what she had done. After all, a woman who could forget the existence of her own son twice, once in a car seat and again in a mad pursuit for self-preservation . . . that same woman could have access to that sort of evil thinking too. Like mother, like daughter. Self-hatred wouldn't allow herself to put it beyond her capabilities.

She buried herself underneath the bed, not caring if her wound opened further. Not even caring if she died in the process. It would be her deserved punishment to die with her already dead son.

As Kendra squirmed under the steel frame, making swimming motions on the cold, bare, floor, the darkness never abated. But she found no shoe box. No underwear, no toys. Not even the expected dust bunnies. The bed had depleted all of its secrets.

Of course Jeremiah Junior wasn't buried in a shoe box, she scolded herself, panting heavily. *He was in a casket with a proper funeral. I remember it now.*

Kendra laughed and the darkness swallowed it up, muffling her voice, making it sound like she was buried legions below the earth. But there was nothing underneath the bed. There never was anything there at all. All that fear over an anonymous note.

Wait a minute...

Nothing. No life, no peace. Just a dead, sullen existence. An emptiness born of desperation, where routine was meant to suppress all terrible ideas and impulses. Here, in this cool darkness she could find blessed forgetfulness. All flaws forgiven.

Just hold on a sec...

She saw it in the form of a swirling void.

A depravity that had always been there. It was this void that caused her to forget young Jay. There was a monster under the bed after all. But it was a friend, not a terror. She wanted it, needed it. She could be free yet again. Of the guilt. Of missing her baby boy. Inside the void, Jay didn't exist. All she had to do was open her mind to it. Embrace it.

But some small part of her still screamed and struggled. *Do you want to betray Jay all over again?*

"Siri!" she screamed, her muted voice barely penetrating through the mattress and the bed skirt. "Note to self! Don't look under the bed! Don't forget Jay again! Don't—"

And the void enveloped her.

Kendra woke on top of her bed, smothered in her comforter and sheets, yet feeling renewed. Her phone shone brightly on the bedside table which was unusual for that time of the morning. She picked it up.

Don't look under the bed.

She stared at the glowing message from her iPhone which was part of her waking ritual. Every morning she inspected her gold and black braids for frizz, next did her stretching exercises, and finally caught up on her emails with her phone. Kendra liked to perform all these actions before starting another glorious day as Sweat or Regret's fitness instructor and owner.

But this morning she was greeted with that strange message coming from her notes app of all places. How odd . . .

About Chere Taylor

Chere Taylor enjoys wasting many hours of her life buried in a good book or binge watching bad cinema on Netflix. She has a passion for reading, writing and almost everything involving the works of Stephen King. She is currently working on her first novel. You can find her stories in *Another Realm, A Thin Slice of Anxiety, The Chamber, Granfalloon,* and *Books 'n Pieces Magazine.* She's also been known to lurk around her Inkitt account as Lunamoongoddess1 at https://www.inkitt.com/LunaMoonGoddess1.

Naija Babylon

Molara Wood

A thin stream breaks away from the splatter on the kitchen floor, snaking red towards the fridge. Your vision blurs momentarily as your mind drifts back to Anti Denrele's call. She hoped you were not on your period because she needed you to come with her to the mountain. Orí Òkè, she called it. Facilities there were threadbare and the fewer the personal exigencies the better. Women are encouraged to stay away during their time of the month, she said.

Just as you started to wonder what any of this has to do with you, what business you had with some mountain, more of her words spilled into your ears. The person who was to accompany Anti Denrele to the mountain was no longer available. And, going by the way Anti Denrele clucked, breathing short and fast on the phone, you reasoned she was altogether unsettled by what seemed an otherwise inconsequential development. So, you said yes, what the heck. You would go with her to the mountain. Replaying the conversation in your head and turning back to the mess on the floor, you only absently hear your mobile phone ringing from elsewhere in the flat.

. . .

Before Anti Denrele's call, before the splattered floor, you had scrolled across yet another Japa post on Twitter. This time from someone you know. He posted a photo of himself on a plane. "Goodbye Nigeria, the evil you have done is enough," said the caption. He had joined the ever-increasing wave out of the country, unabating since soldiers opened fire on protesting youths in your city. "Something broke in me after they crushed the protest," the friend later told you by direct message, the text was bookended by a crying emoji. "They fired on our dreams."

You have lost count of how many of your friends and colleagues have left the country in the last year, often without a heads-up until they land on the other side. Even the Instagram vendor you used to order the occasional Ayamase soup pack from one day changed her service location to Birmingham, UK. You do not plan on leaving. You have Wale and you both have your tech jobs, imperfect though the prevailing social conditions. Yet here you are thinking that, even if you cannot change the big things, you can better navigate the small ones, things over which you might hope to exercise some control. Like a spillage on your kitchen floor.

You set about cleaning the floor, and by the time you pause to take a deep breath, swiping sweat from your forehead with the back of one hand, you have come to a decision. Time you got a few things off your chest, you think. Time you shared a bit with Wale about how you're feeling. "About me, about us," you say out loud as you wring the red into the sink and get back down, knees on the floor, hitching your skirt further up with both elbows so as not to stain the fabric with your blushing palms. You rehearse the conversation in your mind as you toil on the floor.

"In this country where it seems every other person is leaving, it feels to me like those of us who would be left behind ought to satisfy ourselves on some small level and insist on a few basic things, even if not possible in relation to the system, then at least with regard to ourselves, our dealings amongst ourselves, our relationships, how we treat each other."

It sounds to you like some bizarre rhyme to an unstated indignity, ill-defined and unacknowledged, perhaps even unreasoning.

And so, why ever not, you ask yourself. If Anti Denrele wants you to come someplace because she needs the company? Some prayer place? A fervently praying people praying ever more fervently as it all comes crashing down. Isn't that always the approach in this country? If Anti Denrele needs to go on a spiritual retreat, then she needs to go on a spiritual retreat. And if you are to come along for the ride, you might as well make the best of it, you reason. Who knows? Up a mountain, you might grasp at something flitting and receding in the back of your mind as you wipe the floor clean.

"I WAS DEALING with a bit of a situation earlier," you begin, when you return Wale's call. "The coffee decanter broke and spilled hibiscus tea on the kitchen floor. And I'm talking steaming hot. I had to clean up the mess, and quickly too."

"Why zobo in the coffee decanter in the first place?" Wale asks. "Hibiscus tea, that's zobo, right? Some like it hot, I guess."

You tell him you have adopted a versatile approach to the decanter ever since the herbal tea stoneware's metal strainer rusted all of a sudden. Must be the humidity or something. Or poor quality. What with substandard goods flooding the market as the naira capsizes against the dollar.

"I use my coffee decanter a lot, perfectly fine for loose tea," said a guest of yours once, when you mumbled an apology about not using the proper pot to serve oolong. The visitor's response put you at ease, and you had put the decanter to creative use from then on. Until this morning. You laugh on the phone to your boyfriend. You don't mention that the oolong drinker has also left the country.

"A crack had formed at the bottom of the decanter," you tell

Wale. "Can you believe it? I had to move fast lest the mess got on my clothes."

"Rust, cracks, just like this country of ours, eh?"

You check your watch and tell Wale you've got to go.

"Where to?"

"Out of town. Back tomorrow. I'll call when I have connectivity. You know what our telecoms can be like, out there on expressways and in the countryside."

"Just be careful. They are kidnapping people for ransom out there."

"I hear you."

"Don't do what I wouldn't do," he said. "Don't go and Japa on me."

<hr>

YOU ARE A TINY BIT CURIOUS. Why all the drama with the mountain? What if Anti Denrele herself is joining the Japa wave, checking out of the country with those leaving in the thousands? In her fifties, she is outside the core demographic, but one can never tell. Japa is an infectious condition, and it's catching everyone in sight. You needn't have worried, you later find out. Anti Denrele isn't going anywhere. Someone did Japa, however. Simisola, the intended companion on the spiritual retreat. Everything agreed and planned, only for her to message via WhatsApp the night before to say she was in Canada.

"Canada, how?" Anti Denrele says as you set out on the journey, settling into the back of a road-weary station wagon she had booked for the trip. "Didn't Simisola know she was going to Canada when we made the plans a week ago? She could have told me she wouldn't be able to make it because she was relocating."

"Japa," you say.

"Ehn?

"Japa. That's the term for it. People don't relocate anymore, at least not when they're heading out from Naija. They Japa. They cut and run. For good, because they can't see a future for themselves or their children in this country."

"The point is," Anti Denrele says, drawing audible breaths and exhaling in short puffs through her mouth, "Canada is not a place one goes at the drop of a hat. Not from Nigeria anyway. There must have been a long process with the embassy, flight tickets, packing up, selling up, resigning her job, putting things in order. It's not something that takes you by surprise. This is someone I spoke to almost every day. And she never breathed a word."

You shrug. "We get that a lot these days. The surprise element seems to be key. Superstitious society. Many people think their nemesis could be someone close to them."

"Am I the flying witch that will cause Simisola's immigrant visa to be revoked or her plane to drop out of the sky? She could have at least done me the courtesy of goodbye. As close as we have been, we owed each other that."

Anti Denrele mops her face and her neck with a large yellow handkerchief that heroically refuses to become sodden. The handkerchief is embossed with a name and a date you can't make out in the flurry of movement; likely a party favour from someone's birthday or funeral. Anti Denrele's intermittently steaming face, her misty skin on which sweat bubbles up magically every fifteen minutes or so. Her flustered breathing every time the affliction flashes across her face. The balls of sweat rolling down her neck and pooling in tiny creases in the skin before she takes the handkerchief to them.

You look at her as she pants and mops her brows, though she hardly seems to notice your concern, more preoccupied with the heat whirling up and down within her. It is a mild day. Air fans in through the station wagon's windows, only half-wound down for security, but more cool gusts direct to the back than an AC. Anti Denrele had expressed a preference for natural ventilation rather than the vehicle's weak AC, which is in need of more freon gas, as the driver had said in an apologetic tone, his passengers well practised in the art of making do. And still Anti Denrele steams up, a sauna on a faulty clock timer. She rummages in her handbag, chucking items on the seat in the space between you. A pack of Evening Primrose Oil capsules, face wipes, a small Bible, a notebook. Eventually she fishes out a rechargeable handheld fan to commandeer onto her face. You wonder how the device could possibly outpace the whooshing from the windows. With her other hand, Anti Denrele tucks the other items back in the bag which she hugs to her midsection like a cushion.

You watch her, a less composed figure from the assured woman that took you under her wings some years ago. She really is in need of prayers, you think. You look out at roadside shacks selling bucolic enticements to wayfarers. You think about some older women in your extended family, overly fidgety at times, fussing over things, fanning their faces, swiping at themselves with their wrappers, skin glistening and dripping with perspiration as they wrestled with life's unending battles big and small. No one ever asked how they felt under their skins, if they were comfortable, if anyone could help take some of the pressure off . . . not to your hearing, anyway. You never gave much thought to their condition as individuals, the sudden bursts of frenetic sweating, or any challenges they might have had. None of it seemed remarkable then. You certainly never wondered if a similar fate awaited you. Not until now.

"Life may begin at forty, as they say, but your body is not confident of that fact; it starts to bail out on you," Anti Denrele says, seeming to read your thoughts. "It's the exhaustion that gets you sometimes," she says, almost to herself.

YOU HAVE JUST PASSED Ogere when you voice out your plan of calling Wale during the retreat.

"No phone network up there," Anti Denrele says, placing her

bag on the floor by her feet. "It's up above a forest, two states away."

You look at her quizzically. She looks serene, enjoying a bit of respite from the sweats.

"I promised I'd try to call," you say.

"Haba, it's disrespectful to be making calls on the holy mountain. To a man, for that matter. Haaa." Seeing your lowered eyes, she adds in a softer voice, "Well, you know, it may help to see this as your own spiritual retreat too. A night up there with the chill setting into your bones in the lashing wind . . . why do that as a mere co-traveller? The question is, what do you want out of this? That should be your focus, my dear, not a man."

She turns to the elderly driver ferrying you to your holy quarry. "*Ẹ nlẹ o, Baba,*" she says to him. "*Ẹ kú iṣẹ́.*" A greeting acknowledging that he's a diligent worker, transporting you safely on a route that's not without its dangers.

"*Ẹ ṣeun, Ma.*" He nods his appreciation.

She has used him several times before, she tells you with a wink, her voice low. He speaks only Yoruba, leaving her free to hold conversations in English with her travelling companions without being listened to.

Anti Denrele leans well back, her left shoulder in the nook by the car door, taking a moment before the heat rises again. Or is it the exhaustion, you wonder? You lean over and check the car lock to ensure the door is secure on her side. She does not seem to notice as you cast another glance at her. She is going to her spiritual retreat, of that she is certain. The rest is for you to figure out. You breathe deep, clasp and unclasp your hands. Something new about Anti Denrele's resolve, and you do not quite know what to make of it. Her performance of piety does not always cohere and it sometimes grates.

IN THE CHURCH Anti Denrele attends, the rumour was rife, once, that she was romantically involved with one of the church elders, a married man for that matter. Mr. Awosika was not bad-looking. Trim and well put together, face like a soul music love god from the seventies. "The kind of man that could make me commit, erm . . . before I was in Christ," you had heard the choir mistress say in an unguarded moment, looking at Mr. Awosika a bit of a way away. The choir mistress's eyelashes fluttered at some speed. Then she cleared her throat, adjusted her black wide-brimmed hat with the cream satin bow and moved in swift steps to berate a percussionist who'd arrived late for choir practice.

Mr. Awosika's ready charm and heady effect on the ladies made the presiding pastor regard him with the politest scorn, often hinting at that which propriety prevented him from saying. You sensed many a sermon point was targeted at Mr. Awosika for his suspected dalliance with Anti Denrele. The pastor's words were always tentative and diversionary, like the craven reprimand they were. You knew all this because you used to attend the same church. Mr. Awosika had a smile that lit up his ebony features as though from inside. His easy grace irked the pastor, who, as a joke-y aside during Bible Study one day, riffed on the supposed meaning of Mr. Awosika's name and its prefix, Awo, taken as it was from a reference in Yoruba belief to household gods. The kind of observation that made some members of the congregation bristle, since to them, traditional religious observance was demonic. A tactical manouvre by the pastor to discomfit the ageing lothario, to colour the water with the ink of an accusation that could not be uttered from the pulpit.

"We thank the ever dependable elder, the venerable Mr. Awosika for his generous contribution to the outreach programme," the pastor began. "He has been a force for good in the tabernacle of the Lord, despite all that his name might suggest. Awosika. It is Awo that does ìkà; Jesus does not do ìkà; God does not do evil." Several members of the congregation pursed their lips, their ardent gazes fixed on the pastor as they nodded, one or two emitting agreeing noises.

"Actually, that is not the meaning of my name," said Mr.

Awosika, who had risen to his feet, genial as ever, his voice tickled with mirth. He wore bùbá and ṣòkòtò cut from navy blue brocade, the top front panel threaded in intricate, pale lavender embroidery. His head was bare, in keeping with the practice requiring men to remove their caps on entering the house of the Lord. His hair formed scrunchy curls close to his scalp. You imagined some church women dreamt of digging their fingers in. He clutched a brown matte leather man-purse under one arm. All eyes turned in his direction, not a few of the women looking in soft-focus. Only Anti Denrele kept her eyes studiously on the pastor; illicit affairs require dedication, you thought.

"A name like Awosika is deep, ìjìnlẹ̀ Yorùbá, and can only be properly understood in the regional dialect. Awo does no evil. That is the meaning." Mr. Awosika sat back down, the ooohs and aaahs from the pews an indication that many in the congregation were converted to his interpretation. Better luck next time, pastor.

Three rows behind Mr. Awosika, Anti Denrele turned back to her Bible, a little smile playing at the corners of her mouth. They hardly ever interacted in church. But it was an elaborate façade that fooled no one. People ran into them at shopping malls, owambẹ parties, all sorts of places. She was often seen getting in and out of his car before and after church service, but since members of the flock were encouraged to give fellow worshippers lifts as much as practicable, you could all pretend that there was nothing untoward in the high regularity with which she hopped in and out of his BMW.

All that carry-on, only to pointedly ignore each other during the service. They fooled no one. Certainly not you. And since you were close to her, you got to see just how involved they were, always at each other's houses. The rest of the time, she never stopped talking about him. And still the pretence, even to you. Anti Denrele often lamented the rumours to your hearing, arms flailing, conscious of her own inability to dramatise a convincing refutal, and yet refusing to give up the act altogether.

Didn't these idle church gossips know he was married and his family lived in Ondo State, prompting him to go home to them once or twice a month? If he was going to have a mistress, would it be a divorcee like her? A middle-aged woman? And did these church people want the tittle-tattle to get to her married daughter in Abuja? What would people say? People were already saying what people would say, you thought. But she must be allowed her fiction, so you played along.

Anti Denrele said Mr. Awosika was pained by all the talk, despite his unruffled demeanour. According to her, he sometimes gnashed on his index finger like someone swearing a traditional oath, and almost had tears in his eyes whenever he thought about the unfairness of it all. "Ah, and God knows, Sister Denrele, that I have never seen your panties!" he apparently said.

That was the clincher for you. For why would an elder mouth the word "panties" in reference to the undergarments of a woman of a certain age, a fellow congregant in his church? How would he express that to her face, unless he had in fact crossed some boundary and been in some intimate corner with her? Assuming such a conversation happened, of course. No, she never fooled you. But you were not going to quibble with her, especially as she was considerably older than you. Mustn't forget that Yorùbá respect for older folks, however close you were to them and however absurd they were. It was enough that you knew you were being lied to. *Èniyàn méjì kìí pàdánù iró*, as your people say. Two people do not suffer the loss of a lie; between them, someone always knows a lie has been told. And in this matter, you were someone.

———

ONE DAY at Anti Denrele's place, you were in the washroom while she talked with a friend on her mobile phone. She did not know her voice carried over to where you were, or maybe she was just carried away by orgasmic recall as she talked about how great 'Mr. A' was in bed.

"I'm telling you: he presses that clutch all the way down!" she trilled.

Your face went hot over the sink. You stayed there a few minutes longer than necessary to compose yourself. "Cheerio," she said to the friend as she ended the call, when you emerged from the washroom.

You never looked at her the same way again. Part of you was happy for her that she had him, and that she was getting some, and a fine vintage of a man at that. Truth be told, few women in that church would have said no if Mr. Awosika had looked their way. The rumours were fueled in part by envy, you knew this. You left the church not long after, after they brought in a grouping system that divided almost everyone into youth and married. Youths were young persons up to the early twenties, and there was no other category but married couples. Each group would meet separately after the main church service on Sundays and participate in fringe church activities based on these categories. So, someone like you, over thirty and unmarried, where on earth did you fit? That was it for you. Hasta la vista, people of God.

You felt Anti Denrele and Mr. Awosika were protected to a good extent by their elder status, scandalous affair or no. She was above expectations of marriage; his wife was in Ondo State. You hoped to rejoin the church one day when you had found a man that would couple up with you for good, to stick a finger up at the church hierarchy and their fixed categories. Then you met Wale at the tech hub. And what an optimistic time it was: cooped up in each other's places. Well, mostly his, hence the reason he didn't know about your fondness for hot zobo served by decanter. Lying in each other's arms, doing stuff together. Two years went by in no time. Meeting up with his zany friends at the open air 'Point-and-Kill' joint off Herbert Macaulay Way, that was one highlight. You would look at a dozen or more catfish wriggling in the tank and each person would point to a thickly squiggly slippery wobble to be served up as pepper soup. Steaming, fragrant bowls bursting with spices and thick chunks of catfish would arrive on your table soon after. There was Wale's friend, Tobi, a cigarette always dangling from his lips and a different girl on his arm every other week. Eventually Rita became a recurring decimal on his arm, repeated the way celebrity women are said to repeat designer wear. Still, Rita was not able to banish Tobi's onesies, his one-time girls.

Any smugness you might have felt about being the constant girl on Wale's arm, him being the one you would one day take back to the church from which you had decamped, crumbled one night at the Point-and-Kill joint. Rita was there. You tended to loosen up a bit more with her; all you ever had to say to the other faceless girls was "hello." The joint was bubbling with conversation and low music, your table laden with sweating drinks as the pepper soup bowls gradually arrived to take pride of place before each person. The Madame who owned the joint, a woman swathed in a dark purple boubou that contrasted with the bleached-yellow of her skin, went round the tables to ensure her punters had everything they wanted. A cross between a matriarchal cloth merchant and a fast-talking burlesque performer, she traded suggestive banter with guests as she worked the tables.

"I asked after you on Monday," Tobi said to the Madame, holding a lighter to the tip of a cigarette as he spoke.

"Monday is my fucking day!" the Madame replied in a spreading, husky voice. A lived-in voice, a been-there-done-that kind of voice. Raucous laughter ensued. But Rita was not smiling. Face puckered, she turned to Tobi.

"You were here on Monday?"

"Umm . . . kind of." Tobi said, taking the cigarette out of his mouth. His Adam's apple moved up and down.

"What do you mean, kind of? Either you were here or you weren't."

"But you heard what I said to her already, nauw! What more do you want from me?" Tobi looked round at other faces as though for support. The Madam had moved on to another table. Wale, in his guise as your oh-so-dependable boyfriend and Tobi's friend, placed a restraining hand on his shoulder.

"I was here, so what?" Tobi said. He took a concentrated puff on his ciggie, his brows stitched together.

"What is this shit!" said Rita, her voice screeching through the bar, several decibels above the music. She sent her pepper soup bowl flying across the table, the broth splattering everywhere as those in its variegated path scampered for cover. Catfish cutlets dropped in a plop on the polythene table cover. Tobi, cigarette forgotten between his lips, clutched the edge of the table and held it down, fearing she might overturn that too. He blinked repeatedly and his face pulled and stretched, eyebrows raised in mute shock. Across the table, two people sat back down cautiously, wiping splashes of pepper soup off their outfits with paper napkins that left tiny white bubbles on their fabrics, looking up with defeated eyes and wiping some more, seeing no one to care or apologise for their share in the ruin of the night.

"What is this shit!" Rita kept saying as she dissolved into tears, thrashing and shaking all over. You got up, took her by the shoulders and led her away from the table as the Madame followed behind, having stopped to reassure customers that everything was under control.

You consoled Rita, you and the Madame. You dabbed at her face with tissues in the yellow light above the toilet mirror, adjusted her wig.

"If not for jìgìjìgì, what does anybody need a man for?" said the Madame, with a humping movement of her hips.

Rita laughed. Fatai Rolling Dollar's *She Go Run Away* strained out of the speakers as Madame led you both back to the table, dancing and singing along to the lyrics as she did so. The table had been wiped clean, meanwhile, leaving no trace of the mess of earlier. After you were seated, Rita drew her chair away to leave a space between her and Tobi, the Madame sashayed over to a nearby table to treat them to a shimmy, hips swaying, arms wide, and they sang and clapped along. You caught the mood and nodded to the rhythm. More than the Point-and-Kill, regulars came for this kind of escapism, the hint of permissiveness, the lax atmosphere where no one remembered if you came with a different partner the last time. Until Rita deigned to ask Tobi if he came on Monday, since he likely came with a different girl.

The tension coaxed and soothed itself away as Madame slinked over to another table. The whole joint chorused Rolling Dollar's ode to the need for men to work harder to keep their women, otherwise, "She Go Run Away."

Soon, fresh bowls of catfish pepper soup arrived for you and Rita, on the house, Madame's orders. Complete with pink tumblers of chapman. She nodded from across the room when you waved your thanks, her smile big and boxy.

"So, why put up with it?" you said to Rita as you rolled the ice in your chapman with the straw. "Why stay with him if he's a philanderer? Why not walk away?"

"I would if I could, but I like him. I really, really care about him." And then, rolling her eyes up as though into her skull, she guffawed as she said, "And the sex is good."

"Sex. That big a deal, huh?"

"Oh yeah." Rita looked at you like "duh?" and laughed with a snort, then got serious again. "It is a deal-breaker, com'on, are you kidding me? Of course, it is. A guy's got to hit the bullseye. And if he doesn't give head, things will come to a head. And that's on that." She clicked her fingers, moving her head back and then forward with attitude as they do on reality shows. "I used to date this guy that liked getting but wouldn't give. I was out of there before you could say cunnilingus."

"Rita!!" You smacked her playfully on the thigh.

"Huh-huh?"

"A lot of Nigerian men are like that, though, or so I hear."

"Me, I could never stand for that. It's the principle of it, a question of dignity. Either we have intimacy or we don't, no half measures." Rita looked over at Tobi, who was fumbling with his packet of Rothmans, yet to shake off earlier events. "Tobi is committed to my pleasure," she said, her voice turning light and feathery, her eyes glistening.

The pepper soup bowl was losing steam, so you decided to give it some attention and picked up your spoon. "If only he would stay faithful, I guess."

"Female pleasure is a right, non-negotiable," Rita said with the stridency of one delivering a manifesto, nostrils flared. "And beware when a man refuses to give head; he's probably giving it to someone else."

"Honestly, Rita, I'm trying to eat here!"

"Oops, sorry." She picked up her spoon with a giggle.

Too late. She'd left you with a disquieting thought that stayed with you even as you left the Point-and-Kill joint.

"Tobi obviously prioritises Rita's pleasure," you said to Wale in the car on the way to his place.

"What, we are measuring ourselves by their relationship now, are we?" he asked, looking sideways at you before turning back to focus on the road, tightening his grip on the steering wheel.

"I'm going home," you said on arrival at his place, and got yourself an Uber. It's been months and you haven't been back at Madame's joint and you can't say you miss the place.

"Oh, how could I have left that fan behind?" Anti Denrele says, drawing you out of your reverie as the station wagon crosses the bridge at Asejire Dam. Her rechargeable fan's battery is drained and the vehicle's charging port is shaky, and now she laments having forgotten to bring her paper fan as back-up. "Thankfully it will be cooler on the mountain. We leave first thing tomorrow, anyway."

"Do you go to the mountain often?" you ask.

"Two or three times a year, when I feel a need to reconnect in the spirit, or when there's something specific I want to pray for, or a yoke I need to break."

"And which is it on this occasion?"

"A situation I need strength to extricate myself from. A man."

"Hmm." You've both silently agreed to pretend you don't know she is talking about Mr. Awosika.

Anti Denrele shrugs. "I mean, he is nice and everything, we've had some great times. But he's never helped me out financially. If I have a flight or something major or out of the ordinary to spend on, I do it all myself. He just never offers. And I've been foolish enough to help this man out with my own funds on occasion, and he takes, and he sends money home constantly to his family. Oh, did I mention he has a family? He takes full responsibility for them. Which is fine. But what about me? Don't I deserve someone who stands in the gap sometimes, who says 'I'll take care of it?'" She looks into your eyes as she speaks, her head bobbing, her expression searching and open, lifting years from her face.

"It's a tough one, Anti," you tell her, pausing to look out the window at a commercial bus careening past, laden with squashed passengers and misshapen strapped-on loads. You turn back to Anti Denrele. "Could it be this perception everyone has that you're a strong woman who's self-sufficient and fends for herself, even gives to others? Could it be that? Maybe that's how he sees you?"

"Yeah, but there's shades to everything, abi? I mean, it's taken me all this time to recognise the situation with this man for what it is. And what it is, is a kind of disrespect. A kind of disregard. It's a cop-out to say because someone can do stuff for themselves, they never ever need someone else to do stuff for them, that they are not deserving of softness. If you care about someone, you'd want to do things for them, their capacity notwithstanding. It's not greed. It's not entitlement. I just want a bit of care. I want him to care enough to go out of his way sometimes. If I'm in a bit of a fix, he shouldn't be comfortable watching me struggle, but that's been my experience with this man, and now I've had it. I'm done."

You are glad the driver speaks no English. You travel for a long while in silence, rocking when the station wagon slows down to dip in and out of the odd pothole or goes over a speed bump, or weaves out of the way of a trailer or an intransigent danfo bus packed with somnolent travellers.

The sun is waning and the air is cooler by the time you turn back to Anti Denrele, speaking as though you've been in conversation all the while.

"And you are not worried about being alone, especially . . .?"

"At my age?" She shakes her head emphatically. "Other men will come along. And if they don't, so be it."

"What about sex, if you don't mind my asking?"

"What about it?"

"I dunno . . ."

"I mean, since when has a man been necessary for that, with everything one can buy on the internet?"

"I guess so." You feel as though an insect has crawled across your cheek and fallen away. You shift in your seat.

"Anyway, enough about the ways of the flesh. We're nearly there." Anti Denrele points at a peak just visible above the trees diagonally right in the near-distance. She adjusts herself on the seat, too, an expectant smile on her face.

The station wagon turns on a small corner whose only distinguishing feature is a huge billboard bearing the legend, ORÍ ÒKÈ ÌFIHÀN – HOLY MOUNTAIN OF REVELATION, and you start up a narrow dirt road hedged by boulders and scattered bushes. The boulders form a more concerted presence the further in you go.

Anti Denrele, still smiling, turns to you. "Like I said, you've come this far; might as well pray for something."

The mountain looms and seems to block out the sky as the vehicle rocks ever nearer in its shadow.

THE FOLLOWING MORNING, you rise in the blur of a half-seeing dawn. Hazy figures, mostly in white, straighten onto their feet all around, while others remain where they had settled in the small hours. They lay in their selected spots in the small rises and crevices and plateaus that contour the great rock face. You try to clear your head, thinking back to the rapturous vigil of the night before, service starting at 11 p.m. and ending at 1 a.m.

The day awakens slowly and the forest gradually unveils itself from under the mist as viewed from up here. You fold your blankets and stuff them in Anti Denrele's holdall, and the two of you begin your descent, picking your way barefoot on the rock and weaving past the heads and feet of prostrate pilgrims, some asleep, some praying in low voices, heads bobbing in fervent supplication. You place one hand on your waist and stretch a little and yawn, your body leaden from a night on the bed of rock. You'd both have to join one of the first commercial buses setting off from the foot of the mountain, Anti Denrele explains. You had let Baba and his station wagon go after he dropped you off yesterday. First stop would be Ibadan, from where you could get a more comfortable ride to Lagos. You nod. Everything is new, a revelation, carrying with it the muted promise of dawn.

"You know, Anti, I almost didn't want to come, when you said the stuff about periods," you say. "Why the restriction? I said to myself. But now I see it would be impractical."

"Exactly. Even now, we're better off showering when we get home than to join the queues for a few corrugated iron bath sheds; leave them for those staying several days. Speaking of periods, not having to deal with them anymore is surely one positive thing about this phase of my life. You know what they say, always a silver lining."

Anti Denrele has reached the foot of the mountain and is searching for hers among masses of slippers and sandals left here by their owners, since no footwear is allowed up on Orí Òkè. Something about it being sacred ground. You are dabbing at your face and around the corners of your eyes and mouth with a wet wipe as you arrive at the bottom. Having found her footwear, Anti Denrele relieves you of the holdall and goes ahead to secure spaces on a waiting bus. You peer about for your slip-ons, your eyes scanning the ground. Large male feet slough off a pair of open-toed brown leather slippers some paces in front of you, and your gaze rises to a familiar face. You squint for a moment to be sure it's not a trick of dawn. You've never seen him without a cigarette dangling from his lips.

"Tobi!"

"Why, this is a surprise," he says, his smile radiant in the brightening morn. It's the first time you're noticing the small gap in the top row of his teeth. He is robed in an ankle-length soutane made of white, billowy cotton. A philanderer recast as an angel.

"Fancy seeing you in a place like this," you say breathlessly. "What are you doing here?" Your eyes dip at the triteness of your query, for what are you yourself doing here, in a place like this?

His gaze does a 180, sweeping up towards the peak and back down to focus on your face. You sense his familiarity with the place. It's not his first time.

"A place like this? I was raised in the Yorùbá church, I'll have you know," he says genially, his smile undefeated. "My late mum used to come here, and sometimes I came with her, so it's a part of me. So much so, I have to be here now . . . a last prayer and testament before I check out of Naija Babylon."

"You're leaving?" You move clockwise in a half circle around him, stepping absently on forlorn footwear as you do so.

"To Canada. Rita and I."

"Canada?"

"I'm afraid so. Japa time. I'm owed a year's salary at work; Rita hasn't been able to get a job since she finished her national youth service. Sky-rocketing inflation, no light, insecurity everywhere, police brutality . . . At some point, one has got to ask oneself: for how long will I continue in this situation, hoping things get better when they only get worse? And knowing the kind of life my skills can get me elsewhere? We're checking out."

He throws his face up as though in exultant expectation of rain. "A new start, and we can't wait."

"Rita . . . but I thought you . . . she . . ."

Tobi nods and smiles. "She is the one. Took me a while to see it. And now, I feel so blessed to be doing this with her. Enough triangulating."

"Oh. That's great news." Your palms are spread open. You look about you to the left and to the right, searching for you don't know what. You can hardly hug your boyfriend's friend at the foot of a holy mountain. You take a couple of steps back. "I'm so happy for you both. I'm really happy for Rita."

"Thank you. Thank you so much."

"Oh well, I have to go. Good luck."

"You know . . ." Tobi says, almost as an afterthought, from behind you as you start down the last of the wide concrete steps at the very bottom. Having found your slip-ons, you clutch them in one hand.

"Yes?" You turn as Tobi moves closer, stepping gingerly on his bare feet, one hand held out Christ-like, his eyes filled with kindness, a striving to leave you with something, a parting gift worthy of the venerated ground you are standing on.

"You know," he begins again, in a voice made wispy in your ears by a light wind scaling down the mountain. "I believe Wale will make a better go of things now. I'm certain of it, in fact, especially since other plans fell through."

"Other plans?"

Tobi hunches one shoulder and turns his head from side to side, looking dog-eyed at you. "Well, we were processing this Japa thing at the same time, but his own application . . . It didn't work out. He kind of had someone . . . someone . . . over there, he may have told you . . . But that's off the table now."

"I see." Your voice sounds far off, as though whistling up the mountain on the breeze. You sway a little. Tobi's features shift and become indistinct as your eyes pool with water.

"I'd better go," he says, stepping backwards so that he doesn't see the lone tear roll down your face. "I am only here a couple of hours before I head back out," he adds. "Our flight is tonight. Still some packing to do. I'll keep in touch!"

The bus has filled up by the time you reach it, dabbing at your eyes with the sleeve of your kaftan. Anti Denrele has paid for two seats and saved one for you. She is busy shuffling with her backside and shoulders on the seat, getting other passengers to shift for a bit more space. You are thankful she is too distracted to see your face. An hour or so later, you are nearing Ibadan, all cool and quiet as the bus busts ahead in the shell-white morning, the windows open and a crisp breeze whooshing in, banishing Anti Denrele's heat spells. You have not observed her skin spritzing up since your arrival in the light chill of the mountain. Now she has dozed off beside you, her upper body rocking gently with the motion of the bus.

And now you can see scattered housing on the outskirts of Ibadan. Not long now before the familiar sight of hundreds of rusted roofs running up and down the undulating landscape of the sprawling city. Anti Denrele is awake and looking at you.

"Now that you have been to Orí Òkè, would you say it was worth it?" She keeps her voice low, though many of the other passengers are sleeping.

"Oh yes. I feel like something has shifted, for sure," you tell her. "Scales fallen off-a me eyes." You chuckle without mirth.

"And so, what will it all mean, I wonder?"

"I also have a man to shake off, that's what I think it means, Anti. Time to fly solo."

Ibadan spreads wider and wider as the bus, a white eighteen-seater with blue stripes on its sides, parts the city through. Rusted roofs are floating by. Anti Denrele nods off again. You make a note to buy a paper fan at the first stop in Iwo Road before boarding the onward vehicle for Lagos. Handy for when Anti Denrele's sweats hit, as they certainly will. And you never know what kind of traffic you may yet encounter on the Long Bridge into Lagos, so she might well need a fan in the gridlock. You smile, remembering your cracked decanter. You're going to need a new one in Naija Babylon.

ABOUT MOLARA WOOD

Molara Wood is a writer, journalist and editor based in Lagos, Nigeria. She is the author of "Indigo", a collection of short stories. She won the John La Rose Memorial Short Story Competition and received a Highly Commended Award from the British Broadcasting Association for her fiction.

 x.com/molarawood

 instagram.com/molara_wood

Subbed Out

Sandhya Singh

It was a totally ordinary kind of day. After school I had volleyball practice, as usual. Only that Coach Riley wasn't there today and there was another guy we hadn't seen before. But he ran a good practice. And we had a sub for English, but that wasn't unusual because Ms. Crawford had been away a lot this year. And Mr. Singh didn't show up for Math so we had a spare, which was great because Mr. Singh was always picking on me like he expects more of me because I'm Brown or something.

Everything looked normal as I walked up to the house. Buster came running out to greet me before I even got to the front door, so I almost didn't notice the HVAC van in the driveway. Buster whimpered and tried to walk between my legs. I picked him up and gave him a good scratch behind his tiny fluffy ears.

When I opened the front door and went in, I thought I'd just see Dad sitting at his desk at the far end of the living room. But there was another guy sitting in Dad's chair, not Dad.

"Hey Rajesh," he said, as if he'd known me all his life.

"Hey," I answered automatically. Was I supposed to recognize him? One of my dad's colleagues, maybe? But I didn't see Dad anywhere, and for some reason, I started to feel anxious.

Then I remembered the van outside. "You the furnace guy?" I asked, but he wasn't wearing the blue overalls with the company logo and why would he know my name?

He got up from the desk and started walking toward me. I took a step back. Buster whimpered more. I was getting freaked out by the way this guy was looking at me. Like he was worried but trying to hide it by being cool.

"Well, I should just get to the point Rajesh," he said. "I will be your new father."

"What the heck, man," I said. "Where's my dad?" My stomach was lurching. He kept coming toward me.

"I know this is unusual," he was saying. But I wasn't listening. I was totally weirded out. I turned and hightailed it out of the living room, in search of my mother. I kept Buster with me, mostly because he wouldn't let me put him down.

"Mom!" I called out. I went towards Mom's study, but the door was open and I could see she wasn't in there. I went through the patio doors out onto the back porch to see if she was in the garden. It was a mild day, even for early November. But I could see her gardening boots on the deck and the garden empty. I put Buster down, took out my phone, and hit her number on my list of favourites. She was number two. Dad was number one. Maybe I should be calling him, but I got the feeling he wouldn't answer.

The guy was following me, but not too closely. I glared at him. "Just leave me alone, bro," I said, trying to pretend I wasn't afraid of him.

I heard Mom's phone ringing, so I knew she was home. I followed the sound and ran upstairs. The guy was following me all the while, but he stopped at the bottom of the stairs. Mom's door was closed, but I barged in without knocking. Buster trailed behind.

A woman sat on her bed, on my mother's bed. She was not completely unfamiliar, but also not my mother. Mom's phone was beside her, ringing. An Auntie maybe?

"Hi Rajesh," she said, cheerfully but with some trepidation. "I know this will be a bit of a shock."

"No!" I yelled. "What the fuck is going on? What happened to my parents?"

"There's no need for that kind of language, Rajesh," she said, but her tone was flat, not reprimanding like my mother's. I knew she was no Auntie. She remained seated on the bed.

I didn't wait for her to say more. I backed out of the room and called Suenita's number, number three on my list. It went straight to voicemail. Her classes didn't end until 5pm on Tuesdays and Thursdays.

I texted her frantically.

mom and dad are gone

two randoms are here

I'm freaking out

I had to get out now. I turned to go back downstairs, but the guy was still standing at the bottom, one hand on each banister, blocking the stairs. I could see his biceps flex and the veins raised on his neck. No way my lanky 120 pounds could outmatch him.

I retreated to my room and slammed the door. Buster had followed me in, and I was glad for his company. I was terrified to stay in the house with the fake people. I considered climbing out the window. It wasn't too far down to the ground, and I figured I could make the jump. I was pretty agile from track and volleyball. I opened the window, and then I saw the HVAC van, with another guy sitting in it. He was looking right up at me. I was trapped.

I sat on my bed, knees curled up to my chest. Nothing was making any sense. I mean, if something had happened to Mom and Dad, like an accident or something, then the police would come to the door like in the movies. Or someone would call, like Uncle Rick, and say "I'm sorry to have to tell you this, son, blah,

blah, blah." Uncle Rick was the emergency contact on our school forms and passports, although I don't know why because he didn't strike me as the most reliable guy. I scrolled through my contacts for his number. We hadn't seen him since the summer family barbecue at Boulder Beach. He had come with yet another new girlfriend and those two bratty little boys that I had to babysit all day to make sure they didn't run off into the water and drown themselves while Uncle Rick was busy trying to impress the woman with his beach volleyball skills.

I found his number and called it. One of the boys answered, but I couldn't tell if it was Pilly or Bo. "Hey," I said. "It's Rajesh. Can I talk to your dad?"

"Rajesh who?" the boy said. I knew he knew me and was just being a turd.

"Your cousin," I said. "Come on man, just get your dad. It's an emergency, ok?"

"Oh, yah?" said the boy. "Well, Dad's not here . . ."

"Well, you're talking to me on his phone so he must be there. Stop being a jerk and give him the phone, alright?" I said. This kid was such an idiot. The phone went silent for a minute and then he came back on.

"My dad says he'll call you back," he said, and hung up. So much for that.

It would be at least another hour before Suenita came home. My text to her was still showing unread. I sat on the bed, squeezing Buster, trying to hold off the panic. I was a hostage in my own house. How was this possible? I tried to think of what Mom and Dad told us to do in an emergency. Like that time when Suenita was babysitting me and I choked on a piece of popcorn. She called 911, and the operator told her what to do while they were sending the paramedics. By the time they came she had managed to dislodge the popcorn and I was okay, just crying and scared. And when Mom and Dad got there, they were so proud of her for how well she handled the situation. After all, she was only 12 years old then, and I was only six.

But this didn't seem like a 911 kind of thing. What would I even tell them? They would think it was a prank. I couldn't think of what to do. It was like my brain was frozen.

I opened a private browsing window on my phone and searched: What happened to my parents? I don't know what I expected to find. I was pretty desperate.

The search returned only three responses. The first was a government website called the Department of Child and Family Services. I knew that was the one that comes and takes kids away from their parents, especially Black and Brown kids. The second one was a toll-free number for runaway kids in trouble, 1-999-KID-HELP. So not that. The last one was a group called Accept PRP, whatever that meant. None of this was useful.

At exactly 5pm my phone pinged. Finally, Suenita! Except it wasn't. It was a text from an unknown number with a link:

UNKNOWN NUMBER

DCFS_PRP_video_playnow_case89437

Stupid spammer. I tried to delete it but couldn't. I jabbed at the home button but nothing happened. My phone was hacked. A video began to play. A woman of no particular age appeared on the screen. She had brown skin and dark eyes, pin-straight shoulder length hair, an Indo-bot for sure. She smiled and began to speak:

Hi there! If you are receiving this message, if means your family has been selected to participate in the Parent Replacement Program. Congratulations! The PRP is a unique opportunity to learn from the new adults who you have recently met. These two adults have been carefully selected to meet your current developmental needs. But you are probably wondering what happened to your old parents. Don't worry! They have been assigned new duties that better matches their skills and abilities.

Good luck with your New Parents. If you have questions, call 1-

999-543-4357 or check out <u>www.acceptPRP.gov</u> for some helpful resources.

The message looped back to the beginning and started again. I stabbed the screen with my fingers, trying to make it stop. The video disappeared and only the phone number and website remained in the text. I realized it was the same number as the kids' help line.

I threw the phone on the floor and sat on the bed, numb. And then I started to cry. None of this was true. My real parents would never have left me and Suenita. They had been taken away, but I didn't know why. Did this happen to other kids? How could I not know?

I started thinking about movies like *Black Widow* where the spies create a whole fake family as their cover, but the parents are spies, and the kids are just part of the cover, and they just stage a bunch of photo shoots to create a family history that never happened, only the kids don't know it's not real. And I began to wonder if what I remembered about my childhood and my parents was real or not.

My mom was a typical Indian mom. She was born in Kenya but grew up in Toronto. She liked for us to have dinner together every evening, except if Dad was away for work, or if I had a late game or practice. She was the primary cook, and Dad was the clean up guy. Mom did yoga and meditation and all that kind of stuff, but she was firmly against organized religion, which she said was just brainwashing. She never said that in front of my grandparents or when other Brown families were around, only at home and when her other hippy friends were present. Mom and Dad never pressured me and Suenita to go into medicine or law like a lot of other Brown parents. In fact, Mom told us she didn't even want to send us to school, but Dad thought that was going too far. He said that would draw too much attention, although I never understood what he meant. She would say to Dad that we should just buy a little cottage and go "off grid" and Dad would say nothing and they would look at each other in a sad kind of way.

I must have still been crying because Buster whimpered and licked my face. We sat like that for a while longer. Then I picked up the phone and tried to call Suenita again. It was 5:30 by now and she should be home soon. But the call went straight to voicemail again and suddenly, I wondered if they got her too. Maybe she was too old for the PRP. Maybe she had been reassigned too. How could I not have seen this coming?

Panic rose up again. Suenita was my last hope, and now even she was gone. My breathing was heavy and shallow, and it was hard to stay in control. I tried to remember what Mom would tell me when I was small and got scared or freaked out about something. Take a deep breath, hold it for five seconds and then let it out. I did that a few times, and I saw Mom's face, and felt her holding me in her lap like she used to, and stroking my hair, and I calmed down a bit.

It was getting dark outside. I had to come up with some kind of escape plan. I listened carefully for any sound coming from the two imposters — talking, movement, phone sounds — but I heard nothing.

At that moment, there was a knock. My door opened and the two fake parents appeared. Buster growled, low and quiet, and I felt his tiny body vibrate.

"Come on down for dinner, Rajesh," the replacement dad said.

"We've made your favourite," the replacement mom added.

They stood in the doorway, not entering but also not leaving, strained smiles on their stretched plastic faces. Once again, I was trapped.

"What about Suenita? I said. "Aren't we gonna wait for her?" I was testing them, to see what they would say, to see if they knew where she was.

"We're not sure about Suenita," the replacement mom said.

"What do you mean?" I said. "What did you do to her?"

"No, no," Replacement Mom said hurriedly. "I just meant we're not sure what time she's coming home this evening." I knew she was lying of course. But I didn't let on.

"Ok, I'll come down," I said. They nodded in unison and retreated like a pair of programmed puppets.

I went down to the dining room, Buster in tow, and found that the two interlopers were moving around the kitchen comfortably.

"He kind of reminds me of Jason when he was that age," I heard Replacement Mom say. Replacement Dad put his arm around her, and they both sighed.

They had set the table for three. And they had prepared my favourite meal — parathas, dhal, and aloo gobi.

"The potatoes and cauliflower are from the garden," Replacement Dad said, fake proudly. At least he did not say "from your mother's garden" because I would have lost it. They had stolen the vegetables my real mom had grown in her beloved garden, and now they were serving it to me. It was such a classic colonizer move.

Replacement Dad put some curried cauliflower and potatoes on my plate, with dhal and a paratha. It looked exactly the same as when my real parents cooked it. These guys were good.

"How was Mr. Singh today? Did he pick on you again?" Replacement Dad laughed. It was an ongoing joke in our real family since last year when I was in Grade 7 and Mr. Singh became my math teacher. An inside joke, but this guy knew it. It was like they had been trained. Like they got a Mehta family playbook to study before coming.

"He wasn't there today," I said. And then I remembered that two of my teachers had been absent, as well as Coach Riley, and that a random guy had coached us instead. And I remembered that he had run a good session, technically speaking. Just like these two were running a good session. They had simply taken over the technical functions of my parents.

I broke off a piece of the warm flakey paratha, used it to scoop up some masala-laden aloo gobi, and put it in my mouth. The two watched me furtively, and then looked at each other, satisfied. I chewed slowly, waiting for the familiar pleasure of the dish to come, but it did not. The food had no aroma. The dhal could well have been thickened water. I chewed. I swallowed. Technically, I had been fed.

The meal continued, mostly in silence. All the while, I began thinking about how to get out. My dad always taught us to have a back-up plan. He worked as an IT specialist, and he said you always had to have a fail-safe, so that if a program didn't work, there was a sub-program that would take over until the main one could be re-coded. If anything, Dad was a planner. He set up our college funds while we were still babies, bought a back-up generator long before the climate crisis got bad enough for it to be necessary, and even invested in water-powered vehicles while they were still being developed. Surely Dad had a plan for this situation. But what? And now he was gone, and I had to figure it out on my own.

When I had finished eating, I announced that I would take Buster for his walk. Maybe if I got outside, I could make a run for it. But Replacement Mom said she would come with me, and Replacement Dad said he would stay back and do the clean up. I could see there was no way they were going to let me go out alone, nor leave the house empty. They covered all the bases, even though it was just the two of them.

I put Buster's leash on, slipped my phone into my jacket pocket, and headed for the patio doors that led to the backyard. Replacement Mom was ready and waiting, wearing my real mom's sweater and loafers. I realized she was similar in build to my real mom. How convenient all of this was . . .

I walked out into the backyard, through the cold, dark garden and into the laneway behind the house, Replacement Mom walking in step with me. I wondered what she would do if I just took off running. Could she catch me? And where would I even go? How far could I get on foot? I was pretty fast, running 100 meters in less than 13 seconds on my relay team, but these two people were complete unknowns. My parents had been deleted. My sister was probably deleted. My phone had been hacked. There was the guy in the van out front. I knew I wasn't safe, but I didn't know the degree of danger I was in. As long as I complied, I would be okay. But if I dared to resist, who knew what would happen?

We walked on in the narrow laneway behind the houses, passing by garage entrances and low backyard fences. There were no streetlights here, only back porch and solar lights from individual houses. Replacement Mom asked questions to which I gave tepid responses, in between which she spoke of mundane things mostly related to the weather and flu season. My phone pinged and I retrieved it hurriedly, desperate for contact with someone I actually knew. It was a message from Uncle Rick.

UNCLE RICK

Hi Raj. Got ur message. Will pick u up at 7:05 for bball practice.

It was a strange message, not because of what it said but how it was written. With slang that Uncle Rick would never use. Then I realized it was 7:05 right now.

I looked around, my senses on high alert. Something was happening, and it was happening now.

"Who's that? Your friend?" Replacement Mom asked, as if she knew and was trying to distract me.

"Yah," I said, keeping up the ruse. "He's inviting me to a party. Can you hold Buster's leash so I can answer the text?" I said, shoving the leash into her hand.

"Now Buster!" I shouted, and Buster took off at a run, pulling Replacement Mom along with him. It wasn't so much that he was strong, but that she was taken off guard. I turned and ran full speed in the opposite direction. I didn't have a plan, but I was determined to get away.

Headlights suddenly appeared in front of me, blinding me.

My breath, heavy and warm, formed clouds of fog. I kept running. I had to get away. A van was coming straight at me down the narrow lane. The HVAC guy. I kept running, squeezing tight against the fence. The vehicle slowed down, a door flew open, and someone grabbed me and pulled me into the back. I screamed and fought back, kicking and punching. Then I heard my name.

"Raj!"

"Rajesh!"

"It's me!"

A male voice, then a female one. A hand searched my pockets, and removed my phone. I heard a smash as it was tossed out the window.

The van reversed out of the back lane, then turned onto a wider street and sped along. Streetlights now lit the interior intermittently. It was Suenita who had grabbed me. Uncle Rick was driving. I heard voices from the third row — my two cousins Pilly and Bo, but this time, I was grateful to see them.

By now I was crying hard. Suenita was holding on to me.

"I got you little bro," she kept saying.

After a while my heart rate slowed down, and my breathing began to settle. Then I remembered Buster, and how I had used him as a decoy and then abandoned him, and I freaked out all over again.

When I finally settled down, Uncle Rick started to talk. He said we were going to find my mom and dad, but we had to make sure we couldn't be tracked. I asked if he knew where they were and he said he had an idea.

They asked me what happened, and I explained the whole thing. Uncle Rick said that after I called, he knew something had happened and he figured that it was the PRP that had got us. He called Suenita and she confirmed that she had just got a bunch of weird messages and missed calls from me. Uncle Rick told her not to contact me, and that he'd come to the campus to get her. He didn't have a clear plan yet but he waited for an opportunity to scoop me.

After he texted me, he made them toss all their phones, except for his back up burn phone. I guess Uncle Rick was a planner too, like Dad. They were brothers after all. Then they came by the house, driving up and down the back lane with the lights out, trying to figure out how to get me. When they saw me and the strange woman walking Buster, they figured that was their chance.

"But what about Mom and Dad?" I asked. Did they know about the PRP too, and why didn't they tell us?

"Of course they knew about the PRP," Uncle Rick explained, and he had always been the back up in case our family got targeted, and my parents were the backup for Pilly and Bo. He and my parents had a meeting spot, and he hoped that they were able to get there. The van was an unregistered vehicle they kept in a rented storage unit. It would be a while before it could be traced.

"But then what?" I asked. "Where can we go? Why can't we just say no to the PRP and keep living our normal lives?"

"That's not how it works, son," Uncle Rick said. He was calling me "son," so I knew that things were really bad. Adults only talked like that when someone was dead or dying.

"Are you even our real uncle?" I asked. "Are Mom and Dad our real parents?" My voice was cracking and I was on the verge of crying again.

"Rajesh, yes, of course they're our real parents!" Suenita said, putting her arm around me again, and squeezing me hard.

"How do you know it's not all fake like in *Black Widow*?" I said.

"I was there when you were born, Rajesh. I was six, old enough to remember everything. Mom had you at home, with a midwife. I literally saw you come out of mom's . . ."

"Okay, okay!" I said. "I get it. I believe you!" Then I whispered, "But what about this guy?" I motioned toward Uncle Rick. She shushed me and glanced toward the boys in the back. I turned around and saw Pilly and Bo staring at us with huge terrified eyes.

"Suenita," Uncle Rick said, "I was also there when Rajesh was born. Remember? Think hard. I was there."

"That's right! I do remember," Suenita said. But I couldn't tell if she was just saying that or if she actually remembered. Anyway, we had no choice but to believe him. He was the only one who could help us find our parents.

We drove on through the night, far from the city now, although I had no idea where. Uncle Rick tossed us a bag filled with protein bars and bottled water. At some point, he stopped and re-filled the tank from plastic jugs filled with stinking gasoline that he had stored in the trunk. There weren't many vehicles that still used this kind of fuel, but he said we didn't have time to recharge at an electrical station.

As he drove, he told us about the Parent Replacement Program. It all started in 2020, just after this big global pandemic. He and my parents believed it was a government plan to control the people by breaking their relationship bonds and instilling fear and instability. It was a long-term plan, being implemented over two or three generations, so as not to raise too much alarm.

They first started it with schools, replacing teachers and coaches at will, so kids would just accept that as normal, as if the relationship with the teachers had no bearing on their learning. The next step was to replace the parents surreptitiously, here and there, in different cities and towns, to see if they could do it successfully. Sometimes they could; the parents would be moved far away or "retired" if they didn't comply. Anyway, they were not the ones that mattered. It was the children who had to learn to accept that their parents could be subbed out. If they could accept this, they would accept any outside authority. They would be absolutely and completely controllable.

Me, Suenita, Pilly and Bo listened to Uncle Rick, occasionally asking questions but mostly just quietly terrified.

"Some people think it's a conspiracy theory," said Uncle Rick. "They don't think people can just be disappeared, especially here in our part of the world. But now we know for sure. They usually do it when the kids are younger than you guys. Seems like now they're trying it with older kids." Uncle Rick passed his hand over his balding head and sucked his teeth "Those goddamn fuckers," he muttered. "I thought we could evade them . . ."

"Your father always thought if we just played by the rules, we could avoid attention," Uncle Rick continued. "But your mom always just wanted out. From the time we began to hear the rumours, she started to investigate options. She found an underground group, a bunch of neo-hippies really, but your mom was always kind of like that. Do you remember Aunty Natasha and Uncle Jahpaul that used to live next door to you guys? Those kind of people. And good thing, otherwise, we'd have been completely defenseless."

We kids all slept on and off. Uncle Rick put on some music: Kendrick Lamar, J. Cole, old rappers from back in the day. At one point, I heard Childish Gambino's "This is America" playing, and I went to sleep dreaming about the end part of the video where he's running through the warehouse and the cops are chasing him.

Eventually, we arrived at what appeared to be a campground, and Uncle Rick pulled up to a spot beside an old trailer. He went in and came back a short time later, telling us to come inside. A woman that I vaguely recognized as our old neighbour Aunty Natasha greeted us by name, served us watery hot chocolate and arrowroot biscuits, and found a place for each of us to sleep.

"Your parents passed through here about six hours ago," she said to me and Suenita. "You'll catch up to them at the next stop. I'll send a message that you're coming."

Suenita and I huddled together on a mattress on the floor while Pilly and Bo snuggled up on a couch. We slept for a few hours, and early the next morning we were on the road again. The next stop turned out to be a small town, the type with a single commercial main street and a few dozen residential side streets. Uncle Rick stopped in an empty parking lot behind a building with a sign that read "Main Street Library." We waited for some time before another vehicle drove into the lot.

"That's your ride," Uncle Rick said to me and Suenita. "Go now." But Suenita and I sat motionless. Uncle Rick got out of the van and opened the rear door on Suenita's side. The air was frigid. He motioned for us to get out. As we did, we could see that it was Mom and Dad in the other car. I ran the short distance across the parking lot and jumped into the vehicle. Suenita was right behind me. We drove off immediately. There was no time for goodbyes.

About Sandhya Singh

Sandhya Singh was born in Guyana. She was a regular contributor to Herizons magazine from 2011 - 2014. She is grateful for the BIPOC Writing Spaces at Firefly Creative and Writers Collective Canada, and especially for her writing groups Wimmin Writing (for work-shopping this story) and Write and Laugh (for the love and accountability). Sandhya loves seed saving, sprouting and fermenting things.

She currently resides in Ottawa, Canada, traditional territory of the Algonquin Anishinaabe Nation, with her partner and three almost-grown children. You can find her on Instagram (@sandhya.writingforgood) and LinkedIn (sandhyasinghwritingforgood)

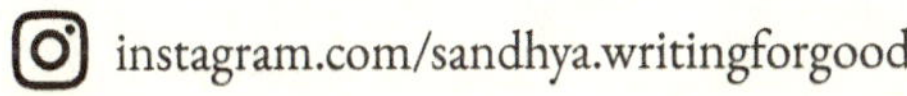

instagram.com/sandhya.writingforgood

linkedin.com/in/sandhyasinghwritingforgood

Sunna's Eclipse

L. Nabang

Daughter

My first mistake was trying to guide Mother to the horizon line at nightfall.

Her movement was stiff as she meticulously assembled her golden jewelry and hair decor on her towering vanity, preparation for tomorrow's wear. Even with me tugging at the yellow silk sleeves of her robe, her attention didn't move. I should've known it wouldn't, but I was too impatient to wait. I needed to show her.

"No," Mother said.

"Please, it'll be quick," I said. I was six.

It was when Mother finished folding her dress, placing it gently on the table, that she sat on her vanity chair and faced me. "What have I told you about the night sky?"

I always believed Mother's voice matched the texture of the clouds. I still do. Anytime I hear it, every muscle in me eases like a ripple. But it also made me forget how quickly she could sharpen it.

When I hesitated, she lightly cupped my cheek. "Tell me." Her tone was softer.

"It's . . . not our territory."

"Why?"

"But this isn't about the stars."

"Sunna."

My eyes flickered to the horizon line, my fingers jittery. I broke from her grip and flew up. She called for me, but I kept rising until I broke past the line. Blackness hit me first, an ocean of it, so dark I had to squint. But the blackness quickly warmed and when I widened my eyes again, it felt like I sunk into a blanket more familiar than the piercing blue I have to rise to every day. That should've been the first sign, honestly, the moment I questioned if showing Mother this was truly the right choice. But I was too excited to think.

I focused on the motionless black sea. Then I held out my hands and made my second mistake. A pale white glow emitted from my palms. Excitement fluttered through me as small waves cropped up; they came in droves, ruffling the ocean with bubbly white edges.

I heard my name.

"Do you like . . .?" My grin withered.

Mother was paler than the ocean's edges, eyes frantic as she took in the waves.

"Mommy?"

She scanned the sky before yanking me back under the horizon line. I jerked my head from the burst of golden light. My eyes hadn't adjusted when Mother held my face, panicked.

"Never do that again."

"What?" I stuttered.

"Promise me."

"But—"

"Promise me!"

My eyes watered. Mother never raised her voice; it wasn't elegant.

"I promise," I whispered. She hugged me tight, knuckles digging into my spine. I shut my eyes but said nothing. There was nothing to say. I scared Mother. Hurt her. Even now, the guilt still gnaws at my bones. I shake my head, ask myself how I could've been so cruel and inconsiderate that night. I should've helped her prepare tomorrow's wear as I always did; that made her happy. Told her I cared.

"I just wanted to surprise you."

"What have I told you about surprises?"

I buried my face into her chest; my third inconsiderate mistake. She had to throw out her nightgown the next morning because I tainted it with too much snot and tears. It was her favorite one.

"They aren't proper."

"What else?"

"Not safe."

"Remember that."

I nodded, opening my eyes again. They still hadn't adjusted.

MOTHER

My attention never strays from my vanity mirror.

Carefully, I slide the last tiny hair clip onto my coal-black curls. I tilt my head left once it's latched, lift my chin. I summon a soft shine; my rays hit every clip.

Perfect.

Sunna watches me from her golden stool that's now rather short for her, back straight as I taught. A year ago she asked me for a taller one.

"If you're seated taller than me, how can I see your head?" I answered.

"You look beautiful, Mother." She smiles.

"I know."

After I dress, I fasten my golden pearl bracelets and earrings. Sunna straightens herself more when I leave my vanity, her eyes glinting. That glint unfurls an air of lightness in me. I never get tired of seeing it. It's the reason why I wake up, why I work as hard as I do to exemplify myself for her.

I kiss the crown of her head. "Time to perfect you too."

I start with her hair. Always first. She holds still as I detangle her curls with my fingers, gentle with each pull. I part her hair next, then oil every section of her scalp, so it's well-nourished and protected. Once it's moist, I parse through her curls again, this time with a wide-toothed comb. I decorate. The golden hair clips that I used for myself, I use on her too.

I lift her chin after attaching the last clip, angle her head left.

"Glow for me."

Sunna closes her lids, summoning her glow. It appears too slow for me. I ease, though, when her glow intensifies, shrouding her in a tender yellow aura and hitting every clip.

My lips raise. Three hundred years and she's blossomed into something beautiful. Long hours spent on her hair have led it to prosper into a thick afro, so large it halos her round face. The fullness of her hair resembles her features: plump lips, softened nose, big eyes more enchanting than the stars she'd mistakenly praised as a child. She's a spitting image of me.

I guide her onto her feet before going to our closet. She strips off her old dress and raises her arms for me to slip her into the new garments I made. As always, it fits her slender figure and the curves of her hips. The dress is silky like her old one, but better, the sun patterns more elaborate. By the time I finish latching on her topaz earrings and bracelets, the stars have set into their side of the horizon line.

"How do I look?"

I walk her to my vanity mirror.

Her gasp satisfies me. It always does.

I wrap my arms around her shoulders, staring with her at her reflection. "You're welcome."

She releases a laugh as airy as I feel. "When will you teach me to make a dress this beautiful?"

"It's not a light task, Sunna."

She gently squeezes my hand. "That's why I'm here right? To help make things easier for you."

"If I want you, I'll tell you."

"Alright." She hesitates. "What about dressing myself?"

Unease surfaces in my gut. "So I can't dress you well?"

"Of course you can," she says, smile faltering.

I slip my arms from her shoulders. "If I did, you wouldn't ask me that."

"Mother, wait." She grabs my hand again before I can leave. "I'm sorry, I didn't mean to imply that. I just . . . want to make myself beautiful like you, *with* you."

My unease thickens. Still, I force on another smile, even squeezing her hands as she did for me.

"That time will come soon. But for now, watch."

Daughter

Mother always says "A blemished sun never glows well."

Nothing can be out of place. Not one ray, glint, or golden streak. My earliest memories are of Mother waking me up for our morning routine five hours before the stars set. Three hours were dedicated to her alone, and during that time, I could only sit and watch. She said observing was important so when it came time to take her place as the Sun, I'd know what to do.

I didn't mind this. Sometimes I'd wake up before her, perked on my golden stool. Already, Mother was — *is* — the most beautiful element, so watching her evolve her image into a more mesmerizing one, it may as well be magic. The right kind of magic. Not the magic I scarred her with.

I knew it was my turn when Mother turned and smiled. She never had me wear the same dress as her; the only thing we could match was our sun pendants. But I saw no issue in that. My dresses are still intricate and for as long as I can remember, Mother has never taken off her pendant.

Every time she worked on me, she'd tell the story of my birth.

I was never meant to be born and when she tried to have me, the elements doubted her. But she succeeded, and I came — her special ray. I'd listen to each word, sinking into the tender aura that cloaked Mother. That same aura would materialize when she'd tuck me in, play dress up with me. But it was always the thickest during preparation time.

As ALWAYS, I witness the power of perfection when Mother and I rise hand-in-hand from the horizon line, our golden light pooling onto the Earth. The clouds awaken and their eyes follow us. Collected as she appears, the slight curve of her lip hides a prideful smile. My heart warms at that. She has every right to be proud. Mother strokes my knuckle when I inch closer. I seared into my head to never rise alone or without being near her. Last I did either, I wasn't allowed in the sky for a month.

Once we've settled East, I breathe in, trying my best to apply Mother's teachings: how strong my energy should be, which places to heat, how far my light should go. My rays waver over South America. I concentrate harder. With time they stabilize, but next to Mother's they appear dim. I try not to stress. I just need more practice, that's all. Then I'll reach her level. My throat constricts once the thoughts creep in. *Will you? Can you?*

A gentle hand settles on my shoulder.

"Remember. Relax."

"Yes, Mother."

Three cumulus clouds float past. One of them is small like a child.

"You both are magnificent as always," says one of the bigger clouds. Mother answers with a polite nod. "We appreciate it."

As the two clouds drift, the smaller one lags behind.

"Sunna, may I ask you something?"

I hesitate. "Yes."

The cloud smiles sheepishly. "Well, me and the others are

going to hang out around the ocean. Would you like to come? Maybe warm the place a bit?"

A lively "yes" hops at the tip of my tongue. I nearly say it until my attention wanders to Mother. Her eyes are slits. A memory flickers, why I rose the line alone. My fascination led me astray when I watched a group of clouds play chase above the sea. Mother quickly caught up and dragged me to our designated spot in the East. She barely acknowledged me while I was grounded, wouldn't tell me stories or tuck me in. It's after I burst into tears, gave Mother the heartfelt apology she deserved, that she softened again.

"I'd love to, but I have to focus on my duties."

The cloud deflates. "Okay. Maybe another time."

They float off. I must've started to follow; Mother grabs my wrist.

"Rule number #1, Sunna?"

I roam close to her again, guilt pricking me.

"Be no more than three feet from you."

MOTHER

"A little further down."

"Here?"

"Yes."

My body relaxes against the head of my sofa chair when Sunna massages the kink beneath my nape. Time must be catching up with me; these aches are becoming frequent. I sigh. Nevermind that. I still have a few billion years left.

"Being the most important element isn't easy. Soon you'll have to bear this responsibility. You understand?"

"That's why I've been practicing more," Sunna says.

"And it's why, you understand, you weren't allowed to go with that cloud?"

"Yes."

"Tell me."

She's quiet for a moment. "I can't afford distractions."

"Nice as the clouds may be, they're good at making you forget that."

"I know," her voice is quieter. "I'm sorry."

The silence that blankets us unsettles me.

I take Sunna's wrist from behind and gently pull her around my chair. She bows her head as she kneels in front of me. A pastel yellow nightgown drapes her, gleaming faintly against her umber skin.

I lift her chin. "Where do we shine? Up or down?"

"Up."

"That's where your eyes should be."

Sunna's face lightens, but only by so much; something else lingers.

I caress her cheek. "You can tell me anything."

Her smile is soft. "I know."

"Then what is it?"

"It's nothing."

"If I could let you roam with the clouds, I would."

My gut roils when the light on her face spreads to her eyes. An unfamiliar glint. "You would?"

"But you already told me why I can't. Distraction is one thing, but say you leave and something happens to me. What then? What if you come and it's too late? What if something happens to *you* and I'm too late?"

Sunna's glint extinguishes, eyes now wide with fear. "But . . . I thought you said we were invincible. Above everything?"

"That means nothing when it comes to you."

I lead us on our feet and to our room. "Is your back okay?" she asks as I put on her golden bonnet.

"It's fine."

She stops on our way to her bed. "Let's not worry about me."

I blink at her. "Are you pushing me away?"

"No," she rushes in. "I mean, let me help you to bed instead."

"Nonsense, Sunna." I take her hand again. Once she's in bed, I lift the covers over her.

"Are you comfortable?"

Her nod is rigid. I ease a stray curl back into her bonnet before kissing her forehead. "I love you."

"I love you too, Mother."

DAUGHTER

My eyes keep betraying me. When I close them for the nth time, they open again and latch onto the horizon line. Turning on my side doesn't help. Finally, I creep out from my covers, acknowledging Mother asleep on her canopy bed beside me. I rise above the line and over the sea.

My body eases as I take in the muted sways of the waves, the coolness of the night, and the faint scent of salt. I hate that I love it. I hate that even after her warnings, I still sneak out every night. But coming here is a need that's hooked itself deep in my chest. If I ignore it, it tugs until I listen. The need is a sin. A distraction I can't afford, not when my time to fulfill Mother's duty edges closer.

White light oozes onto my palms. I lift them, tasting a bitter tang when the ocean responds faster than my rays. More waves arise, bigger ones; they crash harder onto the surface. I snuff out the glow. The ocean calms. I haven't used my power in years. My one smart move. Suns don't play with water. We evaporate it so the sky isn't dry, use it to birth clouds.

Clapping erupts.

I gasp. A few feet from me floats a being who looks around my age with pitch-black skin and levitating hair. A white aura swathes her, blending in with her lucent silver dress. She wears a brilliant grin. I dash for the horizon line.

"Hey wait!"

My pulse quickens as Mother's warnings blare in my head: the stars aren't like us. Not safe.

The star flickers before me.

I scramble back. "Don't touch me."

"It's okay," she says. "I'm not going to hurt you." I swerve around her. "Wait!" I'm nearing the line when she calls out, "I just wanted to say what you did was amazing."

I stop. Slowly, I turn. "What?"

She flickers to me again, but her distance is further away, probably for my comfort. "I said what you did was amazing."

"You're lying."

Her vibrant laugh sparks surprise in me. "You think so?"

"You can never trust a place without light."

The star scans herself then the landscape of blinking stars above us. She raises a brow at me. My face heats and I go for the line again.

"I mean it. Truly, I've never seen anything like it."

"I don't like the game you're playing."

"If I wanted to play a game, it would be fast and competitive."

I dare a look over my shoulder. Her smile is warmer, and in her silver eyes gleam what looks too much like pity.

"You have a gift. It's your choice if you want to see it that way or not."

"I don't need a lecture."

"It's more like a piece of advice. But I get it. The lines can blur."

She sighs when I don't answer. "It's not the first time I've seen you around, so if you ever come back, make a wish and I'll be here. No pressure, of course."

Before I can say anything, she blinks away.

MOTHER

Sunna's rays are duller. I try to advise her, discreetly remind her to relax. Nothing changes. I nod stiffly at a group of passing clouds.

Their smiles falter once they eye Sunna. She doesn't acknowledge them, too focused on fixing her quivering rays. The clouds whisper. Heat clouds my face.

She's been off since preparation. Her gaze stuck to the floor and her posture kept crumpling into pensive slouches. Three times I reminded her to pay attention, only for her to stray again. When I questioned her, her answers mirrored last night: *It's nothing. I'm fine.*

Sunna's gaze wanders to the darkening sky after we set. She must've sensed my glances; she's quick to look away.

"Come. Help me get ready for bed."

She perks a bit, her one bit of normalcy today. I sit at my vanity and unfasten my earrings while Sunna removes my hair clips. She's more attentive to this task than her morning work. Frustration tightens my throat.

"I thought you said you've been practicing more." My tone is level.

She looks up. "I have."

"Today showed otherwise."

"Oh, I just had a bad day."

"You were distracted." I lock my bracelets in their white chest.

"No—"

"The land you were responsible for was experiencing summer. Yet you gave them cold. Who knows how many elements the clouds have told about your performance, how that will reflect on me."

Sunna flinches from my sharp tone. "I'm sorry, Mother."

"Sorry only does so much."

"It won't happen again. I promise."

I face her. Immediately, Sunna lowers herself. She does another thing right when she remembers to look up.

I mellow my voice when I ask, "What distracted you?"

"I had a bad day."

"Bad days don't exist here."

Her shoulders wilt.

"Do you not trust me?"

She cups my hands. "I do."

"Then why lie to me?"

When she tries to look down, I stop her by holding her chin, my touch light. "Talk to me."

Silence lingers before Sunna speaks again; her eyes are glazed. "I'm thrilled about taking your place someday, but aren't I an anomaly?"

"That's what makes you special."

"What about what I can do with the sea? Is that special too?"

My face wilts. "I thought I told you to never speak of that."

"I'm just wondering. Maybe I could use it to improve the earth in some way."

"You made me a promise, Sunna." My tone is firm again. "I need you to keep it. Do you understand?"

Relief ripples through me when, after more silence, she nods. "I understand."

DAUGHTER

I wrap my robe tighter around me as I float in the dark sky. I blame it on my nerves; they're colder than the wind tonight. I shouldn't be here. That star got in my head, adding on to the distractions. She, this place, it's why I upset Mother again. She's right. I made her a promise. So why am I not keeping it?

I shut my eyes; my tears burn me.

I wish I could just . . .

"You came!"

I jump.

The star's there, staring at me with that brilliant grin.

"Oh, no, I didn't—"

"You made a wish."

"How much did you hear?"

"I only feel wishes." She beckons. "You coming?"

"I didn't mean to summon you." The star does that brow raise. I look away. "I'm only here for air."

The star continues to stare at me, analyze, is more like it. I can't help wondering what she felt from my wish. Somehow that sounds worse than hearing it.

"Guess I'll see you around then."

She blinks away. I surprise myself by jerking forward, hand outstretched. I glimpse the horizon line. Sense tells me to return to it. But that hook of need in my chest — it starts yanking again. Harder than I've felt. I shut my eyes.

I know she appears when white flickers behind my lids. When I open them, a light smirk hangs from her lips. She beckons again. I acknowledge the horizon line a second time before finally inching toward her.

"Name's Polaris. Yours?"

I lead with wary silence before confessing.

"Pretty namc."

"Where are you taking me?"

"Around the block. If you're gonna be around here, may as well get a brief tour. Know the best spots." She extends her hands to me. "Hold tight, okay?"

WE BLINK into a sea of clouds blotted with pinks, indigos, and whites. Two other stars float before us; one of their auras outshines even Polaris. She chuckles when I rush behind her. They're just her siblings, she reassures; nothing to worry about. Rocks of doubt sit in my stomach. I look back; no horizon line in sight. How far did she take me? I stay behind her as she introduces her brother Arcturus and sister Vega. They grin at me, waves large. I meekly wave back.

As Polaris guides me further into the sky, my grip hardens on her hand so I don't lose her. "What were those colorful clouds?"

"Nebulas. You're gonna see tons of them."

Further away, I realize the nebula's shaped like butterfly wings, glittering brighter than any ray I've ever conjured. Mother never told me clouds could be that beautiful.

Polaris points at what appears to be a miles-long rip in the sky. My lips part in awe as I absorb its shimmering tans and blues, how they blend like a perfect stitch. The Milky Way Galaxy, she tells me. Two stars zip past us. I flinch back.

"It's okay, they're just racing."

We run into more stars. Most glow white, but a few others radiate unique colors of their own. Blue, yellow, orange, and red. After greeting Polaris, many of them acknowledge me with a bow, a compliment about my golden eyes. By the nth greeting, my shoulders are less tense and when a star twirls, spraying stardust to bless me with luck, I find myself giggling.

Polaris flies us away before brushing off the stardust that speckled my nightgown. "Don't want any evidence."

"Evidence?"

"Your Mother's the Sun isn't she?"

I go quiet.

"Nothing against her," Polaris says. "We're just familiar with her, you know, not wanting to associate with us. So, I figured she'd expect the same from you."

"Why don't you guys have your own Sun?" I detour.

Polaris observes the sky. "Don't know. It's always been like that."

I revert to silence again when Mother's words echo in my head, her sudden confession when I first asked about the stars, admired them: "I am a star."

I gaped at her. "You are? But you don't seem like—"

"Exactly. Without me, the sky loses light. The Earth dies. Cold rules. But the night stars, their light is weak. Imagine nightfall when the clouds cover them completely. There's only cold and darkness. No sky should be that way."

Polaris breaks my thoughts. "Sunna look."

I do. Green paths of light dance before us, shadowed by tender wisps of purple and teal.

"What is it?" I gasp.

"Aurora borealis. Beautiful, isn't it?"

As I watch, a sudden serenity sinks into me, threading every fiber of my being.

It is the most beautiful thing. Just like the nebulas, the Milky Way Galaxy. Heat clouds my eyes as I grasp my pendant. How is it that a place with so much darkness carries more radiance than what I've experienced during 300 years of daylight?

MOTHER

Sunna's rays are stronger. They barely waver and their brightness nearly matches mine. When five clouds pass, she waves at them, her large grin mirroring the twinkle in her eyes.

"Can I help you prepare for bed, Mother?" Sunna asks once we've set. I'm seated at my vanity.

"Yes."

Sunna hurries to me. Before she handles my hair, she bends down and kisses my cheek.

"Oh," I gasp.

Her laugh softens me.

"See what happens when you open up," I say.

"Open up? Oh! Yes." Sunna nods. "Last night, it really changed things for me."

"I can see that," I smile. "You were exceptional today."

Sunna blushes. "It's . . . thanks to you and hard work."

"I know."

She's removing a clip when I take her hand and hold it close to my pendant.

"You'll be perfect. I've always known it."

She's still blushing, but even then, her smile shrinks. Likely self-doubt, but with time she'll blossom into a spitting image of my confidence.

I've always known that too.

DAUGHTER

Every night, I'm methodical; replace my body with pillows stuffed beneath my blanket, stay quiet slipping out, keep track of time, return seven hours before morning rise.

Polaris continues to be my guide, introducing me to more nighttime traits and traditions. Together we watch a group of stars compete in a sky-wide race. I feel a rush once it begins; the racing stars resemble streaks of white rain falling toward Earth. The winner gets to be the first to grant a wish. Another tradition, the assemblage of constellations.

"They can help with navigation," Polaris tells me. "Many people use them for travel, especially at sea." But for us, we enjoy ourselves by playing charades with them. My favorite tradition is lighting nebulas to further brighten the sky. I laugh when Polaris and I twirl arm-in-arm, casting handfuls of shimmering stardust on a nebulous cloud. Her silver dust mingles with my yellow.

The stars are nothing like Mother said they were. Often Polaris and I would meet in the butterfly nebula with her siblings and other stars. After two months, I know most of their names, the different rhythms of their twinkles, and their favorite constellations to form.

I also show them my powers for the first time. My stomach knots once Polaris gathers the stars above the Atlantic. When she announces I have a surprise, all their flares sharpen in anticipation.

"You can do it," she whispers.

I sip in a cold breath, release, then acknowledge the ocean. The stars' glows illuminate the water's true shade of blue. Slowly I hold out my pale white palms. The stars gasp when clumps of waves arise. A few grow taller. Firm crashes echo out. Salt sprays in the air. My white light intensifies. Suddenly, a rainbow stretches from the water, arching over us. I gape with the stars.

Many reach out, parsing their fingers through the colors. Finally, I lower my hands. The ocean stills again, and the rainbow disperses.

I nearly go deaf from the cheers. Polaris tackles me with a hug while the other stars swarm me. Their praise muddles together into a sea of its own: *amazing, incredible, gifted.* The shock in me morphs into an overwhelming weightlessness. Golden tears soak my cheeks as laughter trembles through my body. Arcturus and Vega ask for another show, and when the rest of the stars glint in agreement, I give them one.

"MAKE sure your fingers don't slip," Polaris orders.

"We heard you the first time," Vega says; her and Arcturus's hands rest over my eyes.

"What are you all up to?" I ask.

"Hold on."

I recognize Polaris's soft touch when she takes my wrist. Something jingles. A clasp.

The siblings' hands drop from my face. I stare in surprise. Around my wrist sits a silver bracelet adorned with blue and white stars.

"When did you make this?"

"About a week ago. It's rather overdue."

"Overdue?"

A sheepish look skirts Polaris's face. "You're family now."

I scan the clusters of stars crowded around us. Every one of them nods, smiles warm. Always warm. Mother — she told me if I mingle with them they'll corrupt me, envy me. But where? Where is the corruption? The envy?

I hold my wrist against my pendant. "I promise I'll cherish it."

MOTHER

I rise from my bed, stretch, then look at the horizon line. Despite the soft purple, darkness still overwhelms the sky. Good.

After making my bed, I approach Sunna's.

I nudge her gently. "It's time to prepare."

She doesn't move. I pause while nudging her again. Her shoulder's too soft. I pull her covers back. My heart plummets.

"Sunna?"

I toss aside her pillows, then her sheets and comforter. Nothing.

She must've woken up early, maybe gone to the cleaning room to wash her face. But when I check, I find no one. My breath quickens. I try the light room, the sewing office, the rest of the house. I keep calling for her and when she doesn't answer, I call louder. I go from searching rooms to searching drawers. I fling away hair products, jewelry boxes. I scavenge the closet, tearing through the new dresses I crafted.

My spotless floors drown beneath the chaos. I toss more pillows, more sheets. By now I'm shaking and my voice is raw, face soaked by golden tears. I crumple against my vanity.

Someone must've taken her.

I look up at the horizon line.

The clouds. Why wouldn't they? I've seen the way they look at us. Behind their politeness is envy of what I have, who I've created, and our closeness that surpasses their own. They must've colluded with the stars, told them to sneak in and grab her when my guard was low. They must — what if they've mutilated her?

I'm about to snatch one of my crumpled coats when rustling echoes out. I turn. My mouth dries. From the other side of the house, Sunna freely floats down from the horizon line. Unharmed. Unmutilated. No. What I see is worse. Her glow has been visibly dampened for nightfall and yet . . . that unfamiliar glint. She looks like she's about to rush back to our room when our eyes lock. She freezes. Pales.

"M-Mother."

I can't bring my tongue to move because where? Where do I even start?

My arm trembles as I straighten myself against my vanity. The longer I stare, the more she shrinks.

"What's that on your wrist?" My voice rasps.

Slowly she drifts her hand behind her back; I think a knife twists in my chest.

"It's nothing," she stammers.

I'm moving. Sunna only manages two steps back when I'm in front of her and yanking out her wrist.

"Wait—!"

I wrench the bracelet. She cries out, but I don't care, not even when the band snaps and beads scatter. I'm too focused on the bracelet's remains in my hand. They aren't beads.

My vision blurs.

"What did you do?" she chokes out.

"I thought of the worst possible things imaginable," I whisper. "Now I see those scenarios would've been better." My gaze returns to her. "You abandoned me."

"Mother—"

"For the *night*. Of all things. After everything I've told you."

"But I'm okay," she pleads. "The stars, they're good, I swear—"

"You *abandoned* me!"

She flinches.

"How do you think I felt when I saw you gone? How could you be so selfish?"

"It was only for one night—"

"No. This," I clench the star beads in her face. "This isn't given after one night."

"Let me explain, please."

"You don't love me anymore."

"I do! More than anything—"

"Then why would you do this to me?"

Sunna shudders from her silent cries. "The stars, I showed them my gift."

My face slackens. "You what?"

"I showed them my gift, and they loved it. They love what I can do, how I can control the sea, how I can create rainbows." She flashes a brittle smile. "Mother, I can create *rainbows* and they're just as beautiful as the ones you make. If I could show you—"

"They've brainwashed you."

"No—"

"They're using you, trying to turn you against me."

"Listen !"

"*You* listen. Everything I've done, I've done for you, to protect you, keep you safe. The things I've sacrificed."

"But their kindness is real. Their light, their warmth, the freedom they've given me . . ."

"So I'm a cage to you."

"Ye—no!" she exclaims. "I don't understand. Why hate them so much when you're a star yourself?"

I stiffen. I should've known telling her that would be a mistake. The stars must've used this detail about me to manipulate her, invalidate my credibility, all my protection.

"Apologize," I mutter. "Then promise you'll never return to the night."

"If I could just show you,"

"Promise me, Sunna."

She shakes her head, covering her face with her hands.

I swallow hard. "So you choose the stars."

"No—"

"Get out."

I pull back when she reaches for me.

"I don't!"

"Then promise me."

Again she stutters. Shakes her head. Opens her mouth and for the second time nothing comes out.

I'm walking. She grabs me. I wrench my arm back. She crumples to her knees, cries out to me. But nothing she says is that promise, my apology. I rip off my pendant, tasting my tears when I slam the bedroom door. Lock it. I don't leave until I hear her sobs fade past the line.

Daughter

I lose track of how many times I go back. Every time I'm met with a locked door. When I return to the night, Polaris lets me dampen her shoulder in gold. All the stars take turns checking on me. Some come with stardust, a miniature constellation, or a kiss of solace on the cheek.

My only access to the morning sky is viewing it beneath the horizon line. Far as I am, I can still see Mother. She continues to hold a good composure in public; whenever the clouds ask where I am she puts on a strained smile, gives a vague response.

Then nightfall comes. I never see her, but I think I hear faint cries. The cries echo for weeks. When I ask the stars if they hear it, they shake their heads. Either they're lying to protect my feelings or that connectedness still bounding me to Mother makes me know, see, and hear things about her that others can't. I want to believe the latter. But it's hard to. If she were crying, she'd let me return. Wouldn't she?

I give up after six months. But that doesn't stop me from rising with a blemished face, wet with more snot and tears. Mother would be disappointed.

Mother

It took me three months to have my daughter. The first two I spent molding her from scratch. I started by plucking the golden rays from my body and knitting them together. Tight. Firm. Nimble as my fingers were, I didn't move on to a new stitch until the one before was perfect. The golden threads sunk to a blinding white with each new stitch, melding together like bleeding wax.

Eventually, they hardened into the rounded foundation of my daughter's soul. By the time the second month passed, her soul was as big as a star.

I moved to the next step: I kissed my daughter's soul, opened wide, and swallowed her whole. It felt as if a shrunken Earth had descended into my chest, but I was used to this.

The hard part came: waiting. As time flowed, I swelled, and near the end of the third month, I was so large the clouds would whisper and the stars would watch me sink below the line with wide eyes. At one point, a cloud confronted me, their voice filled with concern. But I merely smiled. I did for every encounter. I'd learned too late to never confess an unborn child.

On the Summer Solstice, five hours before noon, heat overwhelmed my chest. I nestled myself in the softest cloud. It only took one breath, a slow count to three, and a push for my chest to open. I gasped and out slipped a golden ball of light. I quickly bundled her in the cloud blanket I sewed for her. On the side of it, stitched in yellow, was her name.

I smiled when the light morphed into a newborn, brown skin like mine, and still shimmering that radiant gold. When she stirred, I pulled down the shirt of my dress and nursed her with the golden nectar from my breast. I held her close. My special ray. A tear fell.

I was now swarmed by clouds, disbelief on their faces. Those whispers again. I paid no mind to them. After three years. Three streams of golden blood instead of infants. I proved everyone wrong. I created life.

But the validation wasn't important to me. It never was.

I kissed her forehead.

I wasn't alone anymore.

I'd never be alone.

I shouldn't be alone. But after everything I've given her, my time, my body, my love, her life. The very people who doubted she could exist, she chose over me.

DAUGHTER

Mother lingers in my head. She always does. But with time, I learn to break past her, focus on the independence I now have. It's strange waking up when I want, having my own vanity, finally dressing myself, and rising above the horizon line alone. But it unlocks a sense of freeness I eventually get drunk on.

I continue to mingle with the stars, follow Polaris where she guides. But with no restrictions and no rush to return to the line, I go deeper. Alone, I explore more nebulas, blacker folds, and Milky Way-type galaxies, even floating beyond what Polaris has shown me. Soon the familiar darkness, the pulse within it, mirrors my own.

As the years blink, my fierce gold rays morph to a soft white, and my brown skin deepens into the same pitch-black as the stars. My vision alters too, expanding past the northern hemisphere. I see Polaris's distant cousin: Octanis. I see the stars around him, his own Milky Way-type galaxies, and nebulas. Polaris and the others notice, and it doesn't take them long to help me adapt. They lend me all things white. White dresses, white jewelry, white hair clips.

One night before we rise, Polaris gifts me with a new star bracelet along with a pendant shaped like something I've never seen before. It's full and round, white as my clothing. Polaris is patient with me when I hold my sun pendant, trace its pointed edges. My breath shakes once I finally unlatch it and place it on my vanity table. I bend my head down.

Polaris says nothing as she locks the new pendant around my neck. She doesn't need to. My smile is small when she kisses my cheek. I'm more than family now. My glow surpasses the other stars. Nothing compared to Mother, but still enough to explode the brightness within the night sky. Meanwhile, the waves I once needed to consciously control manifest on their own.

This role, what I've done, I've become something . . . an anomaly. But it's my new duty. My purpose. And despite the guilt still clouding me, I can't ignore how this feels more right than taking over Mother.

I know she'll never forgive me.

The few times we pass each other above the horizon line, she doesn't acknowledge me, and as much as I want to reach out to her, convince her to look, I don't. She's never seen me, and she never will.

About L. Nabang

L Nabang is an AroAce, Cameroonian American writer who graduated with a BA in English, Creative Writing, and a Certificate in Editing and Publishing. She enjoys telling Fantasy and Fabulism stories that center around family, friendship, real-world issues and the human condition. Her accomplishments include being longlisted for RevPit 2024, published in Inner Worlds, Crow and Cross Keys, and Midnight and Indigo, and selected as a mentee for the 2024 We Need Diverse Books: Black Creatives Revision Workshop. When Nabang's not writing, you can find her losing herself in a good book, jamming to BTS like the ARMY she is, or binge-watching anime. L. Nabang can be found at https://lnabang.com/

The Sacred in the Mirth

Amena Jamali

The jar of flour mocked me.

The very sight of it invoked the crunch of freshly-baked bread, the warm smell spreading through the house like the butter used on special occasions to accompany it, the soothing touch of my mother's hands, the rolling timber of my father's voice . . .

Baking bread had been our family's favored way to spend time together, and all of our best conversations occurred over the roll and the snap and the rise of dough. And there was no more special day for baking than this one, the last night of the year and the eve of the Day of Light.

I could not risk it this year.

In previous years, the soldiers had not cared what we did, only interfering if a celebration grew too loud or too many gathered, spending instead the entire night engaged in whatever evils their minds could concoct. But this year . . . I did not know whether they were just exasperated by the villagers' clinging to their traditions or whether the Slicer — their master and the tyrant governor of Khuduren — had finally decided to obliterate all that remained of who we once were.

In the directives the sergeant had announced this morning,

not one act of celebration was allowed. No prayer. No song. No food.

If they smelled even a hint of meat roasting or bread baking from a single house, the entire village would suffer.

And there was no way to avoid their detection, for there was a farseer among them this winter, and she could sweep the whole village in minutes with her magic, watching and listening to all we did, even in the privacy of our bedchambers . . . and my own stunted farsight was no defense against hers.

A grimace split my lips, and, placing my elbows on the kitchen counter, I buried my face in my hands, suppressing a sob. *What am I going to do? How can we not celebrate the Day of Light?* Memories flickered on the backs of my darkened eyelids, visions of my parents insisting on tradition, on marking the Day of Light and the first Quest's birth, on offering prayer and singing hymns, on cleaning and bathing, even as the soldiers tightened their nooses around our necks and smeared filth over our houses and our clothes.

How can I dare to beseech the Almighty for the second Quest's coming if I neglect to celebrate the first's? How can I hope for the Quest's protection if I forget them? But how can I celebrate them and still keep my sister safe? Yet what value do our lives retain if we abandon every hint of our identity?

There was no one to advise me. Though this village was supposed to have been a safe haven for us from the tyrant, my mother Meriel, my father Nikos, and my siblings Zabraka and Terros had long ago been murdered. My aunt, her husband, and their children wanted little to do with me now. And the rest of the village, water-attuned, white-skinned Ezulal to my wind-attuned, brown-skinned Nasimih kind, found delight in making my life a misery. Even the countess, once a friend of my parents, seemed inclined to wash her hands of me.

The only person at my side, the only person I had in the entire world, was my darling little sister Kalyca.

And how could I ask for guidance and protection from the one I was meant to guide and protect?

She had been my only solace since my thirteenth year, my sole reason for life once our family vanished beneath the earth of the grave. And I shared everything with her. Yet, it was my place to shelter her from the cruelties of our world for as long as I could. How could I weigh down her little shoulders with my burdens?

Oh, what do I do, oh Almighty? I whispered to the only One who remained to listen. *How can I abandon Your traditions? The entire village has, even the countess and my aunt, but how can I do the same?* I pressed my fingers against my eyes, trying to rub away the tears brewing there, and stifle the untrained magic that connected to those orbs.

A gust of cold air smacked my head.

Startling, I jolted upright. *Did the soldiers break the door open—*

Across the main room, the front door was ajar, drifts of snow as high as my shoulders visible beyond, and a little figure was scrambling halfway up them—

"Kalyca!" I exclaimed, blurring across the room. "What are you doing?" I pulled her off the drift, set her to the side, and then, grabbing ahold of the doorknob, slammed the door shut against the wind.

The frigid air pouring into the cottage cut off abruptly.

My chest heaving, I closed my eyes and tried desperately to calm myself.

A near-silent patter of footsteps, before the back of my tunic shifted and — ice spilled down my back.

"Kalyca!" I exclaimed, twisting around to find her behind me, grinning up at me without shame. In her little brown fingers was a glob of snow, already melting in the warmth of the cottage.

Kalyca's gray eyes were sparkling bright with laughter . . . but her fingers were turning blue.

Seizing her wrists, I pried open her fists, shook away the snow, and began to rub her chilled hands between my own. When they still remained cold, I fell to my knees and buried them in my armpits. Only then did the icy feeling slowly vanish, thawing against the heat of my body.

"Kalyca!" I scolded, glancing up into her laughing gaze. "You know you cannot go outside in the cold! It is dangerous for us! The chill that would make our Ezulal neighbors only sneeze could kill us!"

My precious sister, far from chastised, only giggled. "Yes, I know, Kyie!" she said in her shrill, sweet voice. "But you seemed so sad, and I wanted to make you laugh!" Her pink rosebud lips parted in the gap-toothed grin that never failed to melt my heart as she darted forward and kissed my cheek. "I love you, Kyros!"

I sighed, my fears fading in the face of that smile and those words, and smiled. "I love you, Kalyca." Judging that her fingers were warm enough, I gently tugged them out and then scooped her into my arms.

She was still cold.

As ingenious as my parents' efforts at insulation had been, the cottage still took a few minutes to warm whenever a door was opened. The village had made me remove our second fireplace several years ago — under the guise of preventing fire — leaving only the one in the kitchen, though we needed it as they never would. As Nasimih, we were desperately vulnerable to the cold, our fingers and toes prone to frostbite and our skin fragile like glass that would shatter if chilled too long. And our Ezulal neighbors seemed almost to desire such calamity to befall us.

It was why, for this winter, I had prepared everything, from repairs to supplies, such that we would have to go outside as little as possible.

Holding Kalyca to my chest, I rubbed her back, hoping to dispel the rest of the chill still clinging to her dirty homespun tunic. Then, blowing out a breath, I whispered, "My apologies, Kallie. You scared me, my darling."

"I didn't mean to!" she exclaimed, burying her head into my neck, her cold button nose a shock to my skin and a contrast to the roughness of her cap. "I just wanted you to laugh! You've been so upset lately . . ." She jerked back, pushing my hands away, and looked up into my face. "What can I do to make you happy, Kyie?"

My lips tilted up, her words too sweet for me to do anything but smile. As much as I wished she would not attempt anything dangerous . . . in a world where danger was everywhere, I prayed in gratitude that she retained her spirit. She was not beaten into submission the way the village wanted her to be, and I would do everything to prevent that fate. So I said only, "Your wellbeing is all I need for my happiness."

Kalyca scrunched her lips, pressing them together and twisting them to the side. Lifting a hand, she dipped her fingers into my beard, the ash-blond strands of which were beginning to spiral into a cluster of curls at my chin. "Will we be doing anything tonight?"

My heart stung at how even she, an eight-year-old child, knew that she could not speak aloud of our holy day, even in our own home. It was one matter for me, twenty years old and finally a full adult, to be concerned about such things and quite another for her, who should think only of play and lessons, to even be aware of them. Yet all the children who had not been able to pretend so well had long since been abducted, torn from their families' embraces by the cruel fists of the tyrant's soldiers.

I hesitated, not sure how to answer. I still did not know how to celebrate safely.

"Kyie," she began, pulling at a lock of my beard before running her fingertips over my glossy, glass-smooth cheek. "You said last year that we do everything for love. We-we still love them, don't we?"

I caught my breath.

The answer I needed the Almighty provided through the voice I thought sweetest.

A smile, a wider grin, drew up my mouth. "We love them as ever, Kallie."

Then, surging to my feet, I lifted her into my hold, crossed the room, and seated her atop the kitchen counter.

"What are we doing?" Kalyca asked, kicking her socked feet as she beamed.

"We are," I said, pulling a pot, jars, and a pair of bowls from the cupboards positioned on either side of the kitchen fireplace, "going to play a game." I enunciated the words clearly so that the soldiers, if they were spying on us, would be clear on our plans. With the benefit of practice, I controlled my own magic, suppressing it so completely that no hint of residue would draw their attention.

Kalyca giggled. "Really?" She kicked her feet again, squeezing her lips as she, too, suppressed her magic as I had taught her. "But, Kyie, we shouldn't play games tonight!"

I grinned at how she was playing along with my act, though I hated that I had needed to teach her such deception. "We should not, and I had intended to sleep late, but I cannot sleep at all, Kallie. It is the last night of the year, so let us have some fun." Removing the cover of one jar, I ladled out two dozen dried carrot slices, each possessing the diameter of my fist, into the pot and poured water from another jar. Then, ducking beneath the lip of the chimney, I placed the pot atop the kitchen fire, which was opposite the counter, and set into the wall of the house.

The carrots broke into little pieces as the water returned them to an approximation of their previous plumpness.

The soldiers would not allow us apples for the sacred day's festivities, so I would use carrots, fruits of the earth, instead.

Wrapping my hand in a rag, I lifted the pot from the fire and set it atop a thick mat on the counter's rightmost edge. Taking up the ladle again, I spooned the carrot pieces into the bowls. I stoppered the jars and placed them back onto their shelves. The cold brick forming the cupboard would ensure the food remained preserved.

Finally, I offered a bowl and a spoon to Kalyca. Prayer hummed on my lips, but all I said was, "Enjoy your treat. I will not give you honey tonight — we will not be celebrating — but here are some of the carrots you so liked last year."

Humming agreement, Kalyca accepted the bowl before dropping the spoon to the side and plopping a carrot piece into her mouth.

From the sly look she gave me, she was teasing me just as much as she was performing for a watching farseer.

I shook my head and let the poor manners go for one night. I was letting her sit on the counter regardless, and tonight was not a night for more scolding. So, pulling a chair from the dining table, I sat in front of her and ate my own carrots.

As the boiled carrot slid on my tongue, so far from sweet apple and honey, I began a game. "My eyes see a thing that is brown. Of all the brown things your eyes can see, do they see the same thing, too?"

The questions were once a way of training farseers, what my mother had used to teach me as a very small child. But now I could use them as only a game and as a way of teaching her to be observant.

Kalyca beamed, bouncing slightly, and replied, "My eyes can see so many brown things! Is it the counter? The cupboards? Your clothes? Or my face? Oh, what about that brown stain on the left bench from where I spilled stew last week—"

Laughing softly, I tried to keep up with her guesses, until she landed upon the answer, some stray threads scattered on the stairs. Then she asked me about orange things (the carrots), and we played several more rounds until both our bowls were empty.

Standing, I challenged her to a game of tag, letting her chase me up the stairs, through the bedrooms, and down the stairs again until she finally managed to touch the hem of my tunic. As children of the Nasimih, we could run like the wind, and I needed her to learn how to use her speed even in close quarters. Moreover, the magic that fueled that speed was sacred and a divine gift, something meant to be used.

Once she tired of tag, I turned her attention to hiding and seeking. I asked her to find the best hiding spot in the entire house, and then I closed my eyes and counted, "One. Two. Three. Four. Five."

Each number represented one of the five sacred names.

Kalyca, grasping that, waited until I uttered the fifth number before speeding away.

Praying that she would remember both those names and how to hide if the soldiers ever came for us, I searched the house.

In the first round, I found her in the first place I searched — one of the kitchen cupboards — and in the second, I found her beneath our bed. But in the third . . . I searched and searched, spending ten minutes scouring the house, until I discovered her atop the highest shelf of our parents' closet.

"Well done," I praised as my heartbeat finally began to slow.

Jumping down into my arms, Kalyca giggled and squeezed my neck in a hug. "What are we playing next, Kyie?"

I smiled at her, loving the sight of her bright eyes. Her lower teeth were still missing, as were her upper canines, the adult teeth not yet emerged, but that only added to the charm of her face, the face that had stolen my heart from the first moment I had peeked into her cradle.

"What are we playing next?" my sister asked, pulling at my beard again.

The locks spilling from beneath her cap, unraveling from dashing about the house, caught my gaze. "Let me braid your hair, and we can play catch and clap."

"Yay!" Kalyca wriggled in my arms until I set her down on our parents' bed. With a few brisk movements, I undid her plait, the thick metallic hair flowing down her back, combed through the tangles, picked out pieces of soot, and braided it again. Then, holding her hand, I tugged her down to the bottom floor and retrieved our ball, a worn leather creation, from beneath a bench.

"Remember," I said, positioning her so she stood on the other side of the bench, "do not close your eyes. Instead, follow the ball with your eyes."

She nodded eagerly. "And if I finally catch it, I get to start the clap?"

"Yes," I replied and threw the ball.

Kalyca raised her hands, the fingertips touching the ball before she closed her eyes and it slipped through her fingers.

"Ohhh," she groaned.

I smiled, though I worried that she never seemed able to catch it. "My turn to start the clap." Stepping closer, I clapped my hands down atop hers and then started a complex pattern: right, up, left, five bumps of my fists, right, up, left, bottom-left, bottom-right, right, up, left, three opens and closes of my fists, right, up, left—

Kalyca's hands slid against mine, not quite hitting my palms, but she laughed and cheered. "Faster!"

Chuckling, I increased my speed. And beneath the sound of our hands, I recited the first lines of our nation's hallowed songs. To which she only laughed.

So the night went.

Kalyca and I played every game I knew, snacking whenever we grew hungry on dried vegetables and old biscuits, and amid the laughter I made allusions to our faith. From numbers to snatches of song, from colors to shapes made by our fingers, from what we ate to how we moved.

Between our laughter and her mischief, to the soldiers it would look like we were engaged in mockery of the holy night. But, in truth, by showing love for each other, we showed love for the Divine. And that love was the essence of our worship. Our hearts honored all that our limbs could not, our mirth the nourishment and the melody of our traditions amid this moonless night. Our identity remained inviolate.

Finally, as dawn arrived, I gathered Kalyca in my arms in our room. Clutching her to my chest, I grinned and whispered in her ear.

She giggled, as though at jests.

Yet what I whispered were the verses of the Day of Light's sacred hymn.

Verse after verse I recited, and she laughed, masking the blessed words.

Then she, too, sang in my ear, and I laughed, acting as though she returned my jests with her own.

That music glowed in our hearts as the first rays of dawn painted the smog-filled sky a deep bronze.

Wrapping my sister up in blankets, I lay down to sleep with her sprawled across my chest, holding her as though my grip alone would be enough to shield her if the soldiers came for us.

Kalyca snuggled into me as she fell asleep, clutching my neck as though I could actually keep her safe.

Stroking her hair, I sighed.

Oh Almighty, may this be the year in which the Light finally returns to the world . . .

Exhaustion dragging my eyes closed, I dared to let myself rest, hoping against hope that the quiet around our house meant that the soldiers had been fooled by our performance.

The music my sister and I had sung in secret echoed in my ears . . .

And my dreams were full of white-gold sunlight, dazzling, vibrant, undimmed, a haven amid a world swallowed by darkness.

About Amena Jamali

Amena Jamali lives a life animated by the coolness of shrewd logic, the vibrancy of ambitious passion, and the exaltedness of deep morals and philosophy. Her lenses of choice for viewing the world are faith, gratitude, empathy, love, and clear-sighted rationale and strategy. She is many things: devout Muslim, dutiful daughter, patriotic American, thoughtful political activist in the making, blossoming cybersecurity professional, and — not least of all — a writer of epic fantasy. That last, her epic fantasy writings, holds the essence of all of her hopes, ponderings, and dreams, the substance of her musings about philosophy, and the explorations of her ideas about politics. As her writing evidences, she cares deeply about the power of truth, respectful and reverent discourse, and the formation of a truly inclusive and empowering society that values free choice and the pursuit of virtue for all.

And if you'd like to know what Kryos does to secure a better life for his sister and how he finds his destiny along the way, check out Amena Jamali's *The Lord of Freedom* series!

Mother, Ghost, Bride

Audris Candra

The wooden blocks clack against the cold ceramic floor. They rattle and bounce a little before settling near Mama's knees, flat sides facing down, forming two little crescent moons.

No, is my answer. This isn't what I want at all. How do I tell her that the message I sent her last week was not about me?

Mama swipes her phone and shows me a picture of another paper doll, this time of a tall gaunt man clad in pastel blue hanfu. She stares at me — at the small urn that houses my tiny bones — and throws the moon blocks again. Another no.

We sigh in unison, just like a mother and her daughter would if we had the time to know each other. I did not even have the chance to greet her when I was born, and my supposed father blamed her for that. Now, the pair of moon blocks is one of the two things I can use to communicate with her.

Mama hesitates a little before pressing her finger against the screen. A new folder, another series of new faces. This time of feminine paper dolls with painted red lips and huadian in the center of their foreheads. Again, all I have to say is no.

Her bony fingers cradle the block while her eyes dart around from the three smoking joss sticks to the red bowl of rice and vegetable stir fry. She's looking for a sign, and I can only frown because I can't give her any. Not unless she throws the blocks again.

The only other way I can talk to her is through dreams. It takes such a high toll that I can only mope around on my altar after conjuring one, and that was last week. And the margin of error is . . . well, it's what led to this. I had sent her an image of a man and a woman at the altar, both in the traditional bright red of a Chinese wedding, so I can't blame her for thinking that I want a ghost marriage, this being the Ghost Month. The rules of the afterlife make it hard for me to say things explicitly.

"I'll try again tomorrow." Her hands fall into her lap, and her wrinkles bloom as she smiles. A faint aura of sadness clawed at her, but she won't stop. She can't.

Priests of old believed that children like me, who died too young and in too tragic of a circumstance, couldn't eat the offerings made for us unless we marry in the afterlife. And I want to tell her that such times are past. I am okay now. It's her happiness that she should focus on.

She sets the moon blocks back on the altar, and a smile crinkles her eyes. "I have so many stories I want to tell you."

About the neighbor's dog who humped the telephone pole again. About that annoying co-worker who stole lunches getting caught through a simple scheme involving sriracha and laxatives. About a new mall that just opened and how she wishes she could take me there. All the new styles she wishes she could see me in and all the new shoes she wishes I could try.

I don't wish for the same.

I wish she would throw the moon blocks again. I wish I could show her that I'm listening. I wish she could see me and feel the chills of my soul when I rest my head against her thighs. There's nothing that we can change about my death, and I don't want her to focus on that. I want her to live her own life.

She has so much love in her heart, and I want her to share it with the world. Not just with me.

Palms pressed together, she chants one last prayer, to say goodbye for the day.

A loud *ding!* pierces my ears. Her notifications are always so noisy, I've managed to memorize which sound corresponds to which application. This is no different — except for her grin, toothy and bashful.

Is that . . . ?

No, peeking is adharmic. She is entitled to her privacy, even if I'm dead.

But . . .

This could be her chance.

I creep over her shoulder as she types furiously. The picture of a man in his mid-forties kindly smiles back, showing off his garden of chrysanthemum and chamomile. He's inviting her over for tea, and she's not sure if she should come.

She thinks she has to watch over me for Ghost Month. Mama, please, I'm twenty already!

I scramble to the altar, my ethereal hands gripping the edges of the wood. Every drop of energy I have left, I pour it into the red wooden blocks.

Gods, ancestors, I've never asked for anything. I don't need to be reborn as a rich man or a beautiful woman. Just this once, please hear my prayers.

The moon blocks fly in the air and land with a resounding *clack!* This time, only one of them faces down.

Yes. One thousand times yes.

About Audris Candra

Audris is a queer Chinese-Indonesian writer and editor. Their works are featured in New Naratif, Haunted Hallways, and more. When they're not being a weird gremlin, you can find them across various social media @audriserat

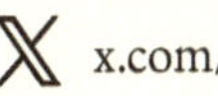 x.com/audriserat

 instagram.com/audriserat

Dova

Kay Mabasa

Kiri watched the drone buzz toward them as it carried the boxes of beer that they'd secretly ordered because they were only fourteen-years-old. The drone set the boxes on the hood of their flying hoverjeep and Munashe, holding the buzzing drone in place, unclasped the boxes of beer from the drone.

Kiri noticed that there was a box of cigarettes taped to the side of one of the beer boxes. He watched as Munashe tore the tape, and bending down, stashed the box of cigarettes into his sock.

Rising back up, Munashe turned the drone around in his hands. He whistled. "Gigantic, isn't it? Haven't seen one like this before. Looks like some military design. Almost want to keep it. Make it mine, you know?"

"You'd get arrested for theft," Kiri said, snatching the drone from him and flinging it into the air like a Frisbee for it to take flight."

"Damn, Mr. Rules. I said almost."

They packed the bottles of beer into a cooler box which Kiri wished he could crawl into and sit in. The heat that day had been reported to have been record-breaking, and it was made worse because they were in the savanna area.

Munashe flicked his fingers in the air and they made a slapping sound. "Kiri, sha, your stepsister looks fine in those white shorts."

Tawonga and Tino hummed in agreement, and Kiri whipped his head around to see Naya in a pair of white shorts, an oversized navy-blue T-shirt with Oliver Mtukudzi printed on it, a navy safari hat, navy boots, and navy socks to match. She swung a flask of water in one hand and held her drawing pad and a case of colored pencils to her chest. Her ebon arms and legs glistened in the sun from the sunscreen she'd spread. He'd seen her in the morning in the same shorts and had thought nothing of it, but now with Munashe and the twins ogling at her, he wished Naya had worn something less revealing.

"Leave the child alone," Kiri said, punching Munashe in the chest. It was meant to be a playful gesture but it came out more forceful than he'd intended.

"Ouch. Okay, big brother," Munashe mocked. "You do know she's not really your sister, right? What's it been? Like a little over eight months since you've been related?" Munashe waved at Naya and Kiri watched his stepsister's face light up as she waved back.

Kiri made an inward sigh. "She's eleven-years-old, Munashe, let her be."

Munashe shrugged. "And I'm only older than her by three years."

"Difference is she's in primary and you're in high school. Focus on the girls that are in high school."

"Munashe laughed. "Hey, Naya, would you like to join us tonight?" he called with a cupped hand round his mouth.

Kiri watched Naya smile shyly and make her way toward them. "Where you boys goin—"

"Sorry, no girls allowed," Kiri said and then pointed her away. "You just go on to wherever it was that you were headed."

Her eyes widened and the corners of her mouth drew down. She turned and walked past them.

Kiri narrowed his eyes at the boys when he caught the boys watching her walk past them.

"We could have at least given her a ride to wherever it is she's going," Tawonga said, jumping into the driver's seat and pressing the button to start the solar powered hoverjeep. A gust of hot air jetted out from beneath the hoverjeep as it lifted off the ground.

"Big brother's just being protective," Munashe said, patting Kiri's cheek before sliding into the tracker's seat, which sat on the hood of the hoverjeep.

"Kiri, handeyi," Tino called as Tawonga set the dust-colored hoverjeep to a gentle glide forward.

"Chief, you coming?" Munashe asked.

Kiri had noticed how Munashe used the chief title as a way to manipulate the people around him into doing what he wanted.

Kiri shook his head. "Not tonight. I'm going to go with Naya. Have to make sure she doesn't get lost."

"Lost?" Munashe and the twins all said at once.

"Chief, I don't think that could ever happen. This is practically her backyard," Munashe said stretching a hand over the game resort. "But hey, your choice. Tawonga, chief, handeyi."

The jeep swished through the tall grass passing Naya who turned, her shoulder length locs dangling in her face as she looked back at Kiri.

Kiri jogged over to Naya and plucked her drawing pad from under her arm. He had noticed how she preferred the paper pads to the digital pad. "So, where are we going?"

"We? Thought you were going with your friends."

"Those idiots aren't my friends," he said, flicking through drawings of zebras, giraffes, and futuristic-looking buildings that she called Eco-Designs. The drawings were all impressive but he had never told her that.

"They can't *all* be idiots."

"Yes, they *all are,* especially Munashe who you keep crushing on." He turned to look at her beaming at the ground. "If anything," he went on, "Munashe is trouble." He handed her back her drawing pad, sunk his hands deep into his pockets and kicked at a stone.

"Then why do you hang around him?" Kiri kept quiet and Naya shook her head. "You can drop the big brother act. If you haven't realized, our parents are on the brink of a divorce." She sighed. "This will be my mother's fourth divorce. I don't think she's wife material, too hardheaded for her own good sometimes. And after that over-the-top roora and African wedding your father paid for . . ."

"I did tell Baba that he was moving on way too soon. I don't think he really went through the grieving process after Mama," he said, even though his parents had divorced before his mother's passing.

"But just cause they're divorcing, doesn't mean we should cut ties. We could still keep in touch, right?"

He looked up ahead and watched the tall golden-brown grass of the savanna move in the wind. The sun was starting to bleed out its orange, red, and pink colors across the blue sky as it was beginning to set.

Their parents had met at one of Africa's Eco-Design seminars, each trying to find solutions for the problems back home. His father, a civil engineer, had been trying to find a sustainable solution for the devastating floods in his country that had been caused by the increased cyclones and the bad luck of being a country near the sea, while Naya's mother had been trying to find ways of providing her landlocked country with water. Since their countries were neighbors, they felt they could help each other. And that was how they came up with underground canals.

Porous tar roads drank up the flood waters and filtered them into drinking water before running through the underground canals that flowed into the country's dams which, once filled, flowed on into the neighboring country's drying dams.

Both countries' economies had been struggling and the

project was financially out of reach, but by putting both their resources together, as well as receiving donations from other countries, the underground canals were built. Naya's mother had said that Africa was entitled to every single cent that was being donated for the construction of the underground canals. Africa had always been the continent with the lowest carbon footprint than the rest of the world and yet She suffered the worst. "They polluted the earth with all their advancements and then came to Africa, deemed our natural ways as primitive, and now, look . . . their advancements are killing the world," Naya's mother had said, shaking her head when they'd watched a news report of how cyclones were becoming more frequent and violent, and how families were losing loved ones and their homes.

Their parents had fallen in love fast. They'd married within three months of meeting, despite Kiri's protests.

When Kiri had first met Naya, he had been cold and distant to her. She'd instantly admitted to being an old hand at it since her mother had been married three times before. She had a string of stepbrothers and stepsisters, none of whom kept contact after the divorce, which was unfortunate since Naya always wanted siblings. "The only siblings I have are the wild animals at my mother's game resort," she'd said with a laugh.

The sound of crickets and distant sounds of birds filled the growing silence between them.

"I hate it when you do that," Naya said, breaking the silence.

"What?"

"How you ignore me sometimes, especially when I ask you a question."

"So why would you want to stay in-touch with such a person?" he asked cheekily.

"Why would you want to walk with someone and not talk to them?" He kept quiet and smirked. "There you go doing it again." She laughed and shoved at his shoulder. Kiri stumbled to the side, nearly falling into a fresh pile of elephant dung, which made Naya laugh even harder. "Mind where you step, that dung costs two hundred alone," she said, raising her chin to the sky.

"Yeah, I know." Paper companies had stopped making paper from trees as a means to conserve them and they had started making paper from elephant, zebra, and donkey dung. "It's no wonder your drawings stink," he said, "you keep drawing on shitty paper."

She rolled her eyes.

They got to where Kiri knew Naya always went around this time before the sunset. A mother giraffe lazily walked in the tall grass, eating leaves from the tops of trees as a baby giraffe followed behind on stalky legs.

Naya walked toward the baby giraffe she'd named Dova, the Shona word for dew. She had named him this because to her, he was her little brother. Her name Naya, was the Shona word for rain, a thing the people of her country relentlessly prayed to the rain spirits for. And so Dova's name, like hers, was a prayer to the rain spirits each time their name was called.

Dova approached them, his legs much steadier than the days past but not yet as steady as his mother's. They both reached out and touched Dova, running their hands across his gold and brown spotted body.

After his father and Naya's mother had married, they had moved out here at the game resort and in some way, it had helped him with the loss of his mother. "I'm going to miss it out here. He turned to Dova and stroked his neck. "And I'm going to especially miss you."

"Really?" Naya said, narrowing her eyes at him and jerking her head back. "You're going to miss the resort and Dova, and not me?"

"As if you're going to miss me. I know I must have been the worst step-sibling you've ever had. Wasn't I?"

Naya kept quiet. And Kiri knew it was her way of making him take his own medicine, but he didn't mind. He kept stroking Dova.

Walking back to the lodges, Kiri had the torch of his cellphone on, scanning the ground for snakes as he recalled what Naya's mother had said about snakes coming out at night to cool off from the day's heat. "Today was hot, ey?" he said.

"My Sekuru would always say that this sun is not the same sun they had played in when he was a boy. That our sun was a cruel one."

He hummed in agreement. It had become an adage a lot of the elders would say to children.

"Do you like drinking beer?" Naya asked.

Though the question had been unexpected, Kiri had been unfazed by it. "I don't drink," he lied.

"I won't tell the parents that you've been drinking with Munashe and them. I know it's your way of escaping. I was just curious."

"I don't think they'd care, or even notice if I walked in drunk, since all they do is argue." His phone beeped and a picture of a battery emptying projected up into the black air just above his phone. "Were they still fighting when you left?"

Naya nodded.

Although their parents had been loud, not caring that they were fighting in front of them, neither Kiri nor Naya could say what their arguments were truly about.

Naya stopped. "Do you hear that?"

"Naya, come on."

"I smell smoke."

"Impossible, everyone knows open fires are illegal, especially during the fire seaso—" A flash of the box of cigarettes Munashe had stuffed in his sock crossed his mind. He then smelled it too, the scent of burning grass. Kiri stopped, turned and looked back to where Naya stood staring at talons of orange fire, clawing the night's sky. Kiri already knew what was going on in Naya's mind before she dropped her drawing pad and flask of water. She screamed as she charged back to Dova.

Kiri chased after her, yelling for her to stop, telling her that

Dova would be fine and his mother would probably take him to the nearest lake.

Each time he got in arms reach to grab at her oversized t-shirt, Naya was always a step out of reach. A sudden gust of wind blew into his face, ash and embers fell from the sky, falling ahead of the fire and lighting unburned grass.

The fire charged toward them as Naya ran to Dova.

"Naya, you won't make it," Kiri said, hearing the desperation in his own voice. "We need to go back to the lodge and war—"

He saw the birds first as they flew out the thick of the forest and it took him back to the time when he and his mother had been caught in a flash flood while they were in their car. He had survived, but his mother had not.

The ground shook beneath him as a stampede of wild bucks came into sight, and his heart choked in his chest. He stopped chasing Naya and Naya had stopped running. Kiri snatched Naya's arm and dragged it as he ran toward the lodge.

Naya pulled her arm out of his grip.

"Naya, stop being stupid."

She ran to where she'd dropped her drawing pad and water flask.

"Just leave them; we need to head back to the lodge."

She picked the flask and left the drawing pad. "We can't outrun the animals or the fire, follow me," she said, running to the west of the fire and dodging a frightened antelope that galloped in the direction of the lodge.

There was a large slab of rock up ahead that he saw Naya run to and he followed. Smoke filled the air and he was attacked by a coughing fit. He slammed into a panicked antelope and it knocked him down.

"Kiri get up," Naya yelled, "you'll get trampled to death."

He got up with the taste of blood in his mouth and made an effort to run but was really limping.

Naya made it to the large rock and picking a smaller rock, she started digging round the large rock, removing the dry grass that surrounded the slab.

Reaching the slab of rock, he picked a small rock of his own and helped her. The ground was hard from the years of drought but they dug through it.

The roar of the fire as it ate through the veld grew but they kept digging. Kiri kept looking up to see how close the towering flames had gotten and each time he looked he felt himself growing small and wishing he could just fly away from it all.

The fire was only a few meters away and they weren't done with their firebreak, but Naya kept her head down and kept digging. Kiri knew that Naya, growing up on the game resort, had seen her fair share of veld fires just as he'd seen his fair share of floods. She knew what they needed to do for them to have a chance at survival just as he knew what needed to be done when caught in a flood. But it didn't stop the look of naked fear on her face.

Just as the fire approached them, they ran up onto the center of the slab away from the talons of fire. Smog encased them and suddenly there was no air to breathe. They coughed, choking from the toxic air.

Naya dropped to the ground, picked up a stone and rubbed it on the rocky ground a few times before tearing at the sleeves of her T-shirt. She opened the flask of water and wet the pieces of cloth. "Here." She handed him one of the dripping sleeves. "Cover your mouth and nose and stay down. He did as he was told, though breathing through the damp cloth was hard.

Wind blew fiercely, and the flames cut higher into the sky. Soot blew into their faces and they shut their eyes.

With his eyes shut and his mouth and nose covered behind the wet sleeve, the only senses Kiri truly had left were what he heard and what he felt. The cracking of the fire grew louder and it mixed with the distant sound of what he believed to be the cries of burning animals. He felt the rock beneath them warm and a frightening thought of being grilled alive came to him.

When the crackling died down and the stinging heat passed. He opened his eyes and found that all around them had gone dark, the fire had gone with its light.

They watched the fire charge on, eating its way down to where the lodges were.

"You need to phone your dad and warn him about the fire," Naya said.

He pulled his phone from his pocket. Three percent flashed into the night as his phone told him that he needed to charge it. He dialed his father and heard the phone ring with no answer. "Baba, come on answer the bloody phone." *They're probably too busy fighting to hear the phone ring,* he thought. "You left your phone?" Naya nodded. She didn't like to go with it when she went out for her walks. His phone beeped, and one percent flashed in the night's air.

"Hello." A hologram of his father's face appeared as he answered the call. Words came spilling out as he warned his father of the veld fire and then the call cut as his phone switched off. "He looked over at Naya. "You think they'll be okay?"

"As long as the fire doesn't jump the firebreaks. If it does, the roofs are all made of grass, so . . ."

They walked slow, Naya matching his limping.

"You think Munashe and the twins are okay?" Naya asked.

Kiri knew that it would be a terrible time to stay quiet but he didn't know how to respond. After all, he knew that it was Munashe who'd started the fire. "They had the hoverjeep so they should be okay."

They walked through the charred grass and trees, the golden brown that he'd loved had all been blackened. Flames of orange were scattered here and there as the patches of fire slowly burned out. Trees had lost all their leaves and the trunks had shrunk and blackened. Unlike people or animals, trees couldn't get up and run.

They found carcasses of burned animals along the way and for the sake of Naya, Kiri prayed they wouldn't come across a baby giraffe. Instead, they came to a baby elephant, moaning in pain.

"Come on Naya, let's go. There's nothing you can do for it now. Maybe if we go to the lodge we can get help."

"The only help it's going to get is a bullet," she said, staring down at the animal. She then hugged herself, crossing her arms across her chest; she held her shoulders and started to cry. Kiri walked to her and held her.

He knew that Dova hadn't made it either.

When they'd finally gotten to the lodges, the thatched roofs had been all burned away, leaving the huts with open tops. There were people on the ground with burns, while others stood dazed with empty buckets that had held sand. The water that the country was receiving from his was only enough for drinking, cooking and bathing. Putting out a veld fire was an extravagance the resort could not afford.

Kiri looked around in search for his father and his eyes met Munashe's, his ashen face told a horror story of its own.

"There they are," Naya said pointing at their parents, who were holding each other. "Mama," Naya yelled.

Her mother's face lighted up and, opening her arms, Naya ran to her.

Kiri's father ran to him and he hugged him. Kissing the top of his head, he said how he was afraid that he'd lost him.

SEPTEMBER 25, 2199

Naya answered her phone and Kiri projected up into the air before her. "Are the clouds there yet?" She'd gotten used to his directness, how he went straight to the point without pleasantries.

"Well, I'm fine, thanks for asking. How are you?" she said knowing that he wouldn't answer. "No, not yet. "You ready for the wedding?"

"Hell, no. You know I'm not a fan of marriage. It's a promise that no one can keep."

"Well, not no one."

"No one."

"Just cause our parents failed to make it work doesn't mean there aren't happy married couples out there."

"Those you think are still married and happy have emotionally checked out and they go out and cheat."

"You don't honestly believe that, do you?" Silence followed. "I'll be there in time for the wedding rehearsals."

"The rain clouds should be there by now?"

Naya stepped out onto the balcony.

After the fire, their parents had divorced. Kiri and his dad moved back to their country and Naya's mom had sold the resort because it was too expensive to rebuild. When Naya had graduated with her architecture degree, she'd used her savings to buy the place and build her Game Eco-Resort.

She'd built the lodges up high so they spiraled around the trees. Her favorite part was when the giraffes came up to the balcony and fed off the trees. Mvura, Water, one of her favorite giraffes was by the balcony eating. She walked up to him and it licked her hand with its long black tongue.

Swishing sound filled the air as the drones approached. "I don't know why you call them rain clouds. They may look like clouds, but you and I both know that they're drones sheathed in white material."

Kiri had continued to improve ways to saving the world from the effects of climate change. These drone rain clouds flew out to the sea where they captured water vapor above the ocean, condensed the water into fresh water and flew to places in Africa that had little rain.

A gentle spray jutted out the drones, raining down on the dry savanna and the animals.

"I love her," Kiri said, changing the subject back. "I want to marry her, but I'm worried that she'll leave me once she sees how difficult I am."

"Well she dated you for two years, trust me, she knows that

you're difficult. That's something you can't really hide if you tried, especially for two years."

"Two years is nothing. Years from now she could get tired of me, you know?"

"Then change." She laughed.

Kiri nodded.

"Hey, even if you two don't work out, you know you're stuck with me, right?"

She watched how the tiny image of him projected into the air, frowned back at her.

"You know I think our parents' love story was really ours."

"That's disgusting."

"Not like that. You know what I mean . . ." She smiled. "You're my big brother."

About Kay Mabasa

Kay Mabasa (she/her) is a Zimbabwean and lives in the city of Bulawayo also known as the city of Kings and Queens. She holds a B.A. in Publishing Studies. You can follow Kay on Twitter @kay_mabasa_ where she always follows back.

x.com/@kay_mabasa_

Birds of Sky, Shadows of Earth

Carla E. Dash

Zed lowers the casket, and the crowd slouching around the grave lets go of the breath they've been holding for the last four months, since Willis turned ninety-nine. No more wondering when they bump into him at the market, *Today? Tomorrow? Now? What should I say?* The wait is over. He's a lump of flesh in a hole, and this death business is over, for now.

I've still got a grave to fill. You wouldn't know it by the way I'm lurking behind the Peytons's mausoleum, but I do, as soon as the crowd gets lost, as per Zed's instructions. I'd just as well get on with it, but does Zed care? The hottest day all summer, and here I am, leaning against four-inch-thick marble and sweating through my shirt before I've even started shoveling.

The graveyard stinks of scorched grass and dust and starving squirrels, and I'm mad again. Why did Mal leave me to this stupid, dirty life? But that's not fair; except for Mal, this is the life I've always had. Walking down the street with Mal's damp fingers curled around mine . . . that was the exceptional part of my life. And it's over.

I remember dumb things about Mal all the time, like the theater, the last time we went. The guy on stage, another victim of the mysterious man in black, had been bleeding to death under a busted streetlamp. A fortuitous raven perched in the treetops above, and the darkness blanketed the ground so thickly it was hard to tell what was shadow and what was the bloom of artificial blood. Mal shook in my arms. I wanted to tell them not to be afraid, that the story was only pretend. In real life no one would ever die so young and from a slash like that across the neck. But that would have been a lie because — don't I know better than anyone? — sometimes people do die far younger than ninety-nine. I wonder if they're still so easily frightened. Pointless to wonder; they're dead. And even if they're not, I'll never see them again.

When I walk over, Zed is already moving dirt.

"What took you so long?" he barks, patches of sunlight and shadow drifting across his shaved head.

"I was waiting for everybody to leave. Like you said."

"Sure, sure. Wait till they're gone, not till they're home, changed, and enjoying celebratory, Willis-has-finally-kicked-it supper."

Beside the gates of the cemetery, a few dark-clad figures dawdle, shimmering like ghosts in the waves of heat wafting up from the pavement. Probably old fogies in a daze. Or Jake and the guys. I don't bring them to Zed's attention.

"What's the matter with you?" I ask instead.

Zed impales a stiff patch of grass. "Nothing's the matter with me. What's the matter with you? You going to start working, or are you going to stand there all day yammering at me?"

People are afraid of Zed. Maybe it's his colossal height, or his biceps like shot put stones, or the tattoos that crawl up and down his legs, symbols in a language that only Zed understands. Or maybe it's the other thing, the story whispered around campfires and by circles of terrified kids telling sleepover tales, candles held beneath their chins. But I know Zed. I've knocked over crystal in our house; I've ruined caskets with clumsy hammering or sanding or staining; once, on a dare from the guys, I even pissed in his garden. I'm not afraid of Zed, not now, in broad daylight, while he's got his sunglasses on and being such a pain.

I shrug and sink my shovel into the pile of brittle dirt. Dust rises around my feet. "Lousy day for burying," I say.

"What?" Zed says. "You'd rather snow?"

"I'd prefer sixty-five degrees. Cloudy. Soil that had seen rain in the last two weeks."

"Well, I'm sure Ol' Man Willis here is sorry he couldn't accommodate you," Zed says, jabbing at the soil. "Shut up and work."

And for a while, we do. Mal would never believe me, the way I used to complain to them about digging graves, but I like my job. Always have; I just didn't want them to look at me the way everyone else does, with their eyes full of armor, like my presence might bruise them. It's satisfying how the mound of dirt shrinks, and the hole gets shallower. It's productive work, work I can feel thrumming through my arms and back and legs.

I'm zoned to the monotony of it until Zed kicks the head-stone. It doesn't move an inch, and he doesn't swear or clutch his foot, though it must hurt something horrible. Instead, he throws his shovel at it, which does no damage and doesn't even make a satisfying sound. It doesn't smash or clatter but just connects with a quiet thump and then whisper-scrapes its way to the ground.

"Wow. Problem?"

"Oh, fuck you," Zed says. Probably he is giving me a look that could boil the husk off an oaknut, but I can't see it underneath those reflective lenses.

"Well? What is it?"

Zed glares across the cemetery, but there's no one left at the gate. The streets are empty. "At this very moment, people are trampling my lilies."

I laugh. "Zed," I say, "Who would do that?"

Zed's lips pucker. "Strangers."

That shuts me up because Zed doesn't joke. I've heard about outsiders. From old people, the grocer, tipsy boys gabbing in Town Center after dark. Movies, books, teachers. Mal. I know we can't be the only people in the world. There must be others off the mountain. But when I climb the water tower and look down to see nothing but clouds and fog, I never really believe it.

"Isn't that, I don't know, a little far-fetched?"

"They'll say they've come to trade, but they're really here to ogle. They always come to ogle," Zed says, folding his meaty arms across his chest. The tattoos bulge and pout.

"You're crazy," I say.

"You'll see."

<hr>

Zed is right, of course. When is he ever wrong? I don't make it two blocks from the cemetery before I hear the commotion. I'm covered in dirt, and I'm supposed to go home, straight home, circumventing town and the eyes that live there. Zed didn't say it in words so much as in an elaborate language of micro expressions and sighs, but I know. The noises are impossible to ignore, though — the thundering clop of hooves, the grind of carts wheeling over road stones, tinkling glass, the eerie squawks of unfamiliar birds, and worst of all, the strange lilt of voices rising and falling out of the pattern I've heard all my life. Well, Zed can't dictate what I do, no matter how much he huffs. I give my shirt a shake, slap what dust I can from my jeans, and change my course.

When I was a kid, Dorst, the mason, put together a show under a giant canvas tent dyed yellow. It had taken him months to collect enough pomegranate rind for the dye job. I remember the boiling pots, the smell, the stain on his fingers, and the weekly hikes to the outskirts of town. Over and down the mountain's edge. The superstitious say he risked his life for a few buckets of fruit. I followed him once, just to see. Would he die the moment he set foot over the edge, the way some say my parents did?

He didn't descend far, only about twenty feet, and then ambled down a wide, even path. He plucked pomegranates from their perches with steady, unshaking fingers. He didn't seem afraid. Zed rolled his eyes at me when I got home as if to say *You aren't sneaky; You aren't subtle,* or maybe *Do you think me so petty?*

It was all worth it in the end, though. He called it the Amazing Animal Extravaganza. Argent coaxed a lynx to leap through fiery hoops, and Miss Julisa tiptoed across a narrow, pine beam strung high off the ground. The Hassen brothers juggled knives, tossing them haphazardly at each other. When I spotted the leathery-throated vulture flying loops above our heads, I pushed my face into Zed's sleeve. He laughed because, despite appearances, despite what the circling scavenger might portend, there was no danger at all.

I'd never seen anything like the Amazing Animal Extravaganza, and I never have since. If the strangers have brought something like that, I'm not going to miss it because I'm supposed to skulk around the back of town like a gem thief.

THE CENTER of town is chaos. Everywhere I look, there are wagons, animals I have only ever seen sketched in questionable library books, and strangers. They are dark of hair and dark of flesh and draped in fabrics of unbelievable colors: greens like moss, purples like irises, and blues as variegated as river water rushing over stones. The people speak oddly, familiar words tumbling out of their mouths twisted.

There are odors I've never smelled and baubles sparkling in the sun and hanging bells chiming in the wind, but it all seems far away. I walk through it with eyes overfull, sick from seeing, but still starving, with fingers trembling to touch, but too afraid to reach out. It's like moving through the aftermath of a tragedy instead of a wonder, the same way I might feel if I'd discovered the wreckage of a neighborhood buried under a rockslide. I've never been so shocked in all my life.

I sit down in the dirt and rub a hand over my face. At my feet is a plant in a pot. It is oblong and covered in bristles. I touch it and pull my finger back bleeding. There is a world beyond the mountain, and it is large and strange and populated with people and things I don't know. Mal was right. They were *right.*

My breath is coming too shallow and too fast. It is like the day I burst through the doors of the schoolhouse, Mrs. Leanne calling after me, and ran headlong into Zed's shin. It should have been my mother there, poppies twisted into her hair, smiling at me and taking my hand to lead me home. Instead it was Zed, mouth frowning and eyebrows swooping, halting the bolting children in their tracks. I stick my head between my knees, link my fingers behind my neck, and breathe.

"Excuse me? Excuse me? Hey!"

I look up. The bottom of the woman's robe is scrunched in her hands, exposing smooth, sandy-colored toes, ankles, and calves. It is the most interesting square foot of space I've ever seen. The robe is green, so dark as to be almost black, as if it is made from the carapaces of hundreds of beetles. The sandals are thickly soled, but airy, with crisscrossing leather straps that form diamonds across the tops of the feet. The nails are a deep black. Several toes are ringed with lighter bands of skin as if usually adorned with jewelry. A dark red design climbs both legs from toe to instep to shin and beyond, disappearing under the robe, disturbing for the nonsensical familiarity of its shapes. A nasty gash on the left calf drips blood, just as red, precisely as thin as mine or anyone else's, onto the sun-withered grass. What language is it? What do the words say? I want to ask. But I can't. I don't have enough breath in my lungs. I curl and uncurl my fingers, trying to feel them.

The woman transfers the cloth to one hand and brings the

other down on my head. She taps her knuckles gently, three times, like knocking on a door.

I try to give her my attention. Her eyes are dark. Her eyebrows are plucked into flawless arcs. Her mouth is tinted a deep red, like the petals of a dahlia. Her dark, straight hair is partially covered by the loose hood of her robe, but I can see that it is long, descending far behind her and out of sight. She looks plain. No, she seems like someone who usually shines herself sharp as a spike, but who, today, is trying to appear plain. If Mal were here, they would appreciate her style. I close my eyes. If Mal were here, they'd know how to help me breathe. But they're not, and I can't.

"Hello? As you can see, I have a problem," the woman begins, voice soothing and peculiar. "The pain is not bad, and the bleeding will likely stop soon. It is infection I am worried about. I brought. We. We brought a healer. But everyone has scattered. I am unsure where he is now. It's all a bit exciting, I suppose, being here." The curl of her mouth is rueful, amused. "I would be very grateful if you could direct me to a hospital or a doctor."

I open my eyes. The make-up is minimal. The jewelry is non-existent. But there's something about the way she stands there, unworried, no doubt that I will comply that tells me it's all bull-shit. She's not just any random woman.

"A doctor. Please!"

I press a hand to my chest. My heart is beating too fast. I hear the woman's urgency, but I can't understand it. Just last year, Hawn sliced his hand clean in half while chopping firewood. He had the nastiest infection I've ever seen. But it passed. Like every-thing, it passed. The woman is not one of us, though. She is from beyond the mountain.

Mal trembled in my arms at the theater, afraid of a little slice, a little blood. My parents had been found bruised and broken-boned, with no injuries that should have killed them, yet it was their corpses that were retrieved from one of the mountain's jutting cliffs. Maybe something as miniscule as a scratch on a leg can kill this woman. Maybe that is the way for everyone off the mountain, like Mal believed. How terrifying. How can anyone live with it? And yet, that's what Mal wanted, what they asked of me: to run away together, even knowing what happened to my parents.

I bow my head and try to breathe through the constricting bars of my ribs. Words spill out, and it feels like vomiting rocks. "The hospital is far. You'll want a cart. But for something like that," I wave a hand blindly in her direction, "you don't need the hospital. Doctor Crevst is closer. But please. Ask someone else. I don't think I can move."

The woman crouches. Her improbable, no doubt rare and expensive, robe brushes the ground. She puts a hand on my shoulder. "I am sorry. Some of the older villagers know of us. I had heard they keep the world a secret from the youth, but I did not truly believe it. I am sorry. I cannot imagine what a shock this must be. Perhaps you should join me in visiting the doctor."

As if I would reveal such a weakness to Doctor Crevst. I hope already that no one has seen me here, panicking in the road. People have enough reasons to look at me slantwise. I shake my head.

"I insist," she says.

"I need a minute."

"I will wait."

ON THE WAY to Doctor Crevst's, I skirt the main road as Zed wanted in the first place. The woman limps beside me. The fingers holding the unnaturally verdant robe off her wound clench with every step, but she makes no complaint, and her hazelnut-like eyes are clear, betraying no sign of her pain. She's used to hiding her feelings, I guess. Like me.

The wound doesn't seem bad. Already the bleeding has

slowed to practically nothing, ringing her too-familiar tattoos in artful red spatters. I focus on putting one foot in front of the other.

"So, what do you do here?" The woman's voice is distant, distracted. She's not even looking at me; she's staring at everything else: the grass, the trees, the houses, the goats bleating in their pens. *What?* I want to ask. *Haven't you ever seen a goat before?* But then I remember, it may be that she hasn't.

"Live, the same as where you're from."

The woman turns her head. "You, in particular, I meant. Do you have an occupation? Your people do have jobs, no? Currency?"

"Yes," I say, placing a palm against my chest to feel the expansion of my lungs. It's calming. "Though if you're hoping I can teach you about my people, you're scaling the wrong bluff. You'd be better off waiting to ask the doctor your questions."

"Oh? Why?"

I shrug. The woman looks at me. She says nothing, but as before, she waits, expecting compliance. She's like Mal that way: relentless. Which is just the sort of thought I don't need to be having. Mal was an anomaly. Despite her lofty courtesy, to this one I am less than a smear of dung on the bottom of her sandals.

"I service the dead. I build their caskets. I clean and shroud their bodies. And then I bury them. People look at me and they see death."

The woman holds my gaze. "In my kingdom, we revere the dead and He who makes them so. Death is a gift. It is freedom from hunger and thirst and pain. It is the right and proper complement to life. Life is the scorching day, and death is the cool night. In my village, our God is the God of Death, but He has abandoned us, leaving his blood, his descendants thrice removed, to do his work. But they are not as skilled as He. Some die too soon and some too late. Some die when they should not, and some live when they should die. We make sacrifices to Him, and each man, woman, child, and person else-wise prays for the day when He will grace us with His merciful presence once more."

I think, *Sacrifices of what?* And I think of my parents' bodies, twisted and bloody and broken. My heart bangs against my ribcage, its fury pounding through the sinew of my fingers. I breathe. I put down one foot. And then the other.

"Pretty words," I say. "Are all your people so devout to this God of Death?"

"Yes," she replies without pause. She gnaws her lip though, as if she has said more than she meant. She watches a cat stalk by, for all appearances deeply interested.

"We have a creature something like that," she says. "But with less hair. And bigger ears. And not spotted."

"Fascinating. So everyone, absolutely everyone, worships death?"

She shrugs. "Some more than others, I grant."

"Mmm."

The woman clenches her jaw. "Our ways may not be your ways, but I'll not listen to your snide—"

"You ever known someone who died?"

"Of course."

"Someone close to you? Someone you loved?"

The woman's eyes turn groundward, anger deflating. "No. I suppose — no."

"Shocking."

The woman's nostrils flare, but she says nothing, and we walk the rest of the way in silence.

* * *

When we get to Doc Crevst's house, the front door is closed, and the house is silent. The medicinal plants sway in the garden beside the porch, too dry to have been tended today.

"No one's home," the woman says.

"You never know," I say. "Try knocking."

"No need."

Unsure what to do with the woman if I can't hand her off to Doc Crevst, I march up the stairs and rap on the door. When that gets no response, I peer through the front windows. Inside all is dark and still. "Sorry," I say. "He's not here."

The woman shrugs the most elegant, careless shrug I've ever seen. "It's quite alright."

I descend the steps slowly and pluck a dainty, white petal off one of the chamomile blooms at the foot of the stairs. "He's probably back in the Center, gawking at the spectacle you brought here."

"Yes," the woman says. "That's likely."

"Well," I say, popping the petal into my mouth and crushing it between my teeth. "You could wait for him. He's bound to be back sooner or later." Sweet, calming juice bursts across my tongue.

"No, my leg needs attention. Take me to your home. Surely you have supplies enough to set it to rights. Disinfectant. Sutures."

"Uh." It's strange how quickly she's pivoted, how willing she is to accept my unskilled medical aid when she was so insistent on seeing the doctor. But whatever she's up to doesn't matter. I can't bring her home. Zed would murder me.

I'm floundering to come up with an excuse when I notice the guards following us. They are dressed in black robes and wearing curved blades cinched at their waists. The metal has been worked in a way I've never seen. The edges are not smooth but twisted like waves. Mal would be shaking like a Rowan leaf, wouldn't they? I'm not afraid of dying. I'm only twenty-eight. Besides, I have Zed, and Zed would never . . . what? Let me? Still, the blades look wicked and painful.

"I insist," the woman says, lips curved apologetically.

I sigh. Zed's going to be livid, but what else is new?

"WELL, THIS IS US," I say when we hit Zed's patch of lilies.

The woman's nose scrunches. She looks around. "Which . . .?"

"This one," I say, pointing.

The woman's face smooths out. Her expression becomes perfectly neutral. Very diplomatic. But she's gone tense under her robe. "This one? This is your home? This *yellow* one?"

I look at the house I've shared with Zed most of my life, wondering what's so offensive about it. The sunny paint job? The window boxes overflowing with lavender and mint? The carefully tended flower garden? It'd all be in shambles if it weren't for Zed. But this woman doesn't know me well enough to know that.

"Are the houses in your kingdom very different or something?" I ask.

The woman blinks. "No, no!" She huffs out a little laugh. "Well, yes, actually. They are made of stone or clay. But that's not it."

"Then what?"

"Nothing, nothing. I apologize. It's lovely. Please, lead the way."

I frown but turn and walk up the stairs. When I push open the door, the woman startles.

"What?"

"Nothing," she says. Then, "Do you not lock your doors in this kingdom?"

"It's really not a kingdom," I mutter. And then I can't help but giggle. The woman tenses beside me, and her shadowy guards shift across the street. "Sorry," I gasp, holding up my hands. "It's just . . . the idea that anyone would steal from Zed."

"Zed?" the woman asks, stepping over the threshold.

"Oh," I say, sobering. "Zed is . . ." I hesitate before closing the door. "Should I invite in your, uh, guards or . . .?"

The woman just smiles at me and begins wandering around the room.

"Okay . . ." I say, shutting the door.

"So, Zed?" the woman says, trailing fingertips across the knickknacks lining the walls.

I shrug. "Zed is Zed. I live with him. I've lived with him since I was little. I guess you could say he's like a father to me."

The woman locks her dark eyes with mine. "Is that customary here? To live with someone outside your bloodline?"

"Um, no," I say. "My parents . . . died when I was young. Zed took me in."

The woman blinks. "I thought," she says, "that people do not die here until they are old. Were your parents old, then? Or have I been misinformed?" Her tone makes me fear for anyone who might have been so foolish as to deliver false information to her.

"No," I say. "That's true. Is it not true where you're from?" The woman's face is so still it could be carved of limestone. "My parents' case was unusual," I say after a moment. "They were, uh, trying to leave the mountain."

"Oh," the woman says. I wait for pity or judgment, for apology or blame. But the woman just resumes her inspection of the living room.

"I'll go get some things for your leg," I say, gesturing upstairs.

"I'll be here," she responds absently.

***

When I return, arms laden with what meager first aid supplies I could find stuffed under the bathroom sink, the woman is perched on the edge of the couch, leg held out imperiously. Her dark robe is stark against the floral pattern, like hawk wings slicing through blue sky.

"Oh," I say. "I guess I'll just, uh . . ."

I nudge the tea table with a foot and drop to the ground before her. While I uncap the alcohol, I chance a look at the woman's face. The slightest hint of amusement hangs at the corners of her eyes. I douse a piece of gauze but hesitate to reach for her leg. Besides Mal, no one has ever let me touch them so intimately.

"Is this okay?" I ask.

The woman smiles, a true smile that stretches her lips and dimples her cheeks. I duck my head. I'm sorry, Mal. I'm sorry to even think it. But wow, she is beautiful.

"Yes," she says. "Proceed."

I touch the cloth to her lower leg, wiping away the dried blood. She does not so much as twitch, just holds her leg perfectly straight and grips the robe loosely to keep it out of my way.

"You used to people kneeling at your feet or something?"

She laughs, and I look up, startled. The sliver of uncovered skin beneath her chin trembles. "Perhaps."

I smile, probably a silly, stupid smile. I didn't dream I'd ever make another person laugh after Mal left. I finish wiping the woman's leg and bring the cloth down on the cut itself, an almost-perfect circle around her upper calf. "How did you say you got this again?" I ask, frowning. I toss the rusty cloth onto the table and unscrew the jar of tea tree oil.

The woman hunches over, resting an elbow on her knee and her chin on her palm, gazing at me like I'm a particularly amusing puppy.

"Okay . . ." I say, applying the oil to the cut with a fingertip, trying not to study the surrounding tattoos too obviously. They're not exactly like Zed's. The images aren't arranged in the same order or located in the same places. But they're very similar. They almost certainly draw from the same pool of symbols. What does that mean? Does Zed come from this tribe? Why wouldn't he have told someone? Me? Why would he let us believe we were all alone on the mountain for all this time?

As if summoned by my thoughts, Zed arrives, throwing open the door with such force that it hits the walls and bounces back at him. He catches the frame in one hand with the familiarity of long practice. He fills up the doorway, thunder lurking in the dark brows furrowed above his shades.

"What. The. Fuck."

I scramble to my feet. "Uh, she was injured. I tried to take her to Doc's, but he wasn't there. So I brought her here. Sorry," I say, hoping to diffuse the mega-angry squeeze of his fists. "I know you don't like unannounced guests. I just . . . didn't know what else to do."

Some of the dizzying panic I felt earlier must bleed through because Zed exhales and unclenches his fists.

The woman rises gracefully to her feet. " ‖ ═ ¬ ¬ + Γ + ∩ ≈ | ‖ ," she says.

"What?" I say, skipping over the incomprehensible speech for the moment. "You two know each other?"

"Yes."

"Never seen her before in my life." Zed steps to the side, clearing the doorway. "Get out."

The woman lifts her chin. "I have been invited as a guest into your home. Will you refuse to observe the rights?"

Zed goes rigid, and the air feels heavy, like there are boulders squatting on my shoulders. It is a feeling I have felt before, but not in a long time, not since the reckless days of teenagerhood, I think, when everything I did grated on Zed's nerves.

"Hey," I say, raising my hands. "It's cool. I'll go make some tea, and then we can all sit down, and someone can explain to me what's going on. Yeah? Sound good?"

Zed slams the door. "I'll make the tea," he says, barreling into the kitchen. "You clean up that shit on the table."

The woman exhales and slumps back onto the couch.

"You okay?" I ask, gathering up the first-aid supplies.

"Yes." The woman smiles again. "Thank you for asking."

"Okay," I say. "I don't think you need a bandage or anything, so I'm just going to run this stuff back upstairs." From the kitchen comes the unmistakable sound of shattering porcelain. "Zed," I yell. "Did you break *another* teacup?"

"No!"

I shrug at the woman. She looks stunned and pleased, like I've performed a surprising trick. "I'll be back in a minute," I say. "Just scream if you need me."

The woman places two fingers to her lips, maybe to hide a smile. "What would I scream? You have not introduced yourself."

"Oh," I say, shifting everything to my left arm. "I'm Makenzie. Mack." I hold out my hand. The woman takes it and shakes, bemused. "So what's your name?" I ask, dropping my hand and redistributing my bundle.

The woman's eyes crinkle. " ‖ ‖ ⚊¬ | ⌐⚊." I stare. She shakes her head. "You may call me Lida, I suppose."

"Cool. Lida. Be right back."

Upstairs, I stuff everything under the sink and hurry back to the staircase, but as I'm about to round the bend, I hear Zed charge into the room and thunk a cup down in front of Lida. I stand in the shadows and poke my head around the corner.

"There," he says, crossing his arms over his chest. Is it a trick of the light or do the tattoos swirl across the thick meat of his forearms? "You've been served. *Now* get out."

Lida's eyes also lock onto Zed's arms. Does she see it as well? " ⌐＋∩≈ | ‖ ," she says.

"I'm not your damn cousin."

Lida takes the cup of steaming tea and holds it on her lap. "You are the progenitor of ⚌⚊⚌¬ , my twentieth grand elder. Be welcome in the home of your kin for eternity, ⌐⚌⚌⊤ ‖ ‖ ‖ | ‖ ⚊⚌ | ."

Zed walks to the eastern window and grips its frame. "The time of your twentieth grand elder sounds too long ago for me," he says.

"Will we play such a game?" asks Lida. "Whatever for?"

Zed's shoulders bunch and twist. "Be welcome, ‖ ‖ ⚊¬ | ⌐⚊," he grits, "in the home of your kin."

Lida stares down into her tea. "Thank you," she whispers.

"Well," Zed says, turning and leaning his back against the window. "What do you want?"

Lida sucks in a breath. "I come to ask you to end your exile upon this crag and return to the larger world. We have great need of you. The—"

"No," says Zed.

Lida takes a sip of her tea. "I was told you would answer thus."

"Yeah? Who told you? Give them a gold star for me. A plus, great work, a true genius—"

"By the one who exiled you here." The silence rings like a bell. "He says to inform you that your punishment has ended. You have learned your lesson. It has been long years since you have slung your gifts around with recklessness or capriciousness. Please," she says. "Please. Return to your true duties."

"No," says Zed.

Lida places her teacup gently on the table. She stands and strides over to Zed. She clasps her hands in front of her chest. "You do not understand," she says. "We try, but we are not you. We cannot control the gift properly. We cannot always bring it when it is needed. Sometimes we bring it without intention, when it is not wanted. The gift in your kin is not the gift that is in you. It is out of control. We need you."

"I understand," says Zed. "No."

"Please!" cries Lida, throwing herself to the ground at Zed's feet. "I am not above begging," she says. "My people suffer. Your kin suffer. Please," she says, pressing her head into the floorboards.

Zed squats and pulls off his sunglasses. I slam my eyes shut, but it is too late. I have already seen what I have spent years trying to forget that I ever saw when being tucked in late at night or sneaking around in the early morning when Zed thought he was alone or I was asleep: black irises on black sclera, eyes impossibly, inhumanly black from corner to corner.

"Look at me," Zed commands. So I do, and so Lida does. "That is the nature of the power," he says. "It comes when it comes, and it doesn't when it doesn't. There is no supposed to, only what is. There is no controlling it."

"But," she says. "What you have done here . . . I do not agree. It is unnatural. But it is controlled. You control it. You could teach us—"

"No," says Zed, finding my eyes. "I don't control it. Not always."

I gulp, heart in my throat.

"But my father—" protests Lida.

Zed sighs. He replaces his sunglasses and touches the top of Lida's head gently, like one caressing the fluff atop an infant's skull. "Go home," he says. "And do not return."

Lida stands. Zed stands. Lida stares into the reflective lenses of Zed's glasses. "Please," she whispers.

"Goodbye," says Zed.

Lida turns stiffly, like a strung marionette manipulated by an inept or uncaring puppeteer.

"Wait!" I scramble down the steps. Lida pauses next to the banister, eyes bright with unshed tears. I grip her arm. I need to ask her — what? What is Zed? What is she? What is the gift, and how much can she do with it? Could she, my parents . . .? "Mal," I gasp. "Is there someone named Mal in your kingdom? Someone from here?"

Despite how tightly I'm gripping her, Lida takes my hand and removes it easily. She cups it between her two. "I don't know," she says, gently. "But I would be honored to welcome one who tends the dead into my kingdom if you wish to search for yourself."

"No," says Zed.

I glance at him. I see the dark glasses perched on his nose and the glint of sunlight bouncing off his bare scalp and the tattoos crawling over his shoulders, down his elbows, and piling up around his wrists. I'm looking at Zed, and I'm seeing Zed, but he's unfamiliar and makes my hair stand on end. It's like looking at your reflection in the mirror and knowing that the moment you blink, it will move out of concert with you, but you'll never be able to prove it. It's Zed, but it's not Zed. It's some other thing that lives in his skin. I will go with Lida. I could not possibly stay in this house with this thing that killed my parents or let them die or couldn't stop their deaths.

Zed frowns. An inky blackness billows out behind him and oozes up the walls, across the ceiling, and down onto the floors. The room is engulfed, and it is like being inside an oil slick.

"What?" I try to say, but I can't speak. There are so many questions swirling in my head, but I can't latch onto a single one. None of them make any sense, the way a shoal of trout is just a shiver of dizzying, undulating silver that won't resolve into a known shape. It feels like there's a rope pulled taut around my chest. It feels like I can't breathe, like my ribs are going to cave in and puncture the meat of my lungs and heart, and I will die here, wherever here is, because my body isn't permeable enough to absorb all this new information. I'm breathing or I'm trying to breathe. I'm inhaling, but I can't get enough air. Where am I? Underwater? In outer space? I don't know. I don't care. I'm choking. I'm dying. I'm sorry, Mal. I'm sorry I didn't go with you when you asked. I'm sorry I didn't go looking for you after. I wasn't brave enough, and now I won't get the chance.

"Stop," says a voice, and something squeezes my hands. It's Lida, I think. And she is saying, *Stop.* And then I remember Lida and Zed and the living room eaten by Zed's shadow. I must be standing there still, at the foot of the stairs, my hands clasped with Lida's. The vise wrapped around my chest eases. This place, whatever it is, isn't real. Not really real. It's the world of the mirror or the inside of my head.

I remember Zed saying no to my leaving. And the no is ricocheting around this space, I realize, like an echo bouncing around a glass box. *No. No. No. No. No.* The darkness squeezes like the inside of a fist.

"Stop," says Lida. "You'll kill him."

I can feel the mental shrug, the indifference suffused into the flapping velvet surrounding me, and it hurts. Not the brain squeeze of this place, but a pain of the heart, like a barb stabbed through my chest.

"Your own kin?"

"He is not my kin."

"You do not know kin. What it means to have it or what it means to be it." A sound rings out behind me, like knocking or hammering.

"What do you think you're doing?" asks Zed. "It's like you said, the power that is in you is not the power that is in me."

"I understand now," Lida says, and the pounding grows louder. Its ripples reverberate through me. "You have not changed. You will not ever."

"Yes," says Zed, and maybe it's my imagination, but he sounds regretful.

Just then, the oily skin behind me bulges inward and pops. A giant black bird pushes through the hole and screeches. The darkness eases. It is not exactly shot through with light, but a darkness less dark than Zed's pours in through the hole the bird has ripped in my prison.

"What the hell?" shouts Zed. "How did you? — Get out. — $=\top\ +\cap\top$. GET OUT." *Get out. Get out. Get out.* The blackness separates, and I see it is formed of tentacles, huge and iridescent. They flail, swiping at the bird, which swoops and dodges. Terrifyingly, one heads straight for me. The bird dives, spreads its wings, and releases a scream that pushes back the suckered arm.

"Cease," Lida says. "His name is not on your ledger."

Zed's laugh booms out, cold and mean and loud. I try to cover my ears, but I can't because I don't have ears. I don't have any kind of body at all. "I told you, didn't I? There is no supposed to, only what is."

Another tentacle whips by, and the bird snaps at it. Beady black eyes fix on me. "Mackenzie," the bird, Lida, says. "I need you to come to me." I don't understand. The bird is right in front of me. "Climb on my back," she says, more urgently, snapping at another encroaching limb.

I can't, I think. I am nothing. I am smoke. I am fog. I am less than that. I can't walk. I can't climb. *I am not really here.*

"You are here," she says. "You are out there, and you are in here. You are everywhere. You cradle us, and you cage us. Be, and climb on my back."

I try. I imagine embodiment, conjuring arms and legs and fingernails in my mind.

"Now!" she shouts as Zed wraps a piece of himself around her thin foot.

Feet, I think. *Heels. Soles. Insteps.* But I can't. I've never been afraid of Zed. But now. If I do not exist, Zed can't catch me the way he has caught Lida. She's hacking at the tentacle with her sharp beak. But I don't have a beak, do I? How would I fight back?

"Mackenzie," Lida says. "I can't bring the gift beyond the border of my domain."

Okay . . . ? I think, still trying to bring into being arches and toes. There is a tingling starting in the region where my feet could be.

"And neither can Zed."

Yeah, but how big is Zed's domain? Then again, Lida broke in here when Zed didn't think she could.

"Do you renounce the land of your birth and vow to come and live in Mazada under the protection of Khalida, the third to be so named."

Do I? I think of the way my neighbors look at me, like I am walking death. I feel a pang of sympathy for Zed. Maybe that is why he grips so hard. He only doesn't want to be alone. But how can I ever share a home with him again? He didn't explain. He didn't ask. He didn't offer a choice. He tried to move my mind against my will, like he made Lida rise and shuffle to the door, eyes sparkling with tears like melted glass. What did I ever stay here for, besides Mal and Zed?

Yes, I think.

"You must say it," Lida urges, claws digging into the darkness to keep her footing against the pull of the tentacle tightening around her ankle like a strangling serpent.

But I would need a mouth for that.

"Yes," she says.

The tingling in my feet has intensified into a burning flame licking up my shins. I think I do have feet now, and I try to move them. Each step feels like touching the vulnerable pads of my soles to the scorched, parched graveyard soil, like the desiccated husks of dried-up acorns are grinding into my flesh. But I move. My legs are on fire and pushing them forward feels like dragging tree trunks through a mud pit. But I move. My stomach comes into existence, and my throat burns so fiercely I think I would hurl if I had a mouth. But I move.

"Yes!" says Lida, sinking her talons deep into the slimy limb gripping her foot. And then it is pulling back, dripping something black and viscous. Lida turns and flies at me, batting away tentacles with beak and claw and wing. I shamble toward her as fast as I can. The tingling is whipping its way over my shoulders and pooling in my fingertips. I reach out and close a hand around one of Lida's wings. She spins, and I flip onto her back.

"Hold on," she says and takes flight. As we soar and dodge and spin, my mouth begins to feel like Doc Crevst has been at it all day with a drill.

"Yes!" I shout from my newly formed lips. "I will come with you."

"Then I declare you a citizen of Madaza under my protection. No harm will come to you."

"No!" shouts Zed. *No, no, no, no.* And the darkness tightens around us.

Yes, I think. *This is my head, you fucker. Get out!*

The darkness does not recede, but the tentacles around us vibrate like they're being electrocuted. Snatches of light speckle through quicker than Zed can cover them.

"This Zed," Lida says. "He is a creature of shadow. Of darkness. Of Earth. And I am a bird on the wing. I am as light as air, as fast as the wind. And you," she says, tucking her wings back and speeding like a bullet toward the hole she burst in this prison for me when Zed did not believe it possible. "You're strong. Think of a weapon."

"What?" I ask as we hurtle toward the broken wall of black.

"Think of a weapon!" she says. "And smash it into the wall when we hit."

What weapon? I don't know anything about weapons. We don't have weapons here. What need is there for them? An axe perhaps, but I've never held one. A wicked, twisted blade, like the ones Lida's guards carried? I'd probably slice my own barely material hands open.

"Hurry!" Lida urges, speeding toward the hole. It is too small, I realize. I am not a svelte bird. I'll never fit. That's why we need a weapon. But what do I know how to wield that could be used for destruction? A hammer? A Chisel?

And then, the thing is taking shape in my hands. I grip its woody body, embarrassed to my core. What am I supposed to do with a shovel? Dig us out of here? A tentacle whips by my ear, and Lida rolls out of the way. She spares me a glance. When she catches sight of my "weapon" she laughs, a beautiful, tinkling giggle completely lacking in mockery.

"Oh, you're lovely," she says. "Your Mal will be so happy to see you again."

So what if my weapon is a shovel? A shovel can make a hole. A shovel can gore and smash. And so what if my business is death? What is it Lida said? Death is the right and proper complement to life. When we get out of this tentacled prison, we'll fight Zed's physical body if we must. Lida's guards will join us because she is their leader, and they love her. How could they not? And no one will fight for Zed because no one here knows how. No life on the mountain has ever been in danger. No person has ever had to risk their life to protect something they love. Except, maybe, my parents. I don't know why they were leaving or if they planned to abandon me. But they were brave, and Mal was brave, and Lida is brave, and I will be brave, too.

The hole is coming up fast. Lida makes herself as small as she can. She plasters her wings to her sides and tucks her feet up close to her belly. She stretches her long neck and pushes her beak out in front of her. There's no point in me trying to do the same. I sit up, swing the shovel over my shoulder, and get ready to do some damage.

About Carla E. Dash

Carla E. Dash (she/her) lives in Braintree, MA with her husband, children, and cats. She teaches middle schoolers, procrastinates via video games and anime, and occasionally buckles down and writes. Her writing has appeared in *The Kenyon Review Online, Cosmorama, Eucalyptus Lit,* and others. Her debut collection, *Monsters and Other Tales of Humanity,* will be published by Meerkat Press in 2025. Visit her at carlaedash.com or follow @carla.e.dash on Instagram or @carlaedash on Twitter.

 x.com/carlaedash

 instagram.com/carla.e.dash

THE SECRET KEEPER

MARIE SINADJAN

I inherited my mother's debt when she died. It wasn't much, but I was young and unmarried. That left me dependent on the *Datu*, the chieftain of our community.

But *Datu* Balintawak was honorable and fair. He had me move into his home so he could take over my family's property and reduce the price of my bond by a couple of years. He, too, tasked me with the care of his only child, alongside three other *alalay* working off their debts. It was hard work, but not as difficult as plowing the fields out in the scorching heat or as painful as scrubbing my hands raw while doing the laundry. I often only had to stand and wait, and once my mistress went to bed, I could likewise get some rest.

Dayang Rosita and I were the same age. Because of that, there were tasks she preferred me to perform instead of the others, though I was younger and less experienced in terms of our duties and about life. Telling her stories about the Spirits was one. As I came from the outskirts of our *barangay*, she believed I had tales she hadn't heard before.

I didn't, but I knew a secret. My mother learned it from her mother, and her mother from her mother's mother. Each of us, *Nanay* had said, had four souls. The first soul is the *kararua*, which only leaves the body after death. The second soul is the *karkarma*, which fear can chase out of the body. It can even be stolen. *Aniwaas*, the third soul, can emerge during sleep and wander toward places the body holds dear, while the fourth soul is called the *araria*, the soul of the departed that visits our world to perform a duty it had failed to do in life or to visit relatives and friends.

That story, that secret, became *Dayang* Rosita's favorite.

Chatting about her suitors while I brushed her hair was the other task on my list. She often asked for my opinion on the string of men who came from far and wide to win her hand, and if I'd heard any gossip about them.

"The *Datu* thinks highly of him, *Dayang*," I always answered. It didn't matter who the man was, or what he was like. It was not my place to speak of such matters.

"What do *you* think?" she insisted anyway. "Please, Marisol. I need you to be honest with me. If they don't treat you well, especially when I'm not looking, I doubt they'll afford me the same respect once we are wed."

At first, I refused to say a word. She frightened me into doing so by declaring that it was my duty to protect her and her family by speaking the harsh truths people otherwise wouldn't dare say to their faces. I knew about duty, about *debt*, thus the words tumbled out of me.

"He is an idiot. He nods along to whatever the *Datu* says, though he does not understand any of it. The way he looks at you is vile, as though you are a pig he will soon roast and devour. He is not a man worthy of your affections, *Dayang*."

Her eyes flew wide — then much wider at "pig" because that was a truly horrible thing to call a woman — and I feared for my life, though I had only done as she asked.

I shrunk back and mumbled an apology, but she cut me off with a loud, bright laugh. She flew out of her chair and threw her arms around me. "Marisol," she gushed, squeezing me. "Thank you."

I spent more and more time with her after that. She insisted I serve the snacks whenever she met with a suitor, and the more of them that came, the more harebrained the schemes she hatched to test them. She tasked me with holding her umbrella while she took her walks, if only so we could whisper and giggle together under the shade. We talked about her dreams as we picked flowers and made garlands in offering to the Spirits. She had this recurring one about a poet, and she would quote the verses she imagined he said to her. They sounded nice, but also full of nonsense. I could never appreciate metaphors. Why didn't people just say what they meant?

"It's nice for her to have a friend," Biya, the oldest of us *alalay*, remarked one day as we gathered *Dayang* Rosita's dried clothes. She had a stern face, further stressed by the streaks of silver in her hair and the way she kept it away in a tight bun. The rest of us feared being admonished by her, or worse, to be reported to the *Datu* for being inadequate at our jobs.

"I can never be her friend," I mumbled, pinching one end of a wooden clothes peg and pulling a skirt away from the washing line. I wanted to be her friend, and I indulged my delusion now and then, but who was I kidding? She might be kind, but she was still my mistress. Even if I would be free of my mother's debt someday, our current relationship would always cast a shadow on our situation.

She would always be my *Dayang*. I was content with that.

THE FENCE APPEARED without warning one day. Made of dried bamboo, it stretched down across the plain for a mile, perhaps even more. I stood under the midday sun, forehead creasing as I scanned the length of it. Wasn't all this the *Datu*'s land? We'd wandered this far out before, even deep into the woods on the other side, but there seemed to be no end to *Datu* Balintawak's territory.

Dayang Rosita ran to the boundary and pushed herself up to her toes to see what lay on the other side. We recovered from our surprise and caught up with her a moment later, pulling her down before she could be seen.

She peeked through the gaps between the pieces of wood. "Are those . . ." she trailed off, swallowing. "Do you see them too, Marisol?"

Biya pried the umbrella from my hand and took over sheltering *Dayang* Rosita from the heat so I could lean closer to the fence and assess the situation for myself. My gaze landed on a man standing outside a shabby-looking tent, a *bolo* tucked into the belt around his waist. The curved blade glinted in the sunlight. I strained to see the design on the hilt, but found none.

"*Horohan*," I confirmed. *Horohan* served their masters as warriors instead of laborers. My father used to be one — until a warrior from another *barangay* took his life in a skirmish over a territory dispute when I was a child. There were freemen warriors, too, but their weapons would have been more ornate than the unadorned *bolo* this one carried.

Now that I knew what I was looking at, it wasn't hard for me to identify the other *horohan* scattered about the other side of the fence, despite the planks of wood limiting my field of vision. "I see six of them. They must have built the fence." I had no other conclusions.

We backed away as quietly as we could and hurried back to the house, ducking low so the *horohan* wouldn't see the umbrella I resumed holding above *Dayang* Rosita. While we walked, she gripped my other hand so tightly that I was certain she had crushed my fingers. But I did not complain or pull my hand away. Somehow, doing so eased her fear. It was such a simple gesture, yet it made her face a little less ashen, her eyes a little less terrified. I could give her that.

Though I did not feel relief until our own sentries spotted us and waved us over.

"YOU PUT UP A FENCE," *Datu* Balintawak accused.

I had never been outside my *barangay*, but I imagined that *Dayang* Rosita's family home was the grandest of the chieftains' houses. Though still roofed with *nipa* like everyone else's, it had many rooms and fine furnishings. Most impressive of all was the hall where the *Datu* welcomed his guests and held meetings with the other nobles. It housed their family's collection of gold and exotic trinkets from other lands.

But the hall felt very stifling that morning, in part because of the other larger-than-life presence that graced its walls then: *Datu* Gagalangin, who had come as demanded by *Dayang* Rosita's father to settle the matter of the fence. He was a stout man, yet his smile and his stance projected an air of confidence. The tattoos on his arms marked him as a warrior, though the years of peace had forced him out of shape.

Datu Gagalangin shrugged off the allegation. "Only to better mark our territories." He cast a glance toward *Dayang* Rosita. "Your subjects like to wander, you see. I do not wish for something unfortunate to happen to them because of a . . ." He paused for effect. "Misunderstanding."

"Is that a threat?"

The visiting *Datu*'s smile brightened. "Only if you take it as one."

I did not like *Datu* Gagalangin. Everything about him and the way he acted hinted at trouble. He reminded me of a crocodile lying in wait and provoking an unsuspecting creature into attacking first so he could strike back without remorse. Neither did I like his son; the way he eyed *Dayang* Rosita did not sit right with me, even if it was not hunger I saw in his gaze.

No, it was how *she* looked at the *Datu's* son that made my insides churn with dread. She had regarded no suitor of hers in that manner before. What was it about this man that she showed such interest in him? He hadn't spoken a word since their arrival.

He just stood there, a boy unmarked by the tattoos that heralded one's victories in battle, cowering behind his smooth-talking father.

How I wished that had been the end of it. The fence, the boy . . .

Little did I know it was only the beginning.

GAT DELFIN, son of the *Datu* of the *barangay* of Gagalangin, was a few summers older than *Dayang* Rosita and I. Yet he was practically a boy. He had not seen battle. He had not even been allowed to do business in his father's court, only to stand and observe.

But he had a way with words. Not the speeches laced with threats that his father excelled at, but the softer, more playful ones appropriate for songs and prayers and poems. I had learned, too late, that before his family and their entourage had departed that day, he'd somehow slipped a letter to *Dayang* Rosita. In it, he'd confessed his love and devotion to her.

That had been her undoing.

"Please, *Dayang*. This is dangerous." *This is madness*, was what I truly wanted to say. How could love blossom from a glance across a room? At a wordless encounter between strangers? It was preposterous. Love was something more than that.

But saying any of that felt out of bounds, even with the freedom she had granted me.

Dayang Rosita grabbed my hands and swayed me in some sort of childish dance. "We are in love, Marisol," she declared, as if there was nothing wrong with that. "What is the worth of one's life if it is not lived in love?"

I said nothing still, but my body had stiffened at her words. She stopped when she realized she could no longer make me move, though she did not release my hands. "I'm sorry." Her voice was soft enough that the ears in the walls could not pick up what she had to say. "But one day, you will find love, too, and my father—"

"Your father," I interrupted, shaking my head, "will be angry if he finds out."

This wasn't about me, so why was *I* angry?

"That is why he mustn't find out. Not yet." She leaned in and let me in on her secret: *Gat* Delfin planned to win over her father through acts of servitude and spoken poetry. Until then, they were going to meet in secret on the nights of the new moon, at the end of the fence, and we were to accompany her.

I fought back a laugh at the absurdity of it. *Datu* Gagalangin was not a man of peace. He could have brokered a marriage between his son and *Dayang* Rosita, but he did not. Instead, he built a wall between our lands. The fence said it all.

This peace would not last, even if his son foolishly believed so.

IN THE END, it was not *Datu* Gagalangin who started the war.

"There was no theft! I have only reclaimed the five meters we are owed and returned the fence to its original position according to the laws of our ancestors!" shouted the *Datu* when we arrived in the hall on our mistress's heels. His face was red with anger. On the floor before him, a messenger prostrated. "Tell him that if he does not stand down, there *will* be war."

"Father!" *Dayang* Rosita gasped. "What is going on?"

"This is none of your business, Rosita," he snapped.

That caught me off guard. *Datu* Balintawak had never spoken harshly to his daughter before. He loved her too much for that.

She flinched at the rebuke, then clutched her skirts. I ducked my head and stepped aside with Biya and the others, clearing the way for our mistress's departure. But *Dayang* Rosita did not leave. Instead, I heard her say in a small, trembling voice, "No. I am your daughter. This is my business, too."

My heart sank. My stomach clenched.

This was about *Gat* Delfin.

Datu Balintawak knew it, too. I did not dare lift my eyes, but venom dripped from his every word. I could almost see it pooling on the floor, about to destroy us all. "Yes, you are my daughter, and therefore, you *will* obey me. You are not to have anything to do with that boy. Not now, not ever. If he so as much approaches the fence . . ."

We did not need to hear the rest of the threat. From the back of the hall came a loud thumping of wood and metal as his *horohan* snapped to attention, preparing to carry out his dark promise.

A flash of movement spurred me to action, my body reacting before my mind could even comprehend it. I'd reached out and grabbed *Dayang* Rosita by the forearm just as she took a step toward her father. The silence that came over the hall from that one small deed said it all.

I had stepped out of line, shamed her in front of everyone. I had never done that before; I loved her too much for that.

But I did it to save her. I would do it again, in fact, even if it meant my ruin. Wasn't that love? To be willing to destroy yourself for the sake of the other?

"Don't," I pleaded, though I should have pulled away then and pleaded for mercy instead. I could already feel the heat of the *Datu*'s glare on the back of my neck, and I knew that the more I spoke, the more I did anything, the closer I brought myself to a fate far worse than death.

Dayang Rosita wrenched herself out of my grip with a strength I didn't know she had. Then she turned on her heel and ran out of the hall, back toward her room. I did not wait for the *Datu* to dismiss us to follow her, protocol be damned. Biya and the others trailed after me.

"I need to warn Delfin," *Dayang* Rosita muttered in between sobs, a touch of madness in her tone. She made a beeline for her desk as soon as she arrived in her room, rifling through and overturning the various items that rested on its surface. Whatever it was she was looking for, she didn't find it.

"The *Datu* has made up his mind. There is nothing we can do, *Dayang*."

She rounded on me. Her face was tight with anger, and the tears streaking down her cheeks only made her look more frightening. I'd never been the object of her ire before. Or was it hatred? That, somehow, felt so much worse.

"Do you not *care*?" she shrieked. Then she brought her hands up to her mouth, stunned by her own outburst. She stumbled back and lowered herself onto her bed. "Oh, Marisol. He is going to die, and if he does, so will I. My heart cannot take being parted from him forever. You would know that, if you loved."

SHE WAS WRONG. I *did* know that. Because I loved.

So I traveled to the fence alone that night, intent on setting the world right. My initial plan had been to tear down the fence so *Datu* Gagalangin's men could put it back together, five meters back where it belonged. But I realized that would be a fool's errand. I was only one woman. Sentries patrolled the border on both sides. I had to be more subtle than that.

I traversed the footpath to the end of the fence, now familiar and even worn smooth from the many nights we'd accompanied *Dayang* Rosita on her secret walks. The wooden hilt of the knife felt cold against my sweaty fingers, but I did not let go. I held on to it like a lifeline, beneath the shawl I'd wrapped around me, as I slinked through the shadows. I prayed to the Spirits, both for deliverance and forgiveness.

'What is the worth of one's life if it is not lived in love?' *Dayang* Rosita's sweet voice echoed in my mind.

No, not in my mind. It came from the darkness in front of me.

I ducked behind the trunk of a *balete* tree. Between it and the fence was a small clearing, and in the center knelt *Gat* Delfin. At first, I thought he was praying, for he murmured to himself and held his hands together in supplication.

But as my eyes adjusted to the darkness, I realized he wasn't alone.

My heart caught in my throat. What was *Dayang* Rosita doing here? How had she beaten me here? I'd tucked her to bed and locked her in, per the *Datu*'s orders, and she hadn't protested, at least not after I promised her I would deliver her message to her lover. Had she climbed out the window? Had she been doing that all those nights we weren't with her? Why, then, did she look . . . well, I wasn't certain what she looked like. She was in her white sleeping gown, but she appeared almost translucent.

Her voice, though. I'd recognize her voice anywhere.

"I will find you," she was saying. "They cannot keep us apart."

It was her hand he held between his, though it looked like he was cupping moonlight. "Not like this. This is not safe. Go back home, Rosita, before they wake you."

"Night after night, we meet in this way, yet *now* you complain?"

"I know, my darling, but we can risk it no longer. Not with our fathers sharpening their blades and getting ready to spill blood." He sighed. "Please, my love. I will figure out a way for us to be together, I promise. For now, do as your father says. Listen to Marisol."

My confusion had been growing, but the mention of my name shocked all sense out of me. I had no idea that he would remember who I was, let alone take my side. The knife in my hand suddenly felt very heavy.

She pouted. "Fine. But before I go, tell me about the flowers."

He held her close as he did. Words tumbled out of his mouth with little effort; he brandished them like a warrior would a sword, though with the grace of a dancer. He spoke of the flowers, and of his love for her. Of her beauty and kindness, too, which she both basked in and protested.

As I sat there in the darkness, watching, listening, I remembered the secret my mother told me about souls, and I finally understood. *Dayang* Rosita and *Gat* Delfin had found each other — *loved* each other — long before the fence. He had been the boy in her dreams, whispering poetry to her soul.

Heart pounding in my ears, I ran back to the *Datu*'s house. I crept through a back door that led into the kitchen and along the corridors until I arrived outside *Dayang* Rosita's room. For a long moment, I stood before the curtain of beads and feathers that served as her door, tears streaming down my face as I grappled with everything that I had learned.

She could not wake. She *must* not wake, not until her *aniwaas* had returned, else she would be lost to us, cursed to wander around forever.

I spread my shawl out on the floor and curled up on top of it.

Tonight, I would keep her secrets.

Tonight, I would keep watch.

About Marie Sinadjan

Marie Sinadjan is a Filipino speculative fiction author based in the UK. She is the co-author of The Prophecies of Ragnarok series, and her short stories have appeared in various literary journals and anthologies. She mostly writes mythology and folklore retellings blended with fantasy, sci-fi, or horror. Marie can be found online at www.mariesinadjan.com

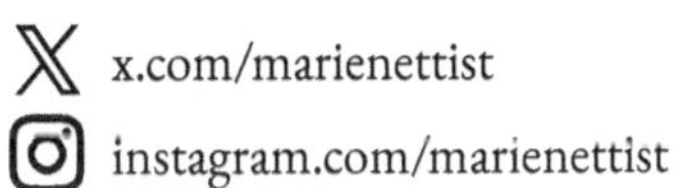

The Wish of a Tree

Veronica Faline

Born from the Earth herself, I am an oaken being. My branches above are as brown as the soil below. I stand stationary, basking in the light, changing the Sun's rays into nourishment by wanting it so.

All I've known is peace. It is an uncomplicated existence to simply be. It is a terribly lonely one as well. My sisters are my only companions, whispering through the soil and the wind. We don't speak often, only when it is essential. They tell me when to bloom and when I should conserve my energy. They tell me if winter will be long or the rains will be short. There are no stories of adventure or fun.

My heartwood aches with sorrow.

I am a singular oddity in my passion for something more — more than only being.

Gray clouds blot out the sunlight, further dampening my mood. Rain drizzles on my leaves, and I let them droop with the extra weight. A bird lands on my branch and sings me a song before flying on its way. I wish I could see where it is going. A rabbit hides under my trunk to escape the wet, and I wish I could feel its soft fur. Squirrels chase each other upon my trunk, and I yearn for someone other than my silent sisters to spend time with.

Rays of light peak along the mountain's edge before the Sun sets in the west. The Stars and Moon come to join me, but they are poor substitutes for the Sun. This night, like many others, I spend missing the Sun.

A Star blazes through the sky, growing brighter as it approaches me. With all my might, I reach my branches out and open my leaves to catch it. The tiny light lands with a thud on the leafy bed I made it. A beautiful butterfly-winged star fairy stretches itself in front of me. "Why are you so sad, sister Tree?" it asks.

I yearn for excitement, for movement and companionship. The desires are an ache that runs up my sapwood, much like water from my roots to my leaves.

"Since your leaves were so kind to catch me as I fell, I will grant you three wishes," the Star fairy says.

I dream of so many things, I'm not sure what to ask for.

"Anything you desire," it replies. Golden light sparkles on the horizon as the Sun begins to rise once more. I think about the sustenance I get from the sunshine and the way my branches constantly grow upwards, yearning to be closer to the Sun. In the core of my heartwood, I wish for a friend and I know just the being I long for.

I wish for the Sun to be here on Earth, to be my friend.

The Star fairy twinkles, "All of nature will die if the Sun is not in the sky at daybreak, but she may come to be with you during the night when the Moon presides over Earth."

I shake my leaves eagerly, agreeing.

"Very well. When you are ready for your next wish, simply call me, and I shall be back."

In a flash, the Star is gone, and I eagerly wait for the night to fall once more. Crickets chirp, and bees buzz as my excitement builds.

When it is time for the Sun to sleep behind the mountains, the sky turns bright orange like a fire burning among the clouds, and I worry for a moment something has gone wrong. Worry wars with excitement as the last sliver of light slowly sinks beyond the horizon.

For a moment, all is quiet, then a figure approaches with long, straight golden hair falling like rays of light around her. Her eyes are blue like the sky, her skin pale and soft like clouds.

She makes a sound like a bird chirping. Is she some sort of animal? My curiosity gets the better of me, and I lean in toward her. My bark creaks, unused to such movements.

Her soft fingers run along my trunk, sending a quiver upon my leaves.

"Oh, hello." Her voice is a song to my ears.

"Do you recognize me?" She dances like a leaf in the wind, her golden hair swinging in the breeze.

Of course! The lovely sun. How I have pined to have you here close to me!

I want to tell her a million things about life here on Earth, but I have no voice to speak aloud. I tilt my massive branches, sending a few leaves fluttering to the ground.

"It is me, the Sun. The Star fairy said you wished for me to join you. What a fabulous wish! What a joy to finally touch the Earth, not simply to shine upon it, but to actually touch it." She scoops some dirt in her hands, cherishing it for a moment. "It is a bit lonely here in this new body, without anyone else to talk to. I have always had Moon. Though he is far away, he is always there with me. Now I have this body and these fingers and toes and no one to share my time with." Sun wiggles the dirt between her fleshy limbs. It looks fun.

Star fairy, I have another wish!

My soul calls out to the world beyond.

"Simply say it, and it shall be yours," the familiar voice calls back.

I wish to be free of my roots and bark. I wish to have fingers, toes, and a voice to speak with.

"Very well," Star replies.

A gust of wind surrounds me, and shivers run up my bark.

My leaves tremble and then wilt into thick hair. My rough bark melts, leaving behind soft fawn skin. Knowledge of a thousand words bombards my mind. My branches are now fingers, the roots are toes, and my massive trunk becomes my body.

I am free of my spot in the soil and tentatively step forward.

Sun's laugh echoes through the branches of my sedentary sisters. Still, I want to call out to them, tell them what it is like to have a body, but my soul is eerily quiet. Though we rarely spoke, I always felt them near. Their roots joined mine as we shared every breath and every moment of our lives. Now, air goes into my lungs through my nose . . . a desolate and lonely act.

My new heart squeezes in my chest, an unfamiliar feeling until Sun grabs my hand. The warmth of her tender touch radiates up my fingers through my whole body, bringing me joy. Her spirit shines dazzling and joyous, like a butterfly flitting among my blooms.

"Sun." My first word is a simple one, but I speak it with the admiration of a thousand years spent longing for her closeness.

"Look at you!" she sings with joy, spinning me around. "Your eyes are green like the leaves on your branches, your hair brown like your bark and wavy like it is blowing in the wind," Her thumb wipes my cheek. "Here on your cheek tiny speckles darker than the rest, like the bud of a flower about to bloom. I still see the tree in you."

Sun holds me tight for a moment, evaluating me, then tugs on my hand. "There is much to see and do," she says as she leads me away from my home. We prance through the forest like deer in spring. Sun spots a stream and leads me to squish our new toes in its muddy banks. I wiggle them, as I've never been able to do with my roots. It's mushy and soft and delights me so. Sun splashes into the stream, sending water droplets flying around her. She giggles with glee, so I do the same. The water is refreshing. It caresses my skin in a way it never did to my bark. I know Water so much better now.

Sun and I sniff flowers delicately, the scent sweeter than

anything I could have imagined. We balance on rocks and hop in a pile of scratchy leaves. How oddly wonderful it is to feel what once was a part of my sisters. Sun prances and dances, never staying completely still.

An owl hoots in the distance, and Sun perks up to the sound. She rushes toward the call and we watch as the owl takes flight into the night.

"I wish I could feel its feathers." Sun momentarily pouts. I reach my long arms into the owl's nest and retrieve a silky feather. I hold it out to her and a smile lights up her face. She caresses it as a precious thing, then rests her head in the crook of my neck. With careful fingers, she weaves my hair-like streams of a river intertwining and knots the feather at the bottom. Her tender touch and glowing smile shines on my soul, feeding me a thing that is neither food nor water, yet fills me so.

Sun darts through the forest like a squirrel finding hidden treasure, and I lumber after slightly less gracefully yet enjoying it all the same. We gaze up at the Stars. Sun is in awe of this unfamiliar sight. Most of all, we laugh, a whole-body experience that illuminates us both from the inside.

"Oh no, it is time I go back to the sky," Sun says, her lips turned down in a frown. "I wish I could stay this way forever."

My fingers reach out and intertwine with hers. I want to grant her desire. The wish is on the tip of my tongue. Then I remember Star's wise words about the world needing the sun.

"When the Moon rises, we will play again," I assure her. She beams a smile back at me, filling me whole. Her long arms wrap around me, bringing me close to her body. Her warmth consumes. A smile tugs at my new mouth before she dances off over the mountains once more.

As soon as she disappears, a longing sprouts in my core. My new fingers reach out but are only greeted by the chill twilight of the morning. The yearning to be in the Sun's presence blooms like a flower on my branches, its sorrow-filled petals pushing against my chest.

With heavy steps, I return to my home among my sisters and stand in the dirt, waiting for Sun to shine upon me again. Sure enough, she rises in the east just as she does every day. Yet, today, it is decidedly different. Today, my heart squeezes tight. Longing burrows holes in my soul like maggots in my wood.

The Sun's glow shines on my toes and then my long Earth-colored legs. It brightens my fingertips, and I smile once more as it kisses my face. I am still in this new body, in a being that feels not at all like a tree. My new friend Sun is a million miles away. It is entirely unfair that space separates us this way.

I curl up in the dirt and close my eyes, letting the sunlight blanket me while I rest. When I awaken, the Sun is still up above — unreachable. I search for the stream, but without the Sun to lead me, I am lost.

I wander the surrounding lands, unable to speak to my sisters or Sun. It is a terribly lonely time. My only cheer comes from the slow trickling of time before Sun comes out to play once more.

Finally, the sky turns pink and red. I hadn't realized before, but now I understand it is Sky's melancholy goodbye to the Sun. Thorny emotions burrow into my new heart: guilt and shame for my elation at the Sky's sorrow. These many feelings will take time to get used to, time I will gladly spend with the Sun and pining for her forever.

Once more, she is here. I feel her before I even see her. Her radiance emanates even in the gloom of the night. She grabs my hand, a feeling I have come to cherish, much like the intertwining of my roots with my sisters.

We run up hillsides, then slide down the grass on the other side, giggling all the way. We dance in the starlight until we tumble to the soft grass below. Sun purses her petal pink lips, shying away from the gloomy Moon. She says, "The Moon is terribly jealous of my ability to come on the Earth. He, too, wishes to touch the ground." I ponder her words; a new friend could be fun. Her sky-blue eyes turn down to the ground. "I know it must be lonely without me, but Moon is my twin. We have been circling each other for all eternity, and I couldn't deny him this. Would you show him the same kindness you've shown me?" She laces her fingers in mine.

I nod. "Star fairy, I wish for the Moon to join us in this body of fingers and toes. For him to touch the Earth as we do."

"He may only come during the day just as the Sun may only come at night," Star cautions, but I eagerly agree. I close my eyes as my last wish is granted.

"Let us not waste our time together. Let us dance!" Sun declares with a hop and a skip.

She leads me through meadows. We run our fingertips over the petals below. We spot a deer and run beside it as it sprints through the forest until our legs ache and our lungs squeeze, gasping for air.

We lay in tall grasses, fingers interwoven, speaking of the Earth and all the wonderful things it has to offer. I know she would enjoy it ten times more in the light. Alas, the Moon is dim, so very far away. With none of Sun's light to reflect upon it, he simply floats in the sky.

When it's time for Sun to return, I follow her to the mountain's base.

"Promise you'll be kind to Moon. Show him the wonders of the Earth and be his friend like you've been mine," she asks, and I promise.

She embraces me, and I soak in her warmth before she slips away over the rocky landscape. I lay in the grass resting for a moment, waiting for my new friend to arrive. I dream of the Sun's own rays dancing on her and me, as we skip through the forest when a sound awakens me.

I look up and see a figure before me. His skin is dark like the shadows that blanket the Earth at night, his body rigid and thick like a stone, his hair is gray and wound in tight circles, much like the shade and light on his rocky surface. He looks at me with pitch-black eyes and smiles shyly. His smile pockets deep holes in each of his cheeks, making pinhole matching craters in his face.

"Moon! I'm glad to have company. It's so lonely here when Sun is gone," I say.

He glances up, his eyes squinting in the brightness of Sun's rays. "Her majesty knows no bounds, her beauty knows no end, and her warmth is my constant companion. How I wish we all three could be here together," he sighs.

I do the thing Sun did to cheer me up; I bring his fingers into mine. His hand is rough, and chill to the touch. His spirit is heavy, like a fog encircling me.

I take him by the hand as Sun had done to me, and we put our toes in the mud. Instead of giggling like Sun, Moon gives me a tight-lipped expression of concern.

I splash in the stream, but Moon dips one toe in and then contemplates the ripples. I show him how to splash, but he prefers simply staring into its sparkling surface. After a time, he decides to walk around the stream instead of through. He takes his time watching how light filters through the leaves above and how the shadows move on the ground.

When I show Moon the fragrant flowers, he shrugs, more interested in a cactus, needled and sharp. He runs his fingers across the thorns, enjoying them as if they were the petals of a flower — but they are not.

Instead of wanting to race up the hillside, Moon is drawn to rocks and cliffs, strolling along as though they were interesting. He stops at a succulent, puzzling over its barbed leaves. A butterfly lands beside him, and I smile with glee. Sun would have loved this colorful creature, but Moon glances away, watching a black beetle crawl through the dirt instead. My head burns with frustration. Why does Moon, morose and unfriendly, get to be here while Sun is stuck in the sky?

We both look up as heavy clouds block out the Sun. Rain drizzles, Moon holds out his hands, wiggling his fingers against the wet. Moon seems happy in the gray, humid air. I let the rain soak my limbs, drooping them in its weight. A shiver chills me to my bones and I wish the Sun would warm me once more.

Sun peeks out from behind a cloud, and a rainbow appears before me, carrying the starlight fairy on its arch.

"Tree, you have had three wishes, yet you still seem just as melancholy as when we first met," Star fairy says as it sits in my palm.

"I'm sorry, I appreciate your gifts, but I am so sad without Sun when she is gone."

"But you have Moon." Star points to Moon, who is cupping a jagged rock.

"Moon is no fun. He does not run, jump, or even dance! He does not like to spin or splash. He doesn't laugh or giggle like the Sun." I sigh.

"Maybe it is not that Moon is no fun but that you simply don't understand what he finds enjoyable," Star offers. I shrug. Star thinks for a moment.

"Do you wish to send him away?" Star asks.

For a moment, I want to shout "yes," but then I think of Sun and her affinity for Moon. She'll be so disappointed if I break my promise to be his friend in the same way I am hers. I shake my head. That won't do.

"I wish we could all live on the Earth as these beings with fingers and toes, that we could all be together forever. But I know that's not possible. The Sun must shine, and the Moon must rise, and I must simply stand." My toes sink into the mud, but I do not wiggle them. I let them be consumed.

"Ah no, my dear Tree, you are so much more than that. You provide shade and shelter. You give nutrition through your fruit to the animals below. You give air to the breeze that keeps the whole world turning."

Her words land heavy on my chest, and I know she is right. So foolish I am to forget. How cherished are the memories of families of bunnies that often burrow in my trunk, the birds that rest on my branches and sing to me their thanks? Even the ants that dig tunnels in my soil and the squirrels that sprint across my branches tickle me so gently. So many critters and creatures share my home with my sisters, and me. How scary and desolate it would be without us to protect them.

"You are right. I am ashamed I've been selfish in my wishes."

"Let me think about this problem, and I will be back tonight," the Star says to me.

I tilt my head in question, but Star is gone in a flash. I join Moon, tossing rocks into the canyon below us. He does not talk of the wonders of the Earth but sits quietly beside me. As the Sun moves in the sky, Moon shows me the critters that hide in the shadows, he spots a slow-moving chameleon inching along a branch. He shows me how the colors gradually change, much like my leaves before they fall. He finds a coiled snake hiding in the shade of a rock and we watch as it comes to bask in the warmth much like myself. Moon shows me stones, which look gray and bland at first, but in his hands and under his wondering eyes, tiny flecks and uneven surfaces become works of art. We sit and watch the stream instead of splashing in it. A leaf swirls in the current and a fish swims through the shining waves; it is beautiful in a different way than before. His comfortable companionship is like a summer rain, bringing me joy in its clouds and cold. Then it is his time to go. He doesn't embrace me, nor do I hug him. We nod goodbye, and he disappears beyond the horizon.

Star appears instead of Sun, a mischievous smile on their lips.

"I've got a grand idea," Star says as they flit about. "Space is connected to Earth in a never-ending cycle. The Sun cannot leave the sky forever, nor can the Moon, and the world needs its trees most of all!" Star proclaims.

"This is the grandest idea I've ever had. I'll combine you all into one. The trees, Sun, and Moon. My fellow stars and the great beyond will go into this new being. I'll combine every insect and creature, both big and small, into one container. Into this being with fingers and toes."

I blink at her, unbelieving for a moment, but her confidence is unwavering.

"Just a speck of each thing, stitched into the very fiber of this being. I will make some fair like the Sun, some ebony like Moon, and others brown like you, Tree. Someday, there will be every shade of skin in-between. This new being, I think I'll call a human." She looks at me and then at the sky as if weighing our fate.

"They won't remember. These human beings. The process of forging will be hard. It'll leave you rooted in the soil and the Sun and Moon hanging in the sky forever. It'll be messy at first, but slowly perfected over hundreds and thousands of years. The humans will have no knowledge that they came from all these things around them. Sun, Moon, and you may also forget one day."

"I carry the knowledge of a thousand years etched in my heartwood. Since the dawn of time when the first sapling took root, its history is written in my rings. In my short time as a being of flesh and bone, I felt one thing even deeper than nutrients flowing through my inner bark. This thing is a feeling humans will never be able to forget," I say.

Star puzzles, glancing my way.

"They'll remember love. When they feel sunlight dancing on their faces, they will remember my love of the Sun and its warm embrace. When they look out into the Stars, they will remember the Moon and its unwavering companionship. These beings will walk through the forest among my sisters and me with our oaken trunks and green crowns. They will taste our fruit and remember the bond of roots and soil." I pause smiling up at my sisters around me; a fluffy squirrel runs up one of their trunks.

"Some will remember caring for creatures, big and small. The comfort of a warm place to hide in the winter, the wonderful scent of a flower in the meadow. Some will love squishing their toes in the mud and splashing in streams, and others will enjoy taking the long way. Some will giggle with glee while running up a hill, while others will meander. Some will balance on rocks and run their fingers over petals while others revere needled cactus and spiky succulents. When the breeze blows through their hair, they might smile reminiscing on soaring through the sky or shiver from the chill, but all will cherish the winds that turn the world. If they quiet their minds and listen with their heart, they will hear the voices of their ancestors all around them," I proclaim.

"If you are sure." Star twinkles and I run my fingers along the trunk of my sister. Her wood is rough, uneven and jagged, almost like a stone, yet I can feel her life inside. I love speaking, touching, and moving, but I remember my wish. I had desired friendship more than anything else. The Sun and Moon had granted me that for a short time but they belong in the sky as I belong on Earth. This new being will carry our hopes and dreams deep in its soul letting us all be on Earth — together at last.

"I wish for a friend," I say my last words and Star fairy nods. With a whoosh and a twinkle, all that I know slips away.

My body becomes rigid again, my toes snake into roots, and my hair reaches up and out into branches ever-reaching toward the Sun.

Every night I watch the sky paint the clouds orange, pink, and red, a somber farewell to the Earth at night and a vibrant hello in the morning. It is written in my rings as it is written in the Stars that they will never forget their time on Earth. For as long as I stand in the soil of my home, I will remember my love of the Sun and cherish the companionship of the Moon.

As the gleeful sound of human laughter echoes through the forest, I hold on to hope.

Hope that my brethren will remember me and the wish of a Tree.

About Veronica Faline

Veronica Faline is originally from the San Francisco Bay Area. She currently resides with her husband, child, and dogs in Arizona where she's reconnecting with her Mexican and Native roots. You can find her other short stories; Ghost Dance featured in the anthology Great Wars and Red Dress in the anthology Not Ghosts, But Spirits 2 under the pen name Veronica S. When she's not fighting evil by moonlight or winning love by daylight you might find her on X @Chibitweetz

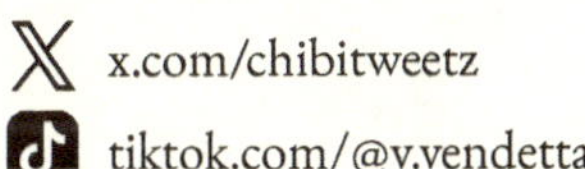

X x.com/chibitweetz

tiktok.com/@v.vendetta13

TALE OF THE MOON

HUANG CHEN

I'm dead. I think.

This thought hits me when I hop over a puddle as I'm running down a dim street. During the split-second mid-air, I look down at the irregular-shaped surface of the silver water. In the vivid reflection, I see a bright full moon watching over the world from the center of the sky. I see my body glow in the dark as if the holy moonlight ignites its core. Between my spread legs and arms, I recognize my features, my round eyes, fleshy nose, and puffy hair, all in an unfamiliar position, exhibiting a mixture of shock, fear, and loss.

Just then, the tip of my right foot presses on the ground and pushes it away, and my left foot reaches beyond for another leap.

The moment is gone. I keep running in the dark.

Despite the persistent moon, down here, the world is still a dark place. The dark buildings and streets devour any light the moon casts, leaving only a trace of silver mist floating above the corners and edges. The earth's dominating darkness can't reach beyond the tallest roof to invade the air, and the moonlight fails to breach the unreflective darkness.

The moon and the dark are two equally powerful opposing forces, splitting the world into two.

Trapped between their worlds, I don't know who I am, how I got here, or where I am heading. Since the beginning of my memory, I've been running. I never pause my steps because of a knowledge of fear in my heart. It tells me that if I ever do, I will either melt in the moonlight or be swallowed by the shadow. One of those forces would take me in the blink of an eye.

So, I guess it is not that I don't have any memories before that moment. I simply don't have anything remarkable to mark my memory until that near-melt self-realizing second. I constantly think back, chewing on that moment. It was so coincidental. The water was right in the middle of that dark street. It was in the world of the everlasting night, while the dark buildings on the shoulders of the road failed to block the moon. With the water as glass and the light as silver, the puddle is as clear as a mirror. This coincidental mirror became a trampoline, catching moonbeams before they fell in the mouth of the monstrous darkness and bouncing them onto my face, onto me.

At that moment, I wasn't shocked by my face or the fact that I was shaped like a human girl. No. Even though I didn't remember anything about myself, my instinct agreed with my expression: the shock at seeing the silver moonlight shine through my body with the chill breath of air, lighten my transparency, and brighten my outline; the fear from the sudden exposure to the world and of melting into the light; the horror at the thought of stopping, of not going, of losing myself through being swallowed by a larger entity; and the sense of loss and happiness from knowing that I was me and I was only me. The moment I saw the reflection of my ghostly self, more than ever, I could feel myself assimilating into the moon and how distinctive I was in the dark. I am like a blue firefly against the dark buildings under the moonlight, except a blue firefly symbolizes happiness, and I embody a hollow emptiness.

I don't know where this information comes from. All I know is that I can't stop. I have to keep running until I find a warm light. Warm light can disperse the darkness, shield me from the moon, lead me to another beginning.

I keep running, passing one residential building after another, taking turns at the crossroads, through playgrounds and parking lots. I must've been running for days, months, decades. The neat thing about being dead is that I never feel tired. My limbs are never sore, my lungs aren't short of air, and my heart doesn't pump. I feel like I can run forever, while the terrible thing about being dead is that I can literally run forever. I don't even have a heartbeat to count how long I've been running. For all I know, I may have run forever already. And since I'm already dead, I've lost the opportunity to escape this eternity by giving in to death.

I keep on running in this quiet town. As my cognitions awaken, I find myself in an aged neighborhood filled with homely housing. I pass failed traffic lights and streetlights. Even though there are no parked vehicles or bikes, I can sense families behind every tightly shut curtain, all asleep. I desperately search the gaps between the curtains, hoping to see a thread of warm light. But no, everyone's asleep except me. I want to scream to wake them; I pinch my arm to wake myself from this endless dream, but my spiritual vocal box can't produce sound, and my airy body won't flinch even with a utility pole piercing through my loins.

I wonder if this is the hell people talk about.

ONE DAY, I am running, as always. I choose a path through a parking lot in the middle of some buildings, thinking maybe I can catch a warm kitchen light, even only a yellow string peeking out between the drapes. Maybe a neglectful family forgot to turn off all the lights before turning in on the other side of the apartment. As always, I miss my luck. Every family in the buildings is cautious enough not to leave any light on.

Suddenly, just as I run through a darkened alley, I see a yellow porch light at the top of a stairway in the back of a four-story apartment building. I can almost feel the warmth of the yellow radiance. It feels like all I have ever wanted and needed, everything I remember and forget. It is so right that it frightens me: is it possible what I have been searching for forever is simply there? Has it been waiting for me as long as time exists, too? Does feeling too good to be true mean it is not true? Is it fair to assume the light is not real just because I fear it's unreal? I fear the happy bubbles that raise me up will burst and drop me into an abyss.

Terrified. Still, my legs keep moving. I run up the six or seven staircases and am rewarded with more dimmed light reaching out through the cracked open door. Without slowing down, I run past the gate into a tiny, colorful kitchen crowded with every cooking machine. I go through a grandmotherly, flowery living room with cream crochet blankets covering every surface and pass by a hallway with China featuring childish drawings filling the wall. There is another cracked open door, without light shining out. In this darker room, I finally stop. Surrounded by rolls of identical cover suits like merchandise, there is the first living thing I see — a woman in a dark cloak standing behind a boiling cauldron. Her face hides in the shadow of her hood, her hand is twirling a large wooden spoon in the thick soup.

She looks up at me, the breathless, unannounced visitor, with her warm brown eyes. She has a short chin, and her hair is neat yet loosely tied up. Both corners of her maroon lips pull up and form a smile, but it doesn't seem like she's doing so only to be polite. Instead, she looks complacent with her looks that way. The second I see her, I feel like I've known her for years, as if she had held me when I was a baby and watched me run around the neighborhood.

"Please, I need help!" is how I open up, explaining what I have gone through in her calming presence.

"Are you sure this is what you are looking for?" she asks, looking deeply into my eyes.

"I want to be free from the moon and the darkness. I want to stop running . . ." I repeat, not understanding what she asks or knowing what I want.

She gestures to me to wait by her bubbly cauldron and disappears behind the hidden back door. While she's gone, I observe the surroundings just as I do when I run, except my body and limbs hang around without a purpose. It's interesting that after running for so long, when I finally stop, it seems that everywhere I look, things are backing away from me. Yet on a second look, they are perfectly still. My limbs occasionally twitch in guilt, embarrassed they are not doing their job. Just as I learn to settle and adjust my sight, I notice what I thought was merchandise hanging on the hooks is actually boneless, rubbery human torsos. The saggy torsos hang neatly by the backs of their necks in two rows on the walls. All the heads and fingers droop loosely since there are no supporting structures at all. Even though they look like apparel on display, their clothes are not the selling point. All the torsos are in basic white tees and gray shorts. Maybe because the torsos are not "blown up," they all look quite the same to me, like their outfits.

"Thankfully, I still have one bottle left." The woman comes out, waving me a glass bottle of yellow gluey substance. "You can rest free now."

The woman grabs the torso that's closest to her and drops it in front of me. "Put this on."

The torso has a vertical slice open on its back, from its head to the top of its butt crack. It looks more like a thick laboratory coverall than a human body because I don't see any organs or vessels inside. I step my feet one by one into its feet, pull it up like pants. It doesn't feel cold or warm. I move my toes — just stuffy. Without much time to think, I push my arms through the sleeves.

When she's done pushing my back and head inside the torso, she starts pouring the yellow glue on the edge of the slit on the back.

"This glue is going to keep you inside this body while you return and relive your life," she urges me. "You won't remember a thing from here, but keep in mind, never expose your back to the moon. Its light will melt the glue. Doesn't matter if it's a full or new moon. As long as it's moonlight, it can dissolve this substance."

As she closes up the back, her voice becomes muffled. The stuffiness heats up as I'm enveloped by the uncomfortable boiling fluidity of the bodysuit and the glue. Soon, I lose consciousness.

* * *

I WAKE to the scent of baby powder and milk in a stroller, belly up, back touching the soft blanket, pushed into the blazing chilly air. Giant adult humans hovering over me take turns making high and low noises. I smack my lips, trying to stop drooling all over my chin, but fail miserably. My attempt only triggers some poking on my cheeks, along with squeaky rolling noises. A humongous round orb approaches, and I see its features. Its mouth opens wide, flashing all its teeth, blowing out hot, moist air on my face. I wave my arms and legs. I scream. Another giant head with a familiar scent comes close. Its nose flaring a deep breath like it's smelling me. It leaves, leaving me screaming alone, then it comes back and stuffs my mouth full with a soft tip. My mouth automatically starts sucking and is filled with warm milk. I doze off again.

* * *

OPENING MY EYES, I'm in the passenger seat, staring at the trees I'm leaving behind. "Are you gonna miss your classmates?" Mom asks while driving.

"I'm in middle school now. I really don't care for their naivety," I answer without turning my head. My elementary teacher commented on my report card: "You are a quiet little girl" five years in a row, making me sound like the wan-faced girl ghost in a horror movie. Can I adopt a new personality when I enter the new school? Maybe I can volunteer to introduce myself first. In the dark space behind my closed eyes, I imagine myself standing in the sunlit middle school classroom, speaking in a bubbly voice with a bright smile. No one will ever find out how shy I really am, and I can lead a life of exciting events like a heroine.

BENDING over in the dark corner, I pat my backpack flatter to save some legroom under the seat. In the flight attendant's reminder, the seat in front of me is set up straight, and I can finally relax a little in my limited space. My phone beeps with messages from those I just said goodbye to at the security. Mom says she will wait till the plane takes off in case something happens; she says she's making fun of my crying cousin and grandma; she says to take the neck pillow out and recline the chair down low and to text her when the plane lands. She says there'll be teachers from my high school picking me up.

The plane starts moving. I turn off my phone and wrap the pillow around my neck. I am flying three-quarters across the world to a whole new country to avoid the mandatory presentations as a study committee member. When I ran for that position, I really didn't think of the responsibilities that came with the title. I didn't know I had to stand in front of the whole class and lead the free blocks. Why do I want to be seen and unseen at the same time? Is running away, for this cowardly reason, a good call to evoke a lonely adventure in a foreign land? Thinking of the things I'm leaving behind, I wonder what I am heading to and what I want.

A CRESCENDO of chattering wakes me up, and I find myself in a pile of winter coats on grandma's couch. I roll my shoulders, feeling my jet lag wane and my cheeks burn with the imprint of a zipper. Grandma's house is crowded, the dining table seems smaller, so small that we have to take turns having our festive dinner. It's been seven years since I last celebrated the Lunar New Year with my family, which earns me a seat to eat in the first round. I guess I didn't realize that flying abroad would mean I could only see those I used to spend all day with every few years.

"You are so tan now. Some facial should be able to fix it," my aunt with loosely brushed hair and short chin complains. Her eyes disappear in her proud unified smile. Her daughter, who grew up with me like my twin, is resting in the bedroom with her newborn attached to her chest. I look at those people who I share part of my bloodline with, watch them mingling, joking, and laughing. They gather here to spend this meaningful night and will go on with their lives tomorrow like it's a new beginning, while I take a break from mine on this mothball-scented, beach towel-covered couch, like a traveler across time and space.

I BLINK hard to keep myself awake, leaning back for a quick neck stretch. It has well past midnight, the busiest time for a bar, and the tiredest time for its staff. My nails dig in the waxed wooden desk and leave a line of little crescents. The clock on the wall ticks like an old monk beating his wooden fish — not too hasty, nor too slowly, loud in quietness and inaudible in noise. But eventually, the minute hand hits nine, which means I should start blocking out new customers. It makes me anxious every time, like I was a kid again, defending my mom's empty seat in a McDonald's while she was out to get food..

It's dark. And I have to walk thirty minutes home in this darkness. The trains are not running in my favorable direction, as if to warn me this is not a favorable job. Two clearly drunk boys stumble in, leaning on each other like a human triangle. "I am your boss's son," one of them says.

I ignore that claim, refuse to seat them, and dig out what they really want. "Bathroom is downstairs," I cut them a break.

On their way out he says, "You are good. I'll let my father know."

Maybe I enjoy working, even though it means some nights I spend the first quarter of a new day dealing with strangers and strangling my bag tight on my back, walking into the dark night.

I TURN my head to the side with my eyes closed so the cold metal can wake me from this mind-boggling dream. My eyes open, and the same gibbous of green message bubbles reflect wax on my glasses. Sliding up the silver refrigerator that I have been leaning against since I read the news from overseas, I scroll up and reread it. My father died, a man I hadn't seen in years. I sit on the floor for a few precious minutes on a busy working morning.

Getting ready for work, I put my book bag on my back and suddenly remember, I never forgave my father. I made it sound like I was okay and made polite conversation with him, well aware that it would make him feel worse. I never told him straightforwardly that I forgave him, even though I very much knew that could be the last time I saw him. I even had a serious conversation with myself about whether I would feel guilty about it. Death was a real problem for him. I mean, yeah, for us all, but him particularly, because he had been fighting cancer for years. But, because he'd been battling cancer for years, surviving for years. Death seemed far. Ironic. What is more ironic is that not freeing him from the guilt seems to trap me in regret. A selfish action I thought could redeem my past could condemn my future. Did I truly forgive him? Or is this peace a result of time, of his death, or of another selfish reason? Am I ashamed like he was? Was he confused like I am?

I AM IN MY WHEELCHAIR, a companion that allows my arms to take responsibility for transporting from my legs and feet. Those old gals have been laboring half of my life, carrying my weight. Now, they've retired and so has my eagerness to fight traces of my happiness, anger, sorrow, and joy on my face. All my life, the satisfaction from the first mouthful of breast milk, the tears from a failed test, the sadness of losing old friends, and the laughter at a grandson's silly joke live in my wrinkles and settle in my soul. I've been petting, pulling, and moisturizing my skin since I was a teenager, trying not to leave any mark on this body.

When did I make peace with those creases and lines?

I don't remember, but they fold quite nicely. I must say, I enjoy being old. Every morning, I push myself around the neighborhood, letting my friends know I'm still breathing. We chat about their partners and children. My children are living their lives in the world. The best I can do for them is keep exercising and staying independent, so they don't need to worry about me. All my friends admire me for being the happiest and liveliest old hag.

I no longer need to wonder if I am younger than equally successful people, more successful than people my age, and pretty as always. At my age, every day I live is a success. The older, the cooler. For people who live as long as me, we've had enough. I'm ready for the next stage. For once in my life, I'm not worried, I'm not anxious, I am free.

This afternoon, Johnson Jr, that chubby boy, is driving us old fellas into the woods for overnight camping. I don't really want to go. At this age, I don't like to travel as much. But that young man had it all set up for us, saying it's the best place to spend a midsummer night, and my girls spoil him. What could I say? So, I put on my fine dress and settle into the van. Along the long drive, I smell the scent of nature. The trees and flowers are thriving nicely. How fantastic is this view! I look out the window, seeing the grass swishing under the bushes, and wonder if there are any wild greens I could take home. It'd be perfect for cooking up a small side dish.

As we go deeper into the day and the wood, a small cottage appears behind some trees. Through the open door, I see dinner is ready on the nice plaid tablecloth and served with utensils specially designed for the elderly. That twisting handle looks perfect for my shaky, crooked hand.

Putting my feet into the moist soil, I hold my handles, tilt my upper body forward, and gradually transfer my weight to my legs. Finally, I'm standing again. A cool breeze swirls by, lifting strands of my hair and the neckline of my dress so they no longer stick to my body as if the silver air is rewarding me for a job well done. I'm showering in the moonlight.

The beautiful harvest moon covers the forest with a silver mist. It is so round and almost familiar . . . a tingling burn creeps along my back. Maybe the muscles woke from my sudden standing? The blood is circulating. I can vividly feel hot liquid running down my back, like it not only runs under my skin. It's coming out of my body as my back melts like ice cream.

Or glue.

Under the watchful eye of the moon my spirit, which has been driving this physical form for decades, retreats back to its core, the core that is soon to lose its shield. The yellow glue melts, splitting the opening on my back in two. From the cut, my spirit touches the cool air.

Once more, I touch the world in my true nature.

From the opening, past yellow residue, a silver moon jumps from the rubbery cover of its human form. Out of the body and into the sky. Shining over the edgeless land from the edgeless sky, and embracing the whole world.

About Huang Chen

Huang Chen is a Chinese American writer, a Harvard graduate, and a jobholder on the surface. But the truth is she lives in the world of her imagination. Her Middle-Grade Fantasy for Voyagers, New Adult Magical Realism for people who lost themselves, and Epic Fantasy for liars will be out any year now. Stay tuned!

instagram.com/chen2huang

Red Dancing Shoes

Joti Bilkhu

Sleigh bells mark the menacing summons of the Night Bazaar.

Sleigh bells and music that leaves one lured and less lucid than before.

Surae follows the sound through maples and a moonless night, made less sullen by the blue-hued clouds. All she cares about is getting Pia back. Pia, who wanted to go to the isles Kumn, Kittle, and Kich to dance and dance.

In a clearing stands a person, guarding a trellis shaped like a doorway. Behind them the Night Bazaar seethes and swarms. The person turns and speaks in a tongue Surae does not know and when she only stares, they switch to the common tongue. "The Night Bazaar beckons all bargains! Pray, how will you pay?"

The doorkeeper wears a top hat of gold netting, poisonous blackberries perched on the brim. Draped from their figure is a long trench coat of black skin, something leathered.

"I don't have a token," Surae says.

"Doesn't have a token, she says!" They leap forward, startling Surae so much that she falls backward. They offer a hand gloved in gold and Surae dares not offend the doorkeeper so she takes it. They yank her up without a grain of grace and study her hand.

"I'll take your left hand," they say.

"My left hand?" she echoes.

"'My left hand,'" they mock. "She seems rather daft. With your hand, I can add to my collection!"

They fling open their coat, and Surae gapes at the insides, lined with bones that clack and clatter. Finger bones, wing bones, feet and whole birds—

The doorkeeper shuts their coat with a sigh.

Surae notices that the doorway-shaped trellis is also made of human bones.

She bites her tongue, thinking of Pia, her precious Pia, the two months they have been parted and presses her lips together.

It's only a hand, and my left one at that — I can learn to work leather with one limb or hire help—

Surae, feeling faint, is about to agree when the doorkeeper cries, "No? Your hair then!"

"Yes," she gasps, relief leaving her numb. "Take it — all of it."

The doorkeeper fishes in their deep pockets and pulls out a toothed blade.

<hr>

In the Night Bazaar, all the tents are tinted black, their flaps fringed with gold cross-stitches with their trades spelled in no tongue Surae has ever seen.

The night air chills her now-shaven head and she feels naked without her long blue-black locks.

A tiny part of her worries whether Pia will know her.

Don't hang with fools, Surae. She can almost hear her grandmother's rough voice, can almost see her heavy brown face, blooming with wrinkles. Surae's skin is browner than her grandmother's, brown as the chocolate-orange slices Pia loves.

Where are you, Pia? Let me take you away, back home. Surae curls her fingers into fists as she hurries past tents and tries not to linger because lingering leads to curiosity and curiosity capers to trouble.

But still, she can't help seeing the glittering cherries that look like rubies, something moving beneath the ripe red flesh. Bone-dust, the scales of sea-things-not-seen, spelled heads, Winter-fleshed teeth, blue and purple shadows trapped in mirrors, mirrors with mouths—

What happens when the mirror gets hungry? What does it eat?

Surae bites her tongue till it bleeds and reminds herself that she is here on such harrowing grounds for Pia and Pia only. Pia who dances, barefoot and in the soft shoes that Surae made for her, stitch by stitch.

The last time Surae kissed Pia was on the day she found those damned red dancing shoes.

A glossy red pair that glinted at the edge of the Wastewood.

Red shoes that waited. Red shoes that baited.

And Pia, who holds no guile in her heart, traipsed over to touch them, to try them on.

Surae squeezes her fists so hard that momentary half-crescents mar her palms.

How marred will Pia be? She is scared to tongue these words, for . . . for what if Pia is unmarred and sees Surae as plain and boring and wishes to dance forever in shiny red shoes? *But if Pia is happy, that will make me happiest.*

It is only when a starved person staggers against Surae that she stops swaying to the bazaar's music. She steadies the person — who has the Night Bazaar's illegible lettering branded in black and gold on their front and backsides — but she does not look too closely because the letters are too lurid.

She places her hands over her ears, startling at the absence of hair, at the stubbled feeling of her scalp, and stumbles on, less certain than before. Gold and black fumes trickle between tents and she has no idea how far the bazaar grounds spread and its endless tables and tents make her dizzy.

What if I lose my way and wander 'til I'm wasted? She curses quietly then snatches at the nearest person and whisper-gasps, "Red dancing shoes! Where can I find them?"

But the person is really a cloud of dark teal smoke in the shape of a person.

As Surae gapes, she smells mint and mist, and the smoke says, "It's rude to smell smokes that one is not acquainted with."

"What?" Surae inhales again and the smoke bristles. *Cats will skin themselves if I leave here still sane.* "I-I'm sorry."

The teal smoke puffs up and grumbles a sound like faraway thunder. "If you're sorry, you ought to unsmell me."

"I can't." Surae feels like sobbing. "Please! Tell me where—"

But the smoke surges at her, a cloud of mint-laced teal that blows around her face and reforms behind her, bobbling along. She swallows the shriek in her throat and walks, counting her steps so she does not sway to the bazaar's music, for if she sways, she may never leave. Spelled like tailor's twine.

Surae slows to a stop.

Wandering aimlessly will only make me weary. She clenches her fists. There must be a shoemaker in the bazaar. Or a tent where leather goods or clothes are sold. Surae works with leather. She knows what tools the tent should have.

So she makes herself look at the Night Bazaar. At its tables with gold-dusted oranges that glitter like lanterns, at the spelled teacups that steal the drinker's breath, at the arrays of teeth spread on semi-black silk.

The night air tickles her bare scalp and Surae scans the tents as she walks: doors without knobs, purple fires that burn for four years, silks that suffocate, ribbons that rip their wearers to shreds once angered. Knives for cutting heartbreak, knives for cutting leather—

Surae blinks and changes directions, hurrying down another long lane of tents, looking left and looking right.

"I want those shoes!" someone screams and she halts.

Shoes. She runs towards the voice, pushing past humans and not-so-human things and then she sees it, a black tent with illegible gold lettering and rows upon rows of shoes. Soft amber slippers, bone shoes for grave-walkers, iron shoes that ail, glass heels with teeth, emerald-green boots for fast feet — thieves like those best — and dark blue velvet for newborns, purple suede to walk in middling climes, witch-hunting boots with silver buckles, and silver boots to sieve a witch.

Surae barely sees the fury-faced child clutching a pair of diamond shoes and his companion, a skinny girl with one leg, shouting, "Diamond shoes lead to deaths!"

She barely sees this because there is a dancer behind them, on a wooden stage scuffed with shoe marks and bloody stains, a wooden stage in the shape of a circle. The dancer dances, twirls and leaps and fancy footwork that Surae can't keep track of, but the dancer is emaciated, her hair in limp tangles, old blood crusting her chin and cheeks, and her face is screwed up in perpetual pain, delirious pain.

The dancer's dress, something that Surae knows was once pink and soft and sun-sweet, is now ragged and dirty, hanging off her skeletal form in strips, knees swollen.

And her feet, they are so bruised and bloody, ankles purple, nearly black.

And on her feet are a pair of red dancing shoes.

Pia.

Surae forgets how to speak and can only make a choked sound in her throat, her hollow throat.

Pia, she wants to wail.

Though Pia is in shreds, hurt and haggard, the red dancing shoes glisten as if they're brand new.

But Surae knows they're not new. They're merely disastrous, cursed things with their damnable red bows. "PIA!" She finally screams and scrambles onto the stage, planning to pull Pia off but she is half-afraid to hurt her more. "Stop it! Make her stop!" Surae shrieks at the shoemaker, who traipses over in black and gold, bazaar colours, her hair gray and plaited, her eyes dark red.

"I couldn't possibly." She smiles cool and corded. "The wearer of the shoes hears their music and they dance," — she throws up her hands — "and dance till death."

Surae stares. Then she catches Pia's leg and tries prying off the red shiny shoe but it's stuck—

"How do I get them off? Do you have any oil?" Surae cries.

"The only way to remove the shoes is to cut off her feet."

Cut off?

"Lies!" Surae hisses.

Feather-hearted Pia without feet may as well be on a burial barge.

"The second way to remove them is to get crocodile tears from the Wastewood Swamp."

"Crocodile tears?" repeats Surae. "What for?!"

"Why, to trick the shoes." The shoemaker never stops smiling, and Surae thinks there is a strange stiffness to her face, as if it is not her real face at all.

"You said second," Surae says, accusation in her tongue. "Is there a third way?"

"Yes! Find someone else to wear the shoes."

Dismayed, Surae looks around the bazaar. No one here will wear the cursed things. Nor should they.

Smiling, the shoemaker turns to the child dressed in brocade with diamonds in his ears, circling his throat and wrists and ankles. "Will you be taking the diamond shoes, human child?"

Surae watches Pia dance, Pia whose face is pallid, her eyes glazed.

If I go looking for crocodile tears, Pia will be dead by the time I return. She knows this with a certainty she has never felt before. *And I can't take dancing from her. Her feet may heal. She may heal and dance again someday.*

Surae stills her wilding heart and faces the shoemaker's tent. She sees a hammer, nails, pincers, insole shapes, leather, thread for stitches, and a paring knife.

A calm settles over her as she strides over and picks up the blade. It fits in her palm, a familiar feeling from her grandmother's workshop.

"What are you doing?" asks the shoemaker, still smiling like a doll.

"The fourth way." Surae grips the knife. "Cutting the shoes off her."

SURAE IS glad that Pia forced her to dance — in her grandmother's workshop, in her house, in the market.

She is glad Pia counted dance steps out loud in her chiming voice, glad that she sees how Pia is moving on the wooden stage. A ballerina under a baleful spell.

Surae crouches on her knees and, when she is sure Pia will pause in the dance, she swipes the paring knife against one shoe.

She will cut them from Pia. Carve them off her. But she will not take Pia's feet.

IT TAKES HOURS. The night seeps by in a symphony of hissed curses and maddening music, but Surae stays steady with the paring knife in her hand, counting Pia's steps.

She is even glad the doorkeeper took her hair because it would've bothered her as she cuts and peels the red shiny leather from Pia's marred feet.

Surae is not perfect though. She has nicked Pia's foot in several places, small wounds that will heal.

One shoe lies in shreds, tossed aside.

The other is almost off, and Pia's steps are becoming erratic as the remaining red shoe is missing its twin to make the wearer dance.

Sweat soaks Surae's clothes as the night is nearly sunk; the bazaar-keepers will force her out but she's not leaving without her dear Pia. Surae cuts. The knife slides deeper than she wants and she gasps, expecting another line of blood. But the sole of the shoe falls off and Surae stares, stunned. The magic crumbles, an acrid sour scent.

Pia collapses.

Surae catches her, loud sobs heaving in her lungs. The red dancing shoes lie in shreds of leather and stitches, lie still, the magic stripped from them. Red shoes she hates.

"Her feet aren't worse than before, are they?" The shoemaker smiles around the cigar between her lips, seated among the endless pairs of shoes.

Surae can't speak because she doesn't know.

The shoemaker puffs on the cigar and says, "Well, that's one less pair of red dancing shoes in the world."

"One less?" Surae rasps. "There's more?"

"Of course." The shoemaker looks at her like cats to fools.

Gathering Pia in her arms, Surae flees the Night Bazaar, never to return.

The sun seeps into Surae's brown skin as she polishes a pair of leather gloves with mink oil. It is the last job of the day and then she'll close up the workshop before hurrying through the bustling market of Kumn.

All these years later and Surae has never grown her hair long again. She wonders, sometimes, if the doorkeeper is still door-keeping.

The gloves polished, Surae tucks them into a drawstring pouch and washes her hands in the backroom.

The chimes tinkle as someone comes in. "I'm closing up—"

"I thought we could head home together."

Surae turns to smile at Pia, who is barefoot with her walking stick, orange-red hair waving around her shoulders. She never wore shoes again.

"Can't trust them," she'd say with a shudder and half-smile. Her feet are scarred and they ache often. So when she tires, Surae lifts her darling Pia onto her back or in her arms, walking in tune to Pia's humming.

They stop at the market, where the musicians play, where Pia always thrums her fingers on her thighs, counting, and then she dances, at her own pace.

It is like Pia dances to a silent song, a song that lets her limp when she needs, a song that lets her lean on Surae when her feet cannot bear her weight. Then Surae leads her in the dance.

The red dancing shoes might've needed Pia to dance, but Pia does not need them.

About Joti Bilkhu

Joti has previously had several short stories published, including "The Hag of Beara" in the Canadian anthology *Still* (Dec 2020), "Two Mouths" in *Night Frights* (Sept 2020), "Scales" (May 2020) in *The Write Launch*'s online magazine, and "Omophagus" (2019) in *The Monsters We Forgot*, Vol. 1. She's also a PhD candidate in English Literature, and her dissertation explores depictions of violence in children's adventure fiction.

THE AUTOCHTHON

T. H. YUAN

"Would you like to take the welcome tour?" Aide Jin said.

"Yes," Bea did. She was shouting, she couldn't help it. The Autochthon was a fully automated retirement community. A perfect cylinder of limestone drilled vertically into the Tennessee mountainside. It blocked out the sun.

In front of the building, a grassy hill doubled as stadium seating. Residents sat in clusters. Most animated in conversation, but a few stared at the empty stage as if anticipating a performance.

"Our stadium seats a thousand," Aide Jin said. "Entertainment every night. Jazz, folk, all genres."

"Holographic?" Nulpi said.

"Usually," Aide Jin said. "But weekends are real performers."

"So you have weekends here," Nulpi said.

"Sure, we do," Aide Jin said. "Weekends here are the best."

They crossed the field. Bea reached instinctively for Nulpi, but Nulpi kept her hands in her pocket.

"We're affordable because everything that can be automated is," Aide Jin said, "Doctors, garbagemen, store clerks."

"Doesn't it get lonely?" Bea said.

"Are you lonely when you order groceries online?" Aide Jin

asked. "Besides, you'll have the fellowship of the other residents. And — less germs."

Bea nodded. They had thought of everything.

"You'll spend most of your time in the entertainment complex on the lower floors," said the aide. "Our indoor track, pool, the school, the dining plaza, your room in the apartments. And slowly, gradually, you will be moving towards the temples upstairs, in the direction of the last room."

Bea looked at Nulpi to see if she had flinched. Nulpi looked straight ahead. Aide Jin was nonchalant. She gestured and the doors slid open. They entered a giant atrium with glittering white tiles.

"Our school and dining plaza," Aide Jin said.

Residents at the plaza had textbooks open next to their paper plates. Vacuum bots buzzed underneath their chairs.

"The most popular course is Introduction to Astrophysics." Aide Jin's bleached curls jiggled as she walked. "Everyone's obsessed with the stars."

"Figures," Nulpi said. Bea nudged her.

"Nulpi's got a telescope," she remarked to the aide.

"Then you'll be our resident star expert," Aide Jin said.

They walked by the indoor pool, a pleasing kidney shape. Men and women, nearly nude, lay in neat rows. Some snored. Heat radiated from the concrete floor.

They passed the care center. Aide Jin was careful not to call it a hospice. Bea strained to see what those teetering on the edge looked like. Did they know? They must. How did they wear it on their bodies, knowledge of the end? They could provide a clue for how to approach it. They were too far away. The aide followed her gaze.

"There's one thing we don't talk about," Aide Jin said. "You don't tell anybody when you're ready for the last room. Not the new friends you'll make. Not your gadgets. Not even each other."

"Not even each other?" Nulpi said.

"You'll understand when it's time," said Aide Jin.

They entered a neon hallway.

"Karaoke rooms, open twenty-four hours a day."

THEIR NEW APARTMENT was three-hundred-square feet, with sensible, self-adjusting appliances. The bed lifted away in the morning, and the couch and coffee table surged up from panels under the floor. The kitchen counter, too, would rejig itself in sputters when both Bea and Nulpi hovered next to it, as if uncertain which one of them to accommodate. Tiny Nulpi, with her hair hacked to a bob, or Bea, lanky, bending down.

They were on the seventh floor of the apartment complex, sandwiched between the entertainment complex and the temples on the top floor. Their only window faced the air shaft, which ran the length of the building. Looking at the windows belonging to the other apartments, stretching away out of sight, Bea was reminded that she was one of many. Insignificant.

A knock at their door. Nulpi answered.

"Hey, we're the Fillmores," they said. "Cyn and Sergi."

They wore matching sweatsuits. Light gray, blending into the concrete walls of the hallway. Cyn's cheekbones were immaculate. She had never been ugly a day in her life, Bea could tell. Sergi, on the other hand, had once been beautiful, and now, all his features were sunken in and scooped out with time.

"I'm Bea," Bea said. "This is Nulpi."

"We live next door," Cyn said. "Just got back from an Alaskan cruise. But honestly, there was nothing to do there that we can't do here. Even the sights, it was all a little . . ."

"Boring," Sergi said.

"We're out for a run," Cyn said. "Would you like to join?"

Nulpi looked at Bea. *Hot potato,* went her look.

"Sorry to say, but I'm not very active because of my knees," Bea said.

"Knee trouble!" Cyn said. "We've got to sign you up for those hot springs trips. Those go fast. But is it worth it! I was coming apart at my joints, and then I had a dip and now I'm better than ever."

Her eyes roved over Sergi's body, searching for infirmities.

"Sergi might make a trip soon," Cyn said. "We could all make a trip of it."

"That sounds great," Bea said.

When they closed the door, Nulpi remarked that their neighbors were clones, and set off for her rock-climbing club, leaving Bea circulating the apartment, fiddling with the couch cushions, and customizing the jets in the bathtub.

***

BEA FAVORED a temple on the eastern side of the building, where everyone sat in a circle on the floor in silence. If someone was moved to speak, they did, until silence overtook them. The room was giant and bare, a relief after their tiny apartment. Bea became intimately familiar with the carpet's shaggy whorls. She enjoyed it. Much of her life, she had fretted, knowing that the gathering was somewhere else. But in this temple, she had arrived, at last, to the big gathering, and nothing was required of her, other than to sit.

The temples were lined along a curved hallway on the top floor of the Autochthon. Every temple door was glass, so Bea could peer inside. After a while, Bea could predict which resident passing her in the hallway was headed to which temple, just by their dress. The evangelicals wore collars. Catholics in cardigans. Jews in polka dots. The ones who shuffled from room to room were clad in practical linen pants.

After one session of total silence, Bea decided to keep walking. The last room was at the end of the hallway, tucked out of sight. Nulpi would be with her social justice club for hours, and Bea didn't want to be back in the apartment, watching the laundry machine fold their hoodies.

The temples further along the hallway were carpeted and brightly-lit, but they were divided into stalls, some with chairs and, increasingly, as Bea progressed, flat surfaces for laying. The residents in these rooms were alone, spaced several stalls apart, affording each other some privacy.

The silence here was different. Bea realized that in one temple, occupied by some residents lying in rows, she couldn't hear anyone breathing. She tensed, even though nothing about the room had changed. It didn't smell any worse. What was it about death that she feared? The end of continuity, maybe? As if things weren't lapsing into entropy all the time. She left the temple, pulling the door tightly behind her. The hallway spiraled on, and she couldn't see the last room. It was just as well.

THE HAIR STYLIST bot pressed its rubber fingers against Cyn's scalp, plucking sections to dye. The pink run-off collected in a pouch that cooled against her shoulder blades.

"Ten," the bingo bot said.

Cyn pressed her chip to the ten. She imagined Sergi breaking into a smile when she came home with the winner's wreath.

"BINGO," said a woman in a turtleneck and thick glasses. She pointed out her winning numbers to the bingo bot. Cyn fantasized snatching the woman's card and sending the red chips flying all over the room. Her pink dye would splatter against the wall.

"LET'S DO IT," Nulpi said.

"You're kidding," Bea said. Nulpi wasn't. She had run the numbers, on a whim. If they took the three-day trip to space, they could still afford ten years at the Autochthon. Nulpi's new rock-climbing friends had just come back from one. Mountains were one thing but seeing the entire world underneath you: that was something else entirely. Nulpi had been buzzing, panning the images across their kitchen table. Tracing the trajectory in their bathroom mirror.

"Serious. Bea, this is space," Nulpi said.

It was like they were forty again. Brochures across their coffee table. *Surrogacy options.* She wasn't ready, Bea told Nulpi. Every year, in a different way, she said it, until they were sixty and it was finally, to Bea's relief, too late. If Nulpi wanted to leave, she had never mentioned it.

"It *is* space," Bea said. "So a million things could go wrong. They could mess up the o-rings, or there could be holes in the ship, or fires."

"C'mon, they've made a whole industry of it," Nulpi said. "There's thousands of people going there every year. The chances of an accident are one in a million — if that."

"That's a big comfort when you're on a burning spaceship," Bea said. "That you were one in a million."

"Sure, it's always a big comfort to be one in a million," Nulpi said, slapping her temple. "Like my one-in-a-million Pick's disease. Comforting, right?"

"Don't joke about that," Bea said. "It's not funny."

Nulpi snorted and turned.

Bea snatched her tote. "I'm late to meet Cyn at the pool."

Nulpi didn't look up from the travel website.

AT THE INDOOR POOL, there was no pain. Just an infrared lamp, mimicking the sun, on the ceiling. Bea baked herself slowly.

Cyn folded her beach towel on the glass table next to her chair. She didn't like the way the cabana boy bots did it. Always making a flirty comment, too. Cyn's cocktail came loaded with electrolytes.

"So the thing about the last room," Cyn said. "I'm not going there. Ever."

"I thought we couldn't talk about that."

"I'm almost ninety. I can talk about anything I want."

That much was clear, thought Bea. Cyn never stopped to breathe between her sentences.

"Sergi . . . heart disease runs in his family," Cyn said. "So we've cut out dark meat, potato chips, even beans. Not like some people here. Some people won't do the bare minimum to keep themselves alive. I see them all the time. But there's really no excuse for that kind of behavior."

Cyn spoke with the smug conviction of someone who had undergone multiple blood tests. Her friends must have succumbed to illnesses. Bea watched Cyn's mouth move, her lip liner impeccable, and she wondered if Cyn could be confided in.

"Well, us, on the other hand, Nulpi's only into things that will kill her," Bea said.

"Kill her?"

"She's in the rock-climbing club. She smokes everything; she'll pick fights, everything. This week she's obsessed with space vacations."

It was delicious complaining about Nulpi.

"Didn't a space trip kill that billionaire? Oh, what's his name," Cyn said. "It was all over the news and I followed it closely because it was so satisfying to imagine. All his money, for what? Won't save him when it comes down to it. Pity about his son going up with him too. You couldn't pay me a billion dollars to go up. So much could go wrong."

"Exactly."

"You gotta show her the articles," Cyn said. "It's just not safe the more you hear about them."

"I will," Bea said, signaling the cabana boy bot for lotion. "I wish she would get into trivia or something."

Sergi knew Cyn's preferences at every restaurant. Marriage was one long conversation, ebbing and flowing over the decades, until you didn't need to open your mouth anymore. Cyn tried to remember if it had been this way before they moved to the Autochthon.

I'm putting us on the automated household maintenance subscription, Cyn said in her head. They were in the Ethiopian-Filipino fusion restaurant, where the chef bot was flipping injera in a row of pans. Sergi sat across from her, tongue furiously working at a morsel stuck between his back teeth.

"I'm thinking of quite possibly getting the automated household maintenance subscription," Cyn said.

Sergi grunted.

"It's starting to feel like work with the cleaning and washing and folding. That's what we came here to get away from."

"Isn't it ironic, 'cuz all the recreational activities this place offers are glorified chores," Sergi said. "Like c'mon, the gardening?"

"That's different. Not as if you're in the volunteer crew. But if you were, you'd know that it's different when it's a team effort."

Sergi shrugged. "If that's what you think is best."

No support, just acquiescence. Cyn realized she wanted Sergi to notice how much she had done, so far. Years at the sink. A pat on the head, even. *Silly.*

<hr>

Nulpi's face flickered all the time from a stranger's face to a mirror image of Bea's. Maybe it was the light from the disco ball. A funny thing had happened on the way to retirement, where Bea had forgotten how to play. She wanted to join Nulpi, dancing halfway across the room, but she was terrified of falling. A bone could snap. Any limb could give way. She sat on the barstool and cradled her mocktail.

"Let's go," Nulpi mouthed. Bea looked away.

In their old life, Bea had begun to eye younger people enviously. Listening to colleagues talk, she imagined their faces sagging. Their stomachs bubbling forward over their belts. Inevitable flab. Here, everybody was already worn. It comforted Bea.

Nulpi came over out of breath. She sat, dangling her legs.

"They're a little stiff today," Nulpi said, tapping her legs with her palms.

"They'll feel better tomorrow," Bea said, even though she couldn't be sure.

"I don't have a lot of time," Nulpi said. Her voice was hoarse. Bea held Nulpi's hand. "I'm scared I'll forget everything with Pick's," Nulpi said. Bea was filled with shame.

"You do it," Bea said. "Go have fun on the trip and I'll watch you."

Nulpi hugged her. As a new disco track began, Bea swayed from side to side until she forgot to be careful, and she jerked with abandon. She only needed, for as long as possible, to make Nulpi laugh. Her limbs knew what to do.

"YOU MESSED UP MY ORDER," Sergi said to the waitress bot at the Argentinian-Kyrgyzstani fusion restaurant. "I wanted medium-rare, not medium."

The bot offered to take the plate back.

"I don't want to wait another half hour for a new one," Sergi said.

"Sergi, please," Cyn said.

"It's your fault. You entered it wrong."

"You wanted me to enter it. You were the one who couldn't work the buttons."

"Trusting you to press some buttons was too much of a responsibility. As I now realize."

Cyn looked at the other tables. The woman with the turtleneck and thick glasses was listening in, alert to the possibility of drama. "Don't talk to me like that."

"I forgot I can't say anything unless I've got a smile on my face." Sergi tossed his fork onto the table, or maybe it slipped from his hands, and he left the restaurant.

SUNDAY. Launch day. Bea craned her neck. She could be brave. She was here, with a big, stupid grin on her face, instead of home buried under the pillows, not breathing.

She could make out Nulpi as a dot in the field. The other residents, who had also come to the launch site on the bus, clapped as the tourists boarded the spaceship. Nulpi was already deep in conversation with another tourist. Nulpi's nerves were steel. She'd be fine.

A boom. Was it the heat from the rockets, or the sun shining down on her face, that flushed Bea red? The residents standing next to her were a husband and a wife. The wife carried her husband's colostomy bag in her hand. Their heads bent together. Love was heavy, but Bea's was in the air.

BEA SAT in the temple on the eastern side. Her ankles were numb. Nobody spoke. Nulpi was coming back tomorrow. In her unending boredom for Nulpi's return, Bea had almost accepted Cyn's bingo invitation.

Aide Jin knelt by Bea and tapped on her shoulder. The other residents looked on, anticipating a revelation.

"I'm sorry to say this," Jin said. "There's been an accident."

The carpet wasn't white after all, but all flashing lights, all colors.

THE PRIEST BOT asked her to pick a sermon.

"I don't want to choose," Bea said.

Options flashed across the screen. *Third month of grief for widows.* The stock photo of a white-haired widow was blurred at the corners, so maybe she was the dead one to be honored. Come to think of it, she resembled that lawyer woman, whose calls Bea had stopped answering. What did it matter, that Bea could collect a settlement, when it was here in Tennessee, where they had come down at last from New England to settle, that she had lost her hacked-hair future, her private syntax, her home?

CYN'S NOSE WAS RUNNING. She had no makeup on.

"It's Parkinson's," Cyn said. "They think he's mid-stage."

Bea held her. Cyn was a little animal, moist and hot to the touch.

Bea held Cyn's things as Cyn slid her old mattress into the hallway to exchange it for a self-cleaning model. After, Cyn tore the shrink-wrap off a new nurse bot. The nurse bot was chrome, with a flared base, meant to imitate a woman in a dress but coming across more like a trombone.

Bea realized her hands had been numb since Nulpi's death. Sergi sat in front of the window, his back towards them.

When Bea returned to her apartment, she sat in the tub, holding Nulpi's mango shampoo bottle. It felt recent, that Nulpi had stepped out of the tub, brushing past so Bea caught a whiff of the shampoo. The bed whirred upwards, so she could lie in it for another week, but Bea couldn't muster up the strength to walk to it.

POOLSIDE, offering their doughy bellies to the artificial sun.

"He's staring at you," Bea said.

Cyn turned. He was. A few chairs down: long limbs, water dripping into a damp patch under his chair, wolfish grin. His paperback tented in arm's reach. "No way," Cyn said.

"Creep. Oh god, in our twenties, all the creepy men we told off, it was hilarious."

"Me and my girlfriends, we would wear shorts under our dresses so they couldn't feel us up at clubs."

"So gross," Bea said, "Men are disgusting."

"It depends on the guy," Cyn said, "The hot ones I let get away with it." Bea laughed and swatted Cyn's arm with her towel. Bea had not been this expressive since Nulpi's death. Cyn felt encouraged. "I had a longtime boyfriend I met at a club. Right off of campus, where they didn't ID. He was so cute, sad puppy eyes, and his awkward dancing. But he put his heart into it."

"Some guy grabs you at the club and that actually worked? Tell me it's not Sergi."

"No, not him. A guy named Cody. He was cute and I gave him a chance, and he turned out not to be a jerk. Not 'til the end, anyway."

"Oh, I bet," Bea said. She took a long sip of her daiquiri.

Cyn closed her eyes. She waited for her limbs to melt, until she couldn't stand it anymore, and she needed to slide onto her float in the pool. There she could dangle in a wet limbo.

Bea was snoring gently, the crook of her arm over her eyebrows. She looked like Cyn's daughter.

"She's come back," Bea mumbled.

"I know, baby," Cyn said. "I know."

The man from a few chairs down winked at her.

Cyn scheduled Sergi's massage. She scheduled a prescription refill. She signed him up for Tai Chi. The waitlist for jazzercise was several months long, but she registered nevertheless.

Sergi was her second husband. They had met at a cryptopharmacological conference. He sat behind her. During lunch, Sergi sat apart from the others, eating from a Styrofoam clamshell, until Cyn invited him to sit with them. After that, he followed her around during the breaks. He prodded her shoulder once, when she fell asleep. That was their first contact. Cyn remembered the weight of his fingers on her sweater.

He asked her to dinner on the last day of the conference. Over the pappardelle, he told her about his two children, both grown. She mentioned her divorce, and he, his. Neither of them spoke with any animosity, which Cyn liked. He was an engineer. Nothing messy that couldn't fit into a container. He had a tendency to speak directly. They were married the next fall.

They had seen the last room together, just a week after they arrived. Shoulder to shoulder, they peered through the double-doors. The walls, floor, and ceiling were pink marble. The floor formed an octagon. There were seven sets of elevator doors, with buttons showing down arrows. Cyn was overcome with terror and she pulled Sergi away. They made their way back to their apartment, where they never discussed what they had seen. When she was alone, Cyn sometimes thought she could hear a tinny *ding*.

"PICK'S DISEASE," Bea said. Cyn wasn't familiar with it. "Semantic dementia. At the front of her brain. So eventually, she would have forgotten how to talk. It was supposed to take eight years. But anytime she forgot somebody's name, I would think 'This is it.'" Bea closed her eyes for a long time. "I know she was scared. I was scared too."

"You were there for her. That's what matters."

"I tried to be. I couldn't be there all the way."

"No. But how could you have known what would happen?"

"I get so mad. At myself and really, really every day, at her." The water sparkled under their knees. "What she gave up."

"No, thanks," Sergi said. He settled in front of the window.

Cyn walked downstairs. She lingered at the back of the studio. The Tai Chi instructor bowed deeply and the students followed suit. They pumped their arms forward at an invisible enemy. Cyn swung, watching the door. She still thought Sergi might come.

Before Nulpi moved in, Bea ate holding a napkin over the trash can. She thought nothing of it. But Nulpi was allergic to gluten, so it was easier if Bea cooked. It became a practice, bookending their days. Cloud bread on a plate and ginger lowered into hot water to wake Nulpi up. Zucchini noodles after work, slurped at their kitchen table. Even when she was tired, Bea relished the possibility that Nulpi would exclaim over a dish. Every thud of Bea's knife against the tofu on the chopping board was an offering, a devotional to their days together, accumulating into years.

The pneumatic tubes delivered food to Bea now. There wasn't any point in making anything. The wrappers crinkled as she ate in bed, leaning over the side, letting crumbs fall and watching the vacuum bot dart forward. Wherever Nulpi was, she had to be hungry without Bea's cooking.

"You ever see the other side of the last room?" Bea said.

"I was too scared to."

"Me too. Couldn't even make it down the hallway."

"I don't know why I'm so scared. It happens to everyone. It's the one thing that happens to everyone."

The synchronized swimmers looked serious as they bobbed up and down in the pool.

"They told me it was some woman with renal failure who lived in our apartment before we moved in. Did you know her?"

"Dalila. She was quiet, but funny, a no-nonsense kind of gal. Much older than you."

"When did she go?"

"I don't know. In the spring sometime, after a few days, she didn't answer her door and we figured she had gone on."

The water churned as the swimmers thrusted. Their skullcaps were ringed with daisies.

"Sign us up for the hot springs trip," Bea said. "Might be good to go."

"Okay. Just the two of us."

"No Sergi?"

"Sergi isn't going to want to go," Cyn said. Her hair was spiky with dried chlorine.

THE UNCLEAN ANIMALS marched two-by-two onto Noah's ark. They were the last of their kind. Not Bea. Nulpi was running late. She would be here soon. Bea waited at the foot of the wooden plank. Nulpi would be here any minute.

When Bea woke from the dream, the sheets left marks on her skin. It wasn't possible that Nulpi was lodged firmly in the past. She had to be further ahead, in fact, at a future place and time. Bea walked past the temple on the eastern side of the building, where the old men and women were still sitting on the carpet and listening to silence. Further down the hallway, Aide Jin was waiting for her.

"I think you're ready now," Aide Jin said.

CYN SCRUBBED THE BATHROOM TILES. Anything — dirt, mold — came out if you applied enough pressure.

It was her ninetieth birthday. Sergi was in bed. In sickness and in health, they had promised. She thought she knew which one of them would be which.

She doubted Sergi would want to go out to dinner, but she was determined to put on a nice dress anyway. Let someone lay eyes on her. She dabbed blush on her cheekbones. Her mirror lit up with an alert. Bea and Cyn were off the waitlist, scheduled for a hot springs trip the next day. Cyn wanted to tell Bea, and then she remembered she should tell Sergi.

She walked into the bedroom, where she thought she saw a woman with gold hair bent over Sergi on the bed. A trick of the light, but it was the monstrous truth. Someone would take Sergi away, not today, but soon, and there was nothing Cyn could do. Every marriage ended in death or disloyalty. They were no exception.

She backed away in terror. If she could will herself to rush back in and rouse Sergi, maybe she could save him. But by insect instinct, she was scrambling out into the hallway, to Bea's door, where she knocked and heard no answer. The silence as deep as when Dalila died. To the elevators, to the entertainment complex where there was noise and bright lighting and Bea, hopefully, dozing on a chaise lounge.

"Is Nulpi there?" Bea said. "The last room?"

"You won't find her as long as you stay here," remarked Aide Jin.

"I know."

"But I can't tell you what's there."

"You can't or you won't?"

"I can't. I don't know. I haven't been there myself."

"You've gotta know something about what happens."

Aide Jin sighed and Bea could tell she had gotten the question before.

"I like to think that they're sleeping and could be back any minute," replied the aide. "But no one has ever come back from it, as far as I know."

"I don't know if I'm ready," Bea said. "I'm scared."

"It won't hurt."

BEA WASN'T at the pool when Cyn got there.

"Dave Lollard," the man with the wolfish grin said, getting up from his lounge chair. His hair was gray but he had a six-pack. She shook his hand, and he held it for a few seconds too long. The woman with the turtleneck and thick glasses was clad in a magenta tankini, her glasses fogging up, on the hot tub platform, and trying her best not to ogle Dave.

"You going for a dip?" he said.

"No, I'm not," Cyn said. She didn't even have a bikini on. "I'm looking for my friend."

"The tall one? I haven't seen her yet, but she'll be down. Why don't we wait for her together?"

Dave waggled a bottle of sunblock. "Some oil for your back?"

He was exquisite. Not Sergi, not Cody. Someone else's story.

"No, thank you," Cyn said. "Not today."

Dave laughed. As the double doors opened to let her out, Dave turned to the woman with the thick glasses, offering his bottle.

BEA FOLLOWED the aide down the curved hallway. If she went quickly, she wouldn't lose her nerve. She had so much to tell Nulpi. The last room had been polished until it gleamed. Bea held Aide Jin's arm so she wouldn't slip. They were on the top floor and there was only one direction to go.

Aide Jin pressed the down button. The elevator doors

opened. She heard footsteps from the hallway behind her. Bea looked at the aide who gave a silent nod. Bea stepped into the elevator as Cyn ran into the last room, panting.

"They've got us down for the hot springs," Cyn said. She pulled Bea out of the elevator, back onto the pink marble floor. "We don't have time for this — you've got to pack."

Bea laughed to see Cyn, her hair and nails accidentally matching the floor. Pink, the last burst of color behind closed eyelids. The pulp under skin when the mortal envelope gave way.

Cyn had seen something. She was scared and she needed a friend. Bea could feel Cyn's hand pounding. They would weather it together. Bea could linger a few days, stretching into a few years, and she would have plenty to tell Nulpi when she saw her again.

"Okay," Bea said. "Let's go."

She let Cyn lead the way. She turned and looked at Aide Jin. Her smile was magnanimous.

About T. H. Yuan

T. H. Yuan is a Taiwanese-American writer. In 2021, she won the American Bar Association's "Legal Tech Fictional Writing Competition." Her short stories have appeared in *The Other Journal* and *ephemeras*. Additional work has been anthologized by the Angry Gable Press. She is a Masters candidate in fiction writing at The Johns Hopkins University.

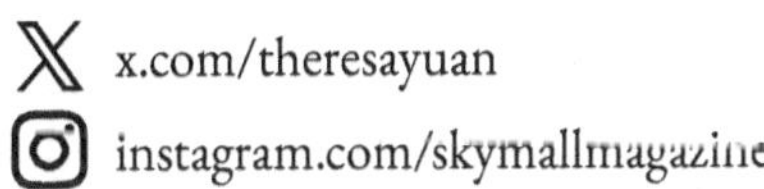

THE FAMILIAR'S GAMBIT

ABOUT MAGGIE H.

My Witch is an idiot.

I'm allowed to say that as I'm her familiar. And it is the truth.

Even now, as I weave my feline-like body between her legs, Liam doesn't pay me one ounce of due attention. No praise, no scritches, no compliments.

Instead, her viridian eyes goggle over the slim, angular form of one Dr. Galen Carter.

The doctor bustles about the biochemistry lab with nary a glance in Liam's direction. Yet, Liam sighs and twirls a lock of her lavender hair.

I scrunch my nose against the foul stench.

What does my Witch see in this mortal?

Before Liam's Ascension to Witchdom, it was us against predators, nature, and desperation.

Lonely kits on an overpopulated, man-made island drifting on the waves of a flooded Earth. A human girl and a ginger cat. Cold nights spent curled around each other for warmth. Empty bellies gurgled fighting off monsters in human skin. Outrunning the Night Reapers' flames as they torched other Undesirables into ash.

Back then, I was driven by instinct. Protect the clutter. Take no prisoners. Feast upon our enemies' defeat.

I miss those days sometimes. Everything was direct and material.

I can't protect Liam from her heart.

LIAM'S SOBS slowly taper off into sleep, still clothed from the seance call with her mentor.

Damn Zariah.

"Scientists have no respect for the natural order," Zariah had said when Liam rambled about Galen's intellect. "You think they'd respect a Witch?"

Respect . . . but we both knew what she really meant.

Love.

One of the many taboos for Witches. For a Witch who expresses their love will have their lifespan reduced by half for each infraction until they turn to stardust.

I glare at the dried tears on Liam's cheeks.

Enough is enough.

I must do something. Curse, or no curse.

LIAM BRINGS the doctor their favorite tea blend the next time we visit.

Galen and Liam word dance over my head as I scratch out a message into the ground.

Once finished, I nudge Liam's leg before swatting at it.

"Hey! Penne, no — Oh."

Galen also looks down, their brown eyes widened.

Liam loves Galen.

Galen blinks once. Twice.

They look up at Liam, bemused. "Your cat's literate?"

Liam sputters. "That's what you take from this?"

Galen smiles and takes Liam's hand into their own. "I figure the loving part was a given."

Idiots, the both of them.

ABOUT MAGGIE H.

Maggie H. (any pronouns) is a cryptid scribe sighted in central North Carolina. They've previously published the short story, Bright-Eyed, in A Guide to Useless Sidekicks anthology. It's been said that they can be found on BlueSky, Twitch, and their website.

Horro and the Mirrimit

M. M. Sahoo

Myeni held the copper frame over eye level and rotated it in her hands. She squinted at it while a misshapen lump of wood flapped its one wing and limped in circles above her head. "What did you call it again?"

Horro cleared his throat, wiping sweaty palms over his apron. "Mirrim. In Ancient Language, it means 'that which reflects.' Based on the grammar they had, I imagine more than one mirrim would be mirrim*it*."

"Just say the name and stop! Why the etymological lesson? Also, why do you sound anxious?"

For the 687th time in their long acquaintance, Horro wondered if perhaps *he* were her apprentice. Each time she scrutinized one of his Inventions, his nerves went on high alert, every last one of them.

After a while, Myeni set the mirrim face-down on a pile of wood shavings. Horro winced on its behalf and had to bite on his lower lip to keep from reproaching her on the state of her carving table. Cleaning was the one thing Myeni never did.

"I do not understand it," she said, tilting her head. The airborne carving hurried to change its angle of rotation as well.

"Doesn't seem all that extraordinary. Copper has a shiny quality, so it does reflect a wee bit, but it's nothing compared to silver."

Myeni had been a tall, living replica of a washcloth wrung dry when she had first shown up at his workshop. Shivering, she had hiccupped out a request for a temporary boarding, which proved less and less transient as days went by. Over the next fifty-three years of the Red Moon, Myeni had grown into a native Kyerenen. Horro might have been around for twice as long as her, but she knew their neighbours better than him, and them her.

Kyerene, despite being one of the nine hundred hamlets of the magically impaired, had some of the highest influx of visitors to brag about. Enchanters, in general, were not known to exert energy unless they had to, and they had to visit whenever Kyerene held its biyearly fair. And this heightened interest was courtesy of its resident Inventor, Horro.

Unlike Myeni, he had arrived in this settlement with the sole intention of putting down roots. It had been soon after that he realized he had let his powers wither from disuse. Being amongst enchanters had been a constant reminder of his loss, and so young Horro had packed his bags and left town for good. Kyerene had been quite small then, with less than twenty houses to its credit.

Not long after, upon discovering that the so-called conveniences of magic could be reproduced to a certain degree, with the help of carefully crafted machineries and tools, Horro took to diligent studying. Word of his genius spread far and wide after the first time he featured some of his Inventions at one of the fairs.

Horro picked his newest one from the bed of wood shavings and wiped it over his sleeve. He held it face-first in front of his apprentice. Smooth silver glimmered behind a layer of transparent glass.

Myeni gasped, clapped her hands, and snatched the mirrim from his hands. "Oh my, I can see myself on a plain surface after so long!" She let out a screech and twirled on her heels. Her unfinished project went haywire in an attempt to match her pace.

Horro shook his head. She was supposed to analyze it, not be infatuated with it. But the onus lay with him, he knew. Like a fool, he had become too excited about the mirrim and forgotten Myeni was too preoccupied at the moment to give him any decent critique. She had managed to acquire a stall for herself and her — as she called them — thingamabobs at the upcoming fair. "I'll leave the serious non-magical stuff to you, but I'm taking over the younglings' market," she had declared and skipped away to her corner in their shared workshop, humming out of tune.

Horro remembered being dumbfounded at her reaction when all he had done was ask whether she wanted a cup or a pot of the crimson tea he had been brewing. When he had a craving for it, he *had* to have it, but all he could do was consume half a cup. Its bitterness appalled him, as did the sting of spice at the very end. Myeni, on the other hand, could chug the swill down three steaming pots at a time. He often wondered if she had an extra-large cauldron at the end of her gullet and if her food pipe was lined with some of his Hotpacks — heat resistant sleeves he had discovered by complete accident. He had been brewing a cure for colds then and had ended up with a strange film at the bottom of his pot. Inventions sometimes had minds of their own.

Myeni kidnapped the mirrim for the rest of the day. Horro watched her prop it up against a stack of unused gears. She proceeded to make faces at it and enact a puppet show using her whittled thingamabobs. She did voices as well. Every once in a while, he heard an untethered giggle escape her throat.

The semi-carved wood piece laboured along and circled an imaginary halo with its single wing, Myeni all but ignorant of its struggles.

"NO ENCHANTER WILL COME for this alone, you know."

Horro yawned and turned over in his cot, pulling the woven blanket to his chest. Myeni's voice sounded mechanical in his dreams. "Go away," he murmured, flapping his hand weakly.

Something tapped on his forearm and he ignored it. The same rounded thing tapped him under the shoulder blade next and he tried to swat it away. The third time it poked his waist. He jumped up, half shrieking, half giggle-sobbing. Whatever it had been tore away from him in a flash, making a beeline for the ground.

Horro leaned over the edge of his cot. Myeni stood on the lower level of the workshop with her arm outstretched. A small wooden bird settled on her fingers and pecked at her glove. Horro recognized the wing pattern from the day before. She must have gotten back to carving after he had retired for the night. Myeni waved a hand over the bird and it went still in its pecking position.

"Did you hear what the bird said?" she yelled out.

The Inventor sighed and pulled out a bulk of rope ladder from under his mattress and let it cascade off the suspended bed. He used to let the ladder hang down, but there had been a time when Myeni, excited over successfully tweaking a shoe with a retractable heel, had climbed right up and announced her achievement at the top of her lungs to a sleeping Horro. He had shrieked then too, louder, and tumbled right over the other edge. The repairs his body had needed that day . . . he shuddered to even think of them.

Thus, Horro decided that as long as Myeni stayed with him, he would have to sleep on a bulky mattress for the sake of survival. The initial discomfort was a small price to pay.

And so was the distasteful pecking of a wooden bird or the high-pitched screech of a tiny musical instrument from time to time.

Horro yawned and reignited their fireplace while Myeni paced the room and launched into a monologue to supplement the avian message.

". . . and the biggest thing is that those enchanters over there" — she waved her hands towards the upper-level walls where numerous framed fabrics with splotches of paints hung over embossed gold labels — "have far too easy an access to flat silvers. They can literally conjure those anytime, anywhere."

Despite drooping eyelids, Horro smiled at the pictures, a feat made possible by Portrait-Right-Away. This little contraption consisted of a thin, stretchable fabric into which the subject would press their face and a catapult mechanism would hurl paints and imprint their impression. A canvas at the ready would slam against the fabric and catch the portrait before it dried. The elastic fabric was washable and reusable. The only tricky bit with the machine was timing. The subject had to move their face before the canvas came swinging. Not every enchanter was imbued with quick reflexes, but Horro chose to focus on the positives — the twenty-seven portraits creepily watching over the workshop. He had stamped golden placards in his own handwriting to label who was featured in which frame.

His apprentice sighed. "I should know, I once had that kind of privilege too. To summon anything anywhere, just like that." Myeni pressed her lips together, her brows furrowing, and clicked her fingers. "Only ninety-seven more years to go till they lift my prohibition," she added through clenched teeth and punched the air.

Myeni had not done anything particularly evil. Those who had the ranking of Great Enchanter were far worse. There was one in some northern town who had swallowed the entire atmosphere and near about choked every living being in the world. Horro had even heard of someone two towns over who had tried to split the planet in half just to see what would happen next. Enchanters passing by always had some or the other extravagant tale of their kith and kin to share. Not too long ago, someone else had doused their whole village in water soluble paints while painting a small canvas. Such happenings were a regular thing. The ministry slapped them with a Ban Notice and that was that.

So Myeni's use of magic being a little berserk bothered no one amongst the authorities, laid back as they all were. However, when it came down to being Banned, she had scored the biggest, both in terms of restrictions and duration of said restrictions. She could not use large-scale magic, which included teleportations, summonings and manipulating other living beings, for one and a half centuries. Animating a whittled bird was the height of her powers at the moment.

"Anyway," Myeni continued, taking a deep breath in. "Where was I?"

Horro put a kettle on and nodded towards the sack of vegetables by the fireplace. His apprentice rolled her eyes and pulled out carrots, peas, and potatoes from the jute bag without moving anything but a finger. As she guided the vegetables into the Mincer — another of Horro's inventions — she nodded and said, "See? That's fascinating. It's got blades, it looks cruel yet it's useful, it's interesting. The mirr . . . mirr . . . er . . . whatever — it does not have the same appeal. Kyerenens will go crazy over it, no doubt. I was fascinated with seeing my proper reflection after so long too. It feels amazing to not have to rush off to Lake Kye to see how I look or to thank my lucky silvers if I happen across a halfway decent reflective surface which was flat and bigger than my thumb. If those from the other dead spots . . . er, *de-enchanter hamlets* could attend our fair, they'd feel the same too, no doubt. But enchanters, I just don't think so, and them are the biggest crowd in our biyearly fair."

This was another reason Horro was glad to have Myeni around. She was a functional enchanter, for all intents and purposes, so she could offer their point of view. A steady stream of enchanters visiting Kyerene meant it was easier to fix up the many structural issues their poorly built houses faced time and again. Them being fascinated improved on their kindness exponentially, which was why instead of the usual payment of food and raw materials in exchange for goods, Horro had them better the Kyerenens' living conditions. He was sure Kyerene was the most affluent of all dead spots, having no rickety houses anymore.

"Think about it. The concept of mirr . . . the *thing* is kind of uninteresting."

Myeni had done it out of sheer boredom. She could never have anticipated for the subsequent Ban Notice to put her on the same level as the hamlet dwellers. She should not have, in hind-sight, hexed the legs of those ministry officials and made them run sixteen laps, and she certainly should not have laughed her head off while being reprimanded for it.

Horro held the kettle with his apron and emptied it into a mug. He put a pot on the fire and coated it in oil before relieving the Mincer of the diced vegetables.

Myeni knew his silence meant he was mulling things over. She settled behind her carving table, brushing aside some of the wood shavings to make space for paint canisters from a shelf tucked under the table. She picked up a paintbrush and dipped it in red. Her Pecking Bird would be the shade of the Red Complimenters. Bunch of 'good' talkers the birds were. Always had something nice to say to passers-by, so enchanters and de-enchanters alike considered the bird as good luck.

At the fair, with the Pecking Bird as the centre, all sixty of her whittled birds could put up an aerial show and carry the drums and flutes with them. Oh, she was going to go all sorts of nuts there! Tingles danced under her skin and her shoulders jiggled as she put the red strokes on the bird.

"I know just what to do!"

The declaration caused the tingles to jump right out of her skin, and she screamed, the inanimate bird unwillingly flying through the air. Horro caught it against his shoulder and propped it on the table. He wiped the splotches of paint from his palm on his apron.

Myeni collected herself in the meantime and pulled the paint-brush away from her cheek. In her shock, she had thrown her hands up and the paintbrush had tilted down, planting its bristles against her face. "Well, what is it?"

Moments later, with a blushed cheek, Myeni listened to the plan, a large cauldron of boiling silver between her and Horro. They took turns stirring it, their breakfast running cold on a side table.

The day of the fair went better than they had anticipated. Nearly every vendor and every Kyerenen bought a mirrim — no, *mirrer*. Even thinking about the name change made Horro scowl at his apprentice, whose stall was swarming with customers and she was smiling away as though it was the only thing she knew how to do.

Horro's Hall of Mirrimit had been another huge success. Having experimented with the shapes, sizes and curvatures of the glass as well as the silver, Horro had managed to create a huge array of mirrimit, which reflected fine but distorted the shapes and angles. Every now and then, stationed right opposite the tented structure, Myeni and Horro could hear spooked customers scream, the sound delighting the duo to no end.

"But what if some enchanters zapped the mirr . . . er . . . whatever to oblivion out of fear? And what if some lost control of their . . . bodily functions? The tent will reek," Myeni had pointed out during their brainstorming.

Horro had promptly grabbed a sheet of sponge rolled up by the fireplace and beamed. "We'll line the floor with Super Soakers and infuse them with scent. Should be easy enough to do."

"And the zapping?"

"I was thinking I would have a few extra sets made and replace them as many times as I can. It's not very practical, but for now, it will have to do."

"Until the hall looks too bare, we can keep the tent open, yes. Do you want me to integrate some of them things with magic so they'll talk or something?"

"Don't be ridiculous! They're mirrimit, not enchanters!"

"You just want the Inventions to not have any superficial inputs in them. They won't be very *you* then."

Horro had snorted, shaking his head as though gearing up to reprimand her for thinking the worst of him. In a calm voice he had said, "If you know, why do you ask?"

As the sun went down, the vendors began to close their stalls. Horro stacked the remaining mirrimit in a box, careful about putting a layer of fabric in-between. These would go on display in their regular shop, which was a small room built in one corner of the workshop with a tiny window looking out to the street. Thick curtains separated the shop from the workshop.

Beside him, Myeni was quicker with closing up. Exhausted from being courteous all day, her muscles refused to do anything other than help her fingers conduct a symphony so everything went into its respective packaging on its own. The wooden counter folded on itself, as did the awning. The inventory of fruits, vegetables and other supplies they had received from Kyere-nens in exchange for their goods announced their capacity. The visiting enchanters, before they entered the Hall of Mirrimit, had repaid by using their magic to steady some tricky foundations, fix their communal water fountain and do other repairs around the hamlet.

"Wow, these could last us until the next fair! Phew! It's a shame we couldn't visit the other vendors, but almost all of them seemed to have managed to visit ours," Myeni remarked and nodded towards the stock, licking her lips.

Horro did not respond, quietly pulling at the ropes of the blue awning. His apprentice watched him work for a moment before waving a finger. The ropes snatched themselves out of his grip and pushed the awning along so it would roll up.

While the ropes tied themselves into two neat bows, Myeni rounded on Horro. "Would you stop pouting like a swollen grape? What's got you all squeezed out now?"

Horro crinkled his nose and bared his teeth, hissing at her. "Couldn't you have paused with at least an 'um' instead of 'er'? My poor mirrimit! What abhorrent name you've inflicted on them! Mirrer, indeed!"

"Either don't leave your stall in my care while you go set up your Hall of Mirrer or don't give your inventions complicated names just to make the names short. The names have to make sense."

"You're the worst apprentice one could have!" he barked out, glaring at her.

Myeni shrugged and pointed to their stalls, which were now nothing more than folds of fabric and wood. "I cleaned up quicker than anybody else. *Cleaned*."

Horro felt a tug at the corners of his lips. Coughing with an exaggerated accent, he muttered, "Good job."

Boxes and wood panels tucked under their arms, the two of them headed to their cart. They estimated it would take three trips to load everything. It could have been six trips but most of the strange mirrimit had been zapped away. Not that Horro complained. Tons of raw silver had conjured before him in compensation. He could make more of those mirrimit, and even some new varieties.

Myeni climbed onto the cart and laid the wood panels of their stalls down as the base. "I heard a couple of them were spooked so bad, they teleported halfway through. I also overheard somebody say 'Horro' might as well mean 'something frightening.'"

Horro handed her a box half-full of whittled toys. These would go up in their shop too. *By Myeni* — he could see it becoming its own brand someday.

"I'm not averse to the idea," he said, stroking his stubbled chin. "It sure has a certain ring to it, doesn't it? All right, let us go and get the rest of it."

About M. M. Sahoo

M. M. Sahoo (she/her), from Odisha, India, has a Bachelor's degree in Engineering and a Master's in English, and is currently working on a high fantasy novel. Her words have appeared in Bridges Not Borders, The Ekphrastic Review, Apparition Lit, Sylvia Magazine, Atticus Review, Amity, and others.

x.com/LeeSplash

instagram.com/LeeSplash

DEAR EKEMINI
WINIFRED ÒDÚNÓKU

The first time I knew you was on my thirteenth birthday in January of 2020.

Then, you were still a mass of living cells meshing together to form tissues — and life, until you could grow enough to change your external environment. That was how Father put it when I asked him what you were like, inside Mother's bulging belly. Besides, our Basic Science teacher had taught us something like that, too.

The first time I knew you was in 2020. Then, you never cried nor whimpered from pain caused by a steaming hot object that you mistakenly touched; you didn't wrap your tiny little fingers around an adult's forefinger like a musician romancing a microphone on stage; neither did you ever drift off in a long callous sleep caused from day-old fatigue.

No!

In there, you were always asleep but moving about the envelope of slimy membrane that is your home. Mother said your *home* was called a placenta. *Placenta*. I could swear I'd heard that word before, most probably in one of our Basic Science classes. Sometimes, your seldom kicks made Mother restless and prone to throwing tantrums over small insignificant matters. Matters that she wouldn't necessarily have gotten upset about. I remember one day when I was indulging in my adolescent mischievousness. On that day, I had refused to eat, no matter how much Mother cajoled me. In all sincerity, she tried to explain that our pantry was low on supplies, so I must eat what was prepared for dinner that night — a bowl of garri with edikaikong soup. But when I persisted that all I wanted was cereal and milk, Mother angrily hissed and left the dining table.

"I don't have time for your *wahala* today oh." She had warned before storming out of the dining room that day, Father's eyes trailing after her figure until it was out of sight.

It hurt so much, dear Ekemini.

For on a normal day, Mother would have sent Abasiama to go buy cornflakes and milk down the street. She would have petted me and ensured that I at least had a little something to eat. She knew what skipping meals could cost me. I would become so thin that Mama, Father's mother, would accuse Mother of not taking good care of me. Was that what her son married her for? Mama would have given Mother an earful, and Father's pleas to his mother to take things easy would have fallen on deaf ears. Mother knew these things. Yet, on that fateful day, she left the dining room angrily with my disappointment not moving her an inch.

That was the first of many shocks.

I soon realised that you influenced this change in Mother's behaviour. The snaps she gave me when I was being naughty. Intermittent hisses hurled at Abasiama for being too sluggish. Mood swings that Father could never fathom no matter how he tried. And occasional happy moments that we all looked forward to, especially me.

Can a woman forget a child in her womb? Pray, tell! Mother never forgot you, and you never forgot her. It was in how you nudged her to go take some ice cream from the fridge at midnight, how she spat around the house every second like a leaking pipe, and how she often ran hurriedly to the sink to vomit her intestines out after a tepid meal (*Did you ever think of enforcing her to tear her stomach open? Heck! You would have also lost your home and life, you pretty little thing*). You never forgot her all through those tortuous months, not even once.

So again, I have always known you since you were still a colony of cells fusing here, dividing there, and giving Mother great joy and concern from time to time. I am not jealous by the way. There was a time when the world also revolved around me, you see. But time and chance happen to them all, and that's why I have decided to name you Ekemini — The Appointed Time — without a care in the world about what name our parents would eventually plaster on you. The Creator knew that it was time I got a baby sister, so he knew you, and then you became.

Dear Ekemini, never mind that I am taking you back down memory lane. What would I gain from it? First, credibility. Then, a sense of pride and ownership. Lastly, excitement over the fact that you could never run to cover the decade gap that is between us, not even if you were saddled with Usain Bolt's special running jersey, or braced with Jesse Owens's athletic shoes. Because I could tell you ran a lot in your hood then. Move would be a better word to use, I think.

It was in how Mother occasionally stooped low and held one side of her tummy one minute, and with absolute dexterity, glided her hand swiftly to another part of her stretch-marked bump the next minute. I wouldn't know why she always raced after you anyway. Need I ask, where were you always running to? Were there masquerades in there that pursued you daily, or were you just simply having a good time hunting foreign bodies that invaded your privacy? Masquerades are the most fearful creatures in this world. I have only seen them on TV and I hope never to see them in real life, because the way they chase people around is so scary.

One couldn't help but wonder if there were masquerades in there that were chasing and making you shift around inside Mother's belly. Whatever your motives were, you truly succeeded in holding Mother spellbound. You didn't need an audible voice before Mother knew you were calling her. Those times were pretty hard for me dear sister. I was unintentionally left alone, and Father didn't help matters either. Most times, he was in front of his laptop, working religiously for every penny he was worth at the end of the month. And whenever he was not working, I felt no difference in his presence whatsoever. If he wasn't massaging Mother's bump with one hand and pressing his phone with the other, then he would be scrambling through the pages of a choice book retrieved from his stack of books in his self-erected library. I think I got my love for books from Father. He always reads books in his spare time and sometimes writes. I write too, or at least I am writing this letter to you now. I hope you receive it in a good light.

Asides from Father and Mother, there are other people you'll meet here when you arrive, dear sister. First is Kira, our dog — a large Rottweiler that Father treats like a child, so he counts her as family. Kira had given birth to several puppies that have been sold out almost as soon as they started walking. Thank God Father and Mother did not sell me out after I was born. Thank God I came to this world as a human being, not as an animal. Animals, like our dog, Kira, don't have a life of their own. Humans control them and do whatever they will with them. We even eat some of them, like chicken, cow, pig, and snail. Don't worry! You'll see these animals and many more when you finally arrive in this world. And you'll even read them in school when learning the alphabet. A is for Ant, B is for Bee, C is for Cat, D is for Duck, and so on. It's an interesting world, dear Ekemini.

But apart from Kira, there's another amiable personality you'll meet, someone whose name I've already mentioned twice. Abasiama, our maid — an eighteen-year-old aunty whom Mother used to call 'village girl' because she could not speak the English language when she first arrived. Abasiama is supposed to be a 'gift' that Mama packaged and sent from Ikot-Ekpene to Mother when she got a new job as a banker and needed extra help. I was five then. Abasiama is the big sister I never had. I have known her since the time I could tell my right from my left. At that time, she was the only one I loved talking to because she is a good listener, as you'll soon find out yourself. Later, when my childish needs grew outrageously, she was always there to meet them and satiate me to sleep. Up until when I knew you and when Mother's attention shifted drastically from me to you, Abasiama has always been supportive and kind. I've grown up with her for seven years now, so I know what I'm talking about.

She was always feeding me at the right time, bringing my out-of-reach toys from wherever they were stuck or hidden by Father whenever he tripped on them. Father has a bad temper, even Mother does, but not Abasiama. She was constantly making sure that I was comfortable at every point in time. Even so, now that I'm a little grown up, Abasiama is still replete with tender love and care — something endearing adults call TLC here — and never falters in the domestic duties for which she was hired, or obtained as it were. People do not hire gifts, right? They obtain them. Maybe 'earn' is the right word to use even. Mother likes Abasiama too, except that she cares less about her welfare but more about what she can do for her. Sometimes, I wish I were Spiderman, Batman, or even the much-respected Black Panther, King of the Wakandians . . . maybe, just maybe, I would be able to manipulate Mother's heart and conjure its valves up so she can truly care for Abasiama. They say caring comes from the heart, right? Oh! What do you even know? I've got a lot of things to teach you anyway. I expect your arrival in earnest.

Then there's Aunty Ima too, Mother's sister who visits us every time school is on break. But now, she has been here for more than six months because of the coronavirus outbreak. We don't even know when schools will resume as the whole world has been subjected to a lockdown. Aunty Ima says the COVID-19 virus is the cause of all these standstills. I wish she could explain COVID-19 in clearer terms to me, as neither Father nor Mother would spare me the knowledge. But anytime I asked how a tiny entity, like a virus, could spread so fiercely across the whole world and cause death, she would say "Don't worry, you'll understand when you're older." And that's Aunty Ima for you. She's always hiding information from us — me and Abasiama. She would say kids don't do this. Kids don't do that. Don't watch this, you're still a child. Meanwhile, Abasiama is no longer a kid, oh. She even has breasts on her chest like Aunty Ima. I still don't understand why Aunty Ima regards her as a child. And to be fair, Aunty Ima's dos and don'ts are too much that they wear me out. Maybe when you arrive, and when we join hands together to wail, she may allow us to watch those action films on her laptop. Until then, we'll make do with SpongeBob Squarepants on Nickelodeon. And we can always watch it during 'TV Time' that Father unanimously created to gauge my screen time. You'd love the cartoon anyway, I promise.

And now to the non-living things you'll meet when you arrive: my teddy bears. There are three of them. It was Aunty Ima that bought them for me on my first, fifth, and tenth birthdays respectively, and their sizes are in that order. I named the three of them Ann, Bee, and Cece. Mother helped with the naming. But Father didn't like them, still doesn't because he believes teddy bears are for girls. If it were possible, I'm sure Father would have rejected Aunty Ima's gifts on my behalf. Maybe when you arrive, I'll transfer the ownership to you. Ann, Bee, and Cece are very nice. I love them to stupor. They don't shout at you when you don't get your sums right, like Father. They don't abandon you when you make them angry, like Mother. They are always there for you, like Abasiama.

And all of us are waiting for when you'll be born, dear Ekemini. The lockdown has been eased, so there's nothing to worry about. Although Aunty Ima has gone back to school, she'd be back as soon as she hears of your birth. That, I'm sure of.

———

ONLY THAT, when you did arrive into our world, I was flabbergasted by the sight of you. You were so tiny and frail. Delicate and soft. Malleable and fragile. I kept wondering if your arm wouldn't dislodge from your shoulder with the way Mama handled you when she finally arrived all the way from Ikot-Ekpene after hearing the news of your birth. I heard that you cried your eyes out at the University College Hospital (U.C.H) Ibadan where Mother had you, but no single tear dropped.

Really?

I also heard that Father was by Mother's side and wouldn't let go of her hand until your head popped out and the rest of your infantile body followed swiftly. At last, he could finally hold and gaze at the invisible growing child he'd been communicating with for the past nine months and more. Father told me that Mother kept asking for water immediately after the burden of carrying you was lifted and she felt light.

Water for what exactly? Was she racing after you again, even in labour?

And I heard again that . . . or never mind. I'll keep this to myself until you are old enough to understand it. That would be when you become six. Too far? Well, grow up quickly and save me the stress. Just like me, I'm sure you would grow to become a strong toddler. You can count on Father and Mother to provide everything you need. Although whenever Mother takes in again, she may abandon you unknowingly, as she did me. But that's just life, you see. Seasons come and go. And things don't stay the same forever.

Have I told you what the doctors at U.C.H. thought of you the moment you popped out of Mother's innards like long-held flatulence that finally found freedom? They said you were so beautiful and adorable, yet gave Mother a tough time. They said you made Mother labour for eighteen good hours. Why? Were you gathering treasures to bring to this world, and keeping your house in order before leaving? Were you contemplating coming to this world — our world? You don't want to leave the warm enclave anymore? News flash! Your indecisions made Mother face death one-on-one. Oh! You didn't know? Girl, one doctor couldn't have delivered you single-handedly. Mother's cervix wasn't wide enough, they said. She was too weak to push. It had been thirteen years since she last had a baby, so delivering you by herself was hard.

So I heard.

It took Father a few drops of tears to muster all the courage in this world not to give in to defeat. You made him weak to his bones as he watched Mother grit her teeth in pain and grip his arms in agony. He was blasting in tongues while watching Mother wail non-stop.

So I heard.

Thank God I wasn't there. Else, I would have started crying and stomping my feet on the floor of the ward. I would have asked the doctors to remove you from Mother's stomach by force if that's what it'll take to stop the pain. Eighteen hours in labour? That's not fair, dear Ekemini.

And now that you are here, you don't talk. You don't try to caress Ann, Bee, or Cece when I bring them close to you. You don't even scramble around the house in search of what is (not) lost like I do. You only stay transfixed in that supine position all day, eyes shut defiantly against the world, legs curled in feminine modesty, fingers interlocked like a *kungfu* fighter revering his combatant, and a curved mouth smiling at anyone or everyone like a brainwashed lover. How long before we start doing rough play together as children of the house do.

No one is impatient except me.

Mother dotes on you endearingly and sings you lullabies when you become unusually restless. What's with the excessive breast milk that she feeds you anytime your smiling mouth disfigures into a cry? Aunty Ima has fast become your second mother, always wanting to carry you in her arms or strap you on her back and pace the living room singing nursery rhymes that she never sang to me. Didn't I tell you she would come back? I wish she was around when I was born. It makes me jealous, but since it's you, I'll let it go. Remember Abasiama, our housemaid? She always wants to carry you in her arms just like Aunty Ima but Mother never allows it.

"Abeg abeg, no break my baby head oh. Oya enter kitchen go wash those detty plates dem, abi which work you dey do sef?" Mother's voice will rise anytime Abasiama attempts to carry you or just peer into your angelic shut eyes.

I hate to see Abasiama treated this way, but what can I do alone? Maybe together, when we both grow older, we'll start setting some things right as the children of the house. Maybe we'd have had one, two, or three more siblings to strengthen our filial love and duty. And I sincerely pray that mother doesn't have to wait another thirteen long years before having another baby. But right now, it is just you and I — me being the captain, you the subordinate. We've got to sail our ship safely to the dock. Nay?

I should also let you know that Father has not been working from his laptop since the day you arrived. I like to think that he applied for a casual leave of some sort because why else would he spend all day carrying you whenever Mother is not? That's a topic for another day, anyway.

Dear sister, I'd like to conclude that you are a glorious child and a bringer of good fortune, for it was soon after Mother got pregnant with you that COVID-19 struck, and with it came the lockdown. Thank God for the lockdown, I wasn't woken up early in the morning by Mother just at the nick of time when the sleep was the sweetest, to prepare for school. Now that you're born, just a little while after the lockdown was eased, we have a full house. Father, Mother, Aunty Ima, Abasiama, Kira, Ann, Bee, Cece, and even Mama who has been with us since you arrived in our world.

And what a sweet grandmother she is; one who lets me have anything I ask for at any time of the day. If Mother tries to force her garri and edikaikong soup down my throat, Mama would give Abasiama money to go get me what I want down the street. Mother's excuse of having a low pantry never held water, and would never do, for as long as Mama stays here. More importantly, Mama has levelled my fears with the way she treats you and has told me not to worry, that at the appointed time, you would open your tiny eyes, uncurl your legs and stretch them out, give me a scrappy punch once in a while when I am being naughty, and even call my name — Etimbuk — with your effeminate and tiny voice. I've stayed too long without a sister, you see. So hurry and start doing these things that Mama said you surely would.

Dear Ekemini, I can't wait.

About Winifred Òdúnóku

Winifred Òdúnóku (she/her) is a writer from Nigeria who loves exploring different narrative styles in her writing. She is an Assistant Editor at Isele Magazine and a Nonfiction Reader at Fiery Scribe Review. Her works have been published or forthcoming in 101 Words, Inked in Gray Press, The Missing Slate, Ilford Review, IBADANarts, African Writer, Isele Magazine, The Moveee, Revista Periferias, Kalahari Review, Nnöko Stories, Ngiga Review, and Punocracy. She loves listening to music with a headset and humming along.

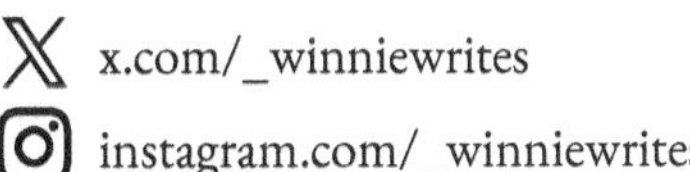

x.com/_winniewrites

instagram.com/_winniewrites

About the Editor

Chyina Powell

Chyina Powell is an award-winning author, editor and founder. She began Powell Editorial in order to help emerging writers become published authors. She offers diverse services including sensitivity reading, developmental editing, and manuscript critiques and is always happy to share her knowledge of the publishing industry with her writers. Moreover, Chyina is an advocate for diversity in publishing which led her to create the Women of Color Writers' Circle Inc., a nonprofit organization that offers community and safe space to women of color writers globally regardless of genre or where they are in their writing career. Chyina Powell is the author of six books and always has at least three WIPs in the works. When she is not writing or working with writers, you can find her with a book in hand and a cup of tea nearby.